"Stop testing me.

"You sit back and watch me with the kids, passing judgment on how well I handle every situation. Can she read bedtime stories to Ruthann? Can she handle Sam's rudeness and Janis's teenage moods? Can she cook supper for the family? Everything is a test."

Caroline stopped and looked at him. "Mitch, I like your kids. They scare me but they also make me want to give them what they need. I'm just afraid I don't have enough."

"You do," Mitch said. "The beauty of love is that the more you give, the more you get back and then the more you have to give in return. It's an infinite loop."

"But a loop is a circle, Mitch. I haven't connected it yet. You're at one end, I'm in the middle and the kids are at the other end. If I can't bind the ends together tightly, the loop will surely break."

Dear Reader,

Is there a woman alive whose heart isn't touched by the struggles of a father to raise his family on his own? Witness the success of last summer's hit move, *Sleepless in Seattle*. The moment little Jonah Baldwin, discussing his widower-father on national radio, announced, "I think he needs a new wife," women across the country—not to mention those in the movie theater—were ready to volunteer.

We at Superromance are sure that Mitch Grogan, hero of *Single... With Children*, will capture your heart, too. Tall, sexy, gorgeous and sensitive—can anyone resist?

And there's more to come. Look for the FAMILY MAN flash on upcoming Superromance covers and fall in love with our other sexy fathers. As always, we'd love to hear how you like these books.

The Editors
Harlequin Superromance
225 Duncan Mill Road
Don Mills, Ontario, Canada
M3B 3K9

Connie Bennett

Single...
With Children

Harlequin Books

TORONTO • NEW YORK • LONDON
AMSTERDAM • PARIS • SYDNEY • HAMBURG
STOCKHOLM • ATHENS • TOKYO • MILAN
MADRID • WARSAW • BUDAPEST • AUCKLAND

ISBN 0-373-70586-7

SINGLE...WITH CHILDREN

ABOUT THE AUTHOR

Connie Bennett, on the challenge and joy of writing about children: "Little ones are easy. Ruthann Grogan just had to be adorable most of the time with occasional bouts of fussiness for realism. Teenagers also ·don't give me much of a problem. I have taught Janis's age group so I am quite familiar with them.

"It was Sam Grogan who was the biggest challenge. Never having had any brothers, little boys are a mystery to me. I knew Sam had to have a definite personality and he had to be able to communicate. Interestingly enough, he's the one I ended up liking the most."

Connie enjoys hearing from her readers. Letters can be sent to Connie Bennett, P.O. Box 14, Dexter, Missouri 63841.

Books by Connie Bennett

HARLEQUIN SUPERROMANCE
373–CHANGES IN THE WIND
416–PLAYING BY THE RULES
436–BELIEVE IN ME
513–TOURIST ATTRACTION
562–WINDSTORM

CHAPTER ONE

IT WAS the kind of voice that drove men wild. The smooth, throaty tones evoked images of Bacall teaching Bogie how to whistle or Kathleen Turner creating body heat with just one sexy, husky word. It created romantic fantasies, promised untold passion and tantalized with its earthy overtones.

The fact that it was coming from a computerized voice synthesizer made it all the more remarkable—and totally inappropriate!

Dr. Caroline Hunter sat on a stool in the research lab and stared in disbelief at the synthesizer module as the voice recited its innocuous test message. When the recording had played through, she switched her astonished gaze to the young technician behind the console. "This is a joke, right, Tony?" she asked hopefully.

Tony Beecroft pushed his thick-rimmed glasses up on his nose and kept a straight face. "Come on, Dr. Hunter. Would I kid you? Everybody knows you don't have a sense of humor."

He was teasing her, but only a little. For a fleeting second, Caroline thought about giving him a poke in the shoulder to prove that she was a good sport who could take a joke, but she resisted the urge. She just wasn't the shoulder-poke-good-sport type. She was a serious, no-nonsense computer designer with a reputation for being ruthlessly single-minded. Since it was an image Caroline had worked hard to cultivate in her male-dominated profession, it didn't take much to squelch the impulse to prove that her reputation was a total fabrication.

"Tony, this is supposed to be a voice for a verbally interactive computer, not a receptionist for an escort service," she said sternly.

"I guess you don't like it, then?"

Caroline shook her head and tried to think of a way to be tactful. "No, I'm sorry. It's a tribute to your skill with a synthesizer, but it's not what I had in mind."

"You don't think a computer named Scarlett OHARA should have a voice to match?"

She pointed at the module. "If we use that voice, we'll have to change her name to Jezebel."

Tony grinned. "Hey! You do have a sense of humor!"

Caroline suppressed the smile that tugged at the corners of her mouth. "If you tell anyone that, you're fired."

"Yes, ma'am," he said, but he was still grinning as he turned back to the console. "All right. If you don't want sexy, try this one on for size." He punched another button and the same test message played through, this time with exactly the effect Caroline had been looking for when she sent Tony back to the drawing board a week ago. Test marketing had shown that the computer's voice tended to grate on people's nerves after extended exposure. All Caroline had wanted was for Tony to lower the pitch and add a bit of resonance.

And he had done exactly that.

"Much better," Caroline said enthusiastically when the second test had played through.

"I thought you'd say that, but I still like the first one better," Tony replied.

"What man wouldn't?" she asked dryly as she slid off the stool. "When can you install the new voice module?"

"I'll have it up and running first thing Monday morning," he promised. "And you can tell marketing that I'll have their test models ready by the end of next week."

"Excellent." Caroline moved around the console and patted the young man's shoulder—it wasn't a friendly poke, but it was about as close as Caroline ever got to allowing herself familiarity with her staff. "Good work, Tony. Just make sure you install the correct module, okay?"

"Would I make a mistake like that?"

This time she couldn't help but respond to his impish grin. "For your sake, I hope not," she said with a twinkle in her hazel eyes. "See you later."

She picked up her old-fashioned clipboard, marched briskly out of the small sound lab and made her way through the sleek, ultramodern facility that had been her home-away-from-home for the last six years. She felt completely at ease within the high-tech walls of MediaTech Laboratories, and that was more than Caroline could say for most places.

A certified genius with an IQ that hovered near one hundred and eighty, Caroline had spent most of her life trying to "live up to her potential." Professionally, she had done that quite well. She was the front-runner in a race to design the world's most advanced computer and as soon as she ironed out the last few bugs from her system, MediaTech would launch the OHARA and set the computer industry on its collective ear. Not too shabby for an egghead who hadn't celebrated her thirty-fifth birthday yet.

Personally, though, Caroline's success had been less than stellar. She had one failed marriage behind her, no friends outside of a small circle of colleagues, a cat that recognized her only at feeding time and a set of parents she hadn't seen in years. Fortunately, her work was her life and she liked it that way. Every ounce of energy and creativity she possessed had gone into giving birth to the OHARA computer, and the enormous satisfaction she felt at her accomplishment was more than enough to compensate for any minor deficiencies she might have experienced in other areas of her life.

Without stopping to chat with anyone along the way, Caroline breezed through the large main programming laboratory and made a beeline for her office, a windowless room with white walls, a desk, two file cabinets, a credenza and one deceptively ordinary-looking computer.

"Good afternoon, Caroline."

The placid, disembodied female voice seemed to come from nowhere. "Good afternoon, Scarlett," Caroline replied as she moved around the desk. "Have you been keeping busy today?"

"Of course. Dr. Caldwell is giving me an astronomy lesson and Dr. Bergman is performing another diagnostic on my primary information data base."

Caroline put down her clipboard and frowned at the blank screen of the computer terminal. "Have you encountered another memory lapse in the data base?" she asked.

"Not to my knowledge," the computer replied. "I believe Dr. Bergman's work is just another routine test."

Caroline breathed a sigh of relief. Scarlett's data base was one of her most complex and critical systems, a carefully constructed encyclopedia of information that gave the computer the ability to reason in a seemingly—and sometimes eerily—human fashion. But for the last few months, Scarlett had been losing bits and pieces of knowledge for no apparent reason. So far, the losses had been minor, but the glitch indicated that there was a flaw somewhere in the design. Despite hours of intensive diagnosis, Caroline still hadn't discovered where the problem lay; one day Scarlett would know something and the next day, that information would simply be gone.

But that hadn't happened again today, thank goodness.

Caroline sat at her desk. "Do you have any questions for me, Scarlett?" she asked.

"Yes, I do." The computer routinely reviewed all new information that was fed into her memory and when she ran across something she didn't understand, she saved her questions for her creator.

"Proceed."

"What is the meaning of 'uppity'?"

Caroline smiled. "Where did you encounter that word?"

"Dr. Caldwell applied the term to me when I informed him that his computations on the distance to the Maxima Quasar were incorrect."

She chuckled. Loren Caldwell was an astrophysicist from Cal-Tech who had recently accepted a contract to "teach" Scarlett about astronomy. The learned scientist wasn't accustomed to having a pupil who was impertinent enough—and smart enough—to correct him when he was wrong.

Caroline reached for her dictionary so that she could give Scarlett a precise definition. "'Uppity' is defined as 'putting on airs of superiority,'" she told the computer.

There was a tiny pause. "Making it synonymous with arrogant or presumptuous," Scarlett said, drawing the logical conclusion.

"That's right."

Another pause. "Am I arrogant, Caroline?"

Without even thinking about it, Caroline reached out and lightly caressed the computer monitor, much as a mother might soothe a child whose feelings had been hurt. Scarlett had no emotions, of course, but she could become easily confused and Caroline always had to tread carefully whenever her brainchild began to question her identity and her "personality."

"You are *intelligent,* Scarlett," she replied. "Sometimes humans mistake intelligence for arrogance."

"Are the words 'intelligence' and 'arrogance' synonymous?"

"No."

"Then it is a question of human interpretation," Scarlett deduced.

"That's right," Caroline said, smiling. Teaching a totally logical computer that humans weren't always logical had been one of the thorniest areas of her programming. "Human interpretation" had become a catchphrase for anything that Scarlett knew she had to accept without completely understanding why it should be so.

Scarlett seemed satisfied with the conclusions she had drawn and went on to her other questions. When they finished, Caroline punched a command code into Scarlett's keyboard and began an on-screen review of the computer's word processing program, one of a dozen software programs that would have to be fully operational before the OHARA computer could be introduced to the world.

"Caroline! What are you doing here?"

Caroline looked up from the terminal, but she was so engrossed in the readout that it took her a second to focus on Bob Stafford, the tall, pinch-faced CEO who was glaring at her from the doorway. "I work here, remember?" she said with a grin when his question finally registered on her. "Are you trying to usurp my role as the absentminded professor?"

"No, you're doing just fine in the part. In fact, you're running more than true to form," Stafford replied, tapping his watch. "Hilliard High School... three o'clock... judging the district science fair... Does any of that ring a bell?"

Caroline fell back in her chair and groaned. "Oh, God... is that today?"

"Yes, it is."

"Do I have to go?" she asked hopefully.

Stafford crossed his arms over his chest. "Yes, you do. My wife is in charge of the fair and I promised her that you'd be there. Her students are counting on you. It's too late to back out now. You're going, and that's that. Now, get a move on before you're late."

Caroline was not looking forward to this, which was probably why she had allowed it to slip her mind. She hated crowds and detested unfamiliar situations because they made her feel socially inadequate. Most of all, she dreaded the idea of having to deal with the teenage competitors she would be judging. But it was obvious that Bob Stafford wasn't going to let her escape. "What time is it now?" she asked.

"It's one forty-five," he answered.

"That is incorrect, Mr. Stafford," Scarlett interjected. "The current time is 1:42 p.m."

Stafford glared at the computer. "Thank you, Scarlett," he said irritably.

"You're welcome, Mr. Stafford," she replied sweetly.

Caroline chuckled. "One of these days I'm going to have to teach her what sarcasm sounds like."

The CEO shot an exasperated glance at Caroline. "One of these days you can teach her to stop splitting hairs. Can you shut her off? I hate it when she eavesdrops."

"You're just paranoid," Caroline quipped, but did as he requested. "Scarlett, end session." Immediately, the lights on the control module above the keyboard faded and Caroline patted the monitor. "Sleep well, honey."

"Oh, for heaven's sake," Stafford snapped, coming toward her desk. "Next thing I know you'll be singing her lullabies."

"That was a joke, Bob."

"No, it wasn't," he argued. "You do it all the time. It's a computer, Caroline, not a child."

She knew that very well and didn't need anyone to remind her of it. "Bob, that computer and I are going to increase MediaTech's profits by several billion dollars over the next few years, so if I want to treat Scarlett like a child, I suggest you indulge me."

Stafford's lips pursed into a frown that told Caroline she had made her point. "All right. You can anthropomorphize that inanimate object all you want, but in exchange, you have to do something for me."

"What's that?" she asked suspiciously.

He tapped his watch again. "Judge the science fair. Today."

"All right. All right." Caroline dug into the bottom drawer of her desk and retrieved her purse. "Tell me, Bob, how did I ever let you talk me into this?"

"Because I'm a persuasive, silver-tongued devil that you just couldn't resist," he replied sourly.

The notion was so ludicrous that Caroline had to laugh. "No, as I recall, you played on my sense of civic duty with a line of malarkey about MediaTech's responsibility to foster the growth of a new generation of scientific minds." She shook her head. "I must have been crazy to agree. Bob, I don't know anything about handling children."

"For God's sake, Caroline, you don't have to counsel them on their personal problems. You're just judging their computer projects."

"I know that, but kids are so... fragile," she replied. "I remember what these competitions were like—the tension, the pressure, the disappointment..."

Stafford frowned. "I didn't think you went to public school."

"No, I didn't. My parents didn't believe in public education, but they believed in competition. They entered me in every science contest in the nation and two of them abroad." She didn't add that it had been a grueling ordeal that had contributed greatly to her feelings of being an oddball, because she had been barely ten years old when she started competing against teenagers who were preparing to enter college.

As a result, Caroline hadn't made any friends among her fellow budding scientists. In fact, she'd never had any friends her own age until after she had completed her third doctorate degree at the age of twenty-two. By then, she had caught up in age with the other graduate students and had learned a little more about integrating socially.

In all that time, though, she had never been around children, and as a result, the very idea of confronting a roomful of them terrified her.

"Caroline, this contest is no big deal," Stafford told her.

She stood and took her jacket off the back of her chair, knowing it was pointless to explain to a man with four children and ten grandchildren that it was entirely possible for a thirty-four year old woman not to know anything at all about how to handle kids. "Well, if it's no big deal, why didn't you do it instead of volunteering me?"

"Because I don't know anything about computers," he answered.

She grinned at him. "That's quite a confession coming from the man who heads one of the largest computer research companies in the country," she said wryly. "Don't let our competition over at The Richmond Group hear you say that."

Stafford frowned, something he was exceptionally good at. "You know what I mean. I lack the broad base of knowledge needed to judge the merits of a variety of computer projects like the ones these kids are doing."

"In other words, you're a bureaucrat."

"Exactly."

She slipped into her jacket. "All right, I'll go, but the next time you grouse at me because we're behind schedule,

I'm going to remind you of how much of my time you've forced me to waste.''

"Who says it will be a waste of time? Gloria tells me that some of these projects are extraordinary. There are a lot of brainy kids out there, you know."

"That's what worries me," she muttered. "I don't suppose I have time to stop somewhere along the way for a crash course in child psychology, do I?" she asked hopefully.

Stafford checked his watch. "You're due at the high school in an hour. I know you've earned degrees in less time than that, but considering the crosstown traffic, this might be pushing it a little."

"All right. I'll bluff my way through it somehow," she said with a grin, but she looked a lot more confident than she felt as she headed for the science fair.

HIS DAUGHTER WAS going to win. Mitch Grogan was absolutely certain of it. He had carefully evaluated all the other entries in the computer division of the science fair, and not one of them could hold a candle to the extraordinary project Janis had created. Even discounting parental prejudice, Mitch knew that Janis couldn't lose. Before the afternoon was over, she would be holding a first-place ribbon, a thousand-dollar scholarship, and a chance to progress to the prestigious state finals, then the nationals...then, who knew? The Westinghouse Scholarship, maybe, and her pick of the finest colleges in the country. MIT, Stanford, Harvard, Yale?

It was almost too much to hope for, but Mitch knew Janis could make it happen. She'd have to, because God knew that Lieutenant Mitch Grogan couldn't afford to send her to one of those colleges on a cop's salary.

This science project that she'd worked so hard on was going to be Janis's ticket to the education she deserved, but convincing her that she was going to win was another matter entirely. She was so nervous that it made Mitch ache just to watch her. She was standing beside her project, demonstrating it to other parents who were checking out the competition just as Mitch had done. She seemed confident and enthusiastic, but her father could hear the strain in her voice and see the tremor in her hands. She was just plain scared. The official judging was over, but Janis wouldn't be able to relax until they announced the winner.

It was a lot of pressure for a fifteen-year-old to handle, and Mitch wished the contest coordinators would get on with it.

The batch of spectators passed on to the next booth, and Janis slipped off the headset that was an integral part of her project. She came out from behind her display, hurrying toward Mitch, who had been trying to maintain a discreet distance from his daughter.

"Dad!"

Mitch would have to have been blind to miss the excitement that was suddenly sparkling in her eyes. "What is it? Did I fall asleep during the presentation? Can we go home now?"

"No-oo," Janis said in the disapproving tone she always used when she thought her father was being silly. "It's her!"

"Who?"

"Her!" Janis pointed, then quickly withdrew her hand. "No, don't look! She's coming this way."

Janis shoved her father, forcing him to change direction, and Mitch tried not to laugh. His composed, serious daughter was suddenly wiggling with excitement and trying to look inconspicuous at the same time. Not exactly compatible activities. Fortunately, no one else in the crowded, noisy room seemed to notice. "Would you mind telling me who it is I'm not supposed to be looking at?'' he asked her.

"Caroline Hunter," Janis whispered.

"A movie star?" he asked, though he knew better. It would take more than a famous actress or even a rock star to get Janis this excited.

Janis's blue eyes rolled up in disgust. "A movie star at the district science fair? Get real, Dad. That's *the* Caroline Hunter. You know, the big computer designer? She was one of the judges for my division of the contest. I told you she was going to be here."

That was certainly true. In fact, she'd told Mitch so many times that the name Caroline Hunter would have been seared into his brain even if he hadn't known who the eminent scientist was.

Since Janis hadn't appreciated his movie-star joke, he decided he'd better redeem himself. "Is this the same Dr. Hunter who's trying to invent the first optical computer?" he asked.

"That's right." Janis took another quick peek at the scientist, then glanced away, afraid to be caught looking at the judge. "It's called Optical Heuristic Algorithmic Reasoning Architecture. They say that the OHARA is the closest anyone has come to creating true AI."

"Artificial intelligence," Mitch translated.

"Right. It has the reasoning capabilities of a ten-year-old."

Mitch grimaced. "Oh, great. Just what the world needs—another ten-year-old."

Janis giggled and looked up at her father. "I'm sure the OHARA isn't as rambunctious as Sam, Dad."

Mitch grinned at her, pleased that she'd gotten the joke. "For Dr. Hunter's sake, I certainly hope so. I wouldn't wish your brother on my worst enemy."

"Tell me about it." Janis rolled her eyes again—an often-used gesture that Mitch hoped she'd eventually outgrow.

"What did Dr. Hunter say about your project?"

Janis chewed nervously on the underside of her lip. "Not much. I mean, she couldn't say too much, could she? Not until the judging is over, anyway. But she asked a lot of questions and she seemed . . . well, impressed, I guess."

Mitch placed a comforting hand on her narrow shoulder. "I'm sure she was impressed—and so were the other judges. How could they not be?"

Janis sighed and glanced forlornly at the odd-looking box that sat on her display table. "I hope so, Daddy. IVAR just has to win."

"What else did Dr. Hunter say?" Mitch asked, hoping to distract Janis with something more pleasant than her fear of losing.

She brightened. "She was nice. You know, like a real person, not somebody famous and stuck-up."

Mitch had to smile. How many teenagers would call a scientist famous? "I'm sure she is nice," he said generously.

"And she had her first doctorate degree before she was nineteen. I read all about her in *Future Technologies* magazine just last month."

She said it with the same reverence most teens reserved for a cover story in *Teen Life* about Madonna. But then, Janis wasn't most teenagers. She was . . . well, her teachers called her gifted, her classmates called her Egghead, and her younger brother, Sam, called her a dork whenever he thought he could get away with it.

To Mitch she would always be his little angel, his firstborn, but he wasn't quite sure how he'd fathered a full-fledged genius. His wife had been intelligent and Mitch was no slouch in the brains department, but a genius daughter? It just didn't compute.

He couldn't deny that he was proud of her, though. She was a well-behaved, conscientious, straight-A student...a little on the serious side most of the time, with a sharp tongue and not much of a sense of humor, but overall a great kid whose heroes just happened to be famous scientists instead of movie stars.

Janis took another peek over her shoulder and sighed with relief. "Okay, you can look now," she said, turning. "She's down at the end of this row talking to my science teacher, Mrs. Stafford. She has short dark hair and she's wearing a gray suit."

"Who, Mrs. Stafford?"

Janis sighed heavily. "No, Dr. Hunter."

"That was a joke, Janis."

She paused a moment. "I knew that. Now, look before she comes this way. But be subtle."

Mitch made a big show of turning very casually, even whistling an off-key tune for good measure. Janis poked him and him told not to be silly, so he stopped whistling. What his daughter lacked in a sense of humor, she made up for in other ways, he reminded himself.

The high school gymnasium was packed with science-display booths, anxious teenage competitors, proud parents, and teachers, so it took Mitch a moment to pick out the woman in the gray suit. When he finally found her, she wasn't exactly what he expected.

As head of the Computer Crimes Division of the Hilliard Police Department, Mitch had been on the fringes of the California Silicon Valley computer industry for the last ten years, so he was acquainted with a number of so-called computer geniuses. Dr. Caroline Hunter wasn't like any he had seen before. For one thing, she was female—an uncommon occurrence in the computer industry, even in these days of women's liberation. For another, she was well-groomed and dressed in an understated but very attractive style.

The public's concept of a computer nerd was, for the most part, pretty accurate, Mitch had learned. They were usually eccentric in the extreme and proud of it. In fact, one of the wealthiest, most powerful computer geniuses in the world still needed his mother to pick out his clothes and remind him when to take a bath. He was so intelligent that the real world held no challenge for him, so he had created his own world inside a magical mathematical box called a computer.

According to rumors floating around the industry, Caroline Hunter was doing the same thing. If she had her way, computer technology would soon be taking a gigantic leap forward—a leap that would make MediaTech one of the richest corporations in the world.

Mitch hoped she'd had the foresight to insist on a profit-sharing plan when she'd taken the job.

"Well?" Janis asked expectantly. "What do you think? Isn't she beautiful?"

Since Mitch couldn't see anything but the profile of her slender body and angular face, he really couldn't make that kind of a judgment. "She seems attractive."

"Oh, come on, Dad! She's positively gorgeous! And she's—"

When she stopped abruptly, Mitch looked down at her. "She's what?"

Janis leaned toward him. "She's single. Well, divorced, actually. But she's not married."

Mitch couldn't believe what he was hearing. It had been four years since his wife had died, and in all that time Janis had never once expressed the slightest interest in seeing her father with another woman. In fact, the first time he'd gone out on a date, Janis hadn't spoken to him for a week.

Of course, that had been nearly two years ago, and Mitch hadn't had much time for women since then. What widower with three children and a demanding job did?

"I'm sure Dr. Hunter is quite capable of finding a husband without your help, Janis," he told his daughter patiently.

Janis looked at him in disgust. "You're right. And she's not your type, anyway. She's flat-chested and she's got an IQ."

"Watch your mouth, young lady," Mitch snapped, glaring at her. Obviously she still hadn't forgiven him for his brief flirtation with Bambi Brightwood two years ago.

"What are you two squabbling about this time?"

Mitch turned as his father strolled up. Mitchell Grogan, Sr., was a retired schoolteacher in his mid-sixties, a widower like his son, and Mitch's salvation. Pop lived with him and took care of the kids while Mitch worked.

He gave his father a subtle wink. "Janis is playing matchmaker, Pop. I think she wants me to flirt with one of the judges so she'll have a better chance of winning first prize."

"Da-ad!" Janis wailed. "I would never cheat to win!"

Mitch put his arm around her and dropped a kiss onto her forehead. "Lighten up, Angelface. I was just joking."

"Well that's not funny," she said, wiggling out from under his arm. She went into her sullen-teenager mode, and Mitch knew better than to try to cajole her out of it.

Besides, it finally hit him that he had another daughter to worry about. "Pop, where's Ruthann?" he asked with a frown as he glanced around.

Pop looked bewildered. "I left her with you."

Mitch felt his heart skip a beat, but he refused to give in to panic. Yet. "No, she got fussy right after you left, so Sam said he'd take her to you."

"She was distracting people who were trying to look at IVAR," Janis explained.

Pop's graying eyebrows went up as he looked at his son. "And you trusted Sam with her?"

"A momentary lapse," Mitch replied tersely. "You hadn't been gone a minute. I didn't think it would take him long to catch up with you."

"Well, I never saw them," Pop replied. "I was looking at the other displays."

"Oh, Lord," Mitch groaned. "Sam's probably trying to sell her on the black market. All right, let's spread out and find them."

"Dad, they're going to announce the winners soon," Janis protested.

"Not for another—" Mitch checked his watch "—fifteen minutes. Now start looking. You and Pop check in here and I'll work my way to the lobby."

"Done," Pop said.

They separated with Janis muttering dire threats against her brother, and the search began.

CHAPTER TWO

MITCH MOVED quickly through the crowd, muttering a few oaths himself. But they were all directed inward.

This was his fault. He wasn't competent to raise three children alone. He was cop. A flatfoot. A simple, ordinary Joe who had bought into the American Dream and most days felt as if he were about to be smashed flat by it. This certainly wasn't what he'd bargained for when he and Rebecca had gotten married.

The plan had been simple: they were going to have exactly two children—Becky would stay home and take care of them, then maybe go back to college once the kids were in school. Mitch was going to work his way up through the ranks of the police force and do his damnedest not to let his marriage disintegrate under the pressure of his job.

Of course, he had fully expected to have to do the bulk of the disciplining because Becky was a limp noodle when it came to saying no. He'd been prepared to teach his son baseball, deliver the standard father-son birds-and-bees lecture and fret over his daughter's first date.

What he hadn't counted on was a third pregnancy and the devastating complications that had resulted in his wife's death.

Now Mitch was doing it all alone, except for his aging father. Days like this one pointed up what a lousy job he was doing of it, too.

Keeping his eyes low to the ground, Mitch hurried through the room, feeling a growing desperation. There weren't many young children at the fair, which increased the odds of spotting a four-year-old with blond curls and sky blue eyes. But on the other hand, Ruthann Grogan was a world class hide-and-seek player. If for some reason she didn't want to be found, a search could take hours.

Mitch didn't even let himself think about the grim possibility that something sinister had happened to her. Before he'd moved into the white-collar world of computer fraud and theft, he had investigated crimes that had curdled his blood. He knew too well what a dangerous world it was for children.

Sam was only ten years old, but he was a tough, shrewd kid, perfectly capable of taking care of himself. But would he take care of his sister? That was a question Mitch didn't want to answer. Sam was responsible only when it suited his purpose. He wouldn't deliberately let harm come to Ruthann, but he was so easily distracted that it wouldn't take much to make him forget that he had taken responsibility for his sister's safety—or to forget that she even existed, for that matter.

That's why Mitch didn't feel much relief when he finally spotted his son with a couple of other boys milling around near one of the four exits of the cavernous gym.

"Sam!"

The boy's head jerked up and he looked around. He said something to his friends, then moved through the crowd toward his father. "Yeah, Dad, what's up?"

"Where's your sister?"

Sam frowned. "Which one?"

"Ruthann," he said, grinding his teeth.

"She's with Pop."

"No, she's not. You were supposed to take her to him, but you didn't."

"Yes, I did," Sam insisted. "He was looking at some dorky display about electricity and Ruthann ran to him."

Mitch got the picture. "So you figured that was the end of it and just walked off?"

Sam's face clouded over when he realized what big trouble he was in. "Uh-huh."

He clamped his hand down hard on his son's shoulder. "She didn't make it to Pop. She's missing."

"Uh-oh."

Mitch was too angry and too worried to waste time scolding Sam. "Go find your grandfather," he said tersely. "Tell him to report a missing child to the officials and have them make an announcement, then you stay in here until we find her. I'm going to start searching the halls."

"Okay, Dad."

The search went on.

CAROLINE WAS completely out of her depth. She had made it through the judging without feeling too much like an idiot because there had been some excellent computer projects to keep her focused. Dealing with the teenagers hadn't been as bad as she had feared and Caroline had begun to think that maybe the day would turn out all right, after all.

But that was before she had ended up with a blond-haired, blue-eyed toddler on her hands.

Or, more accurately, the child had her hands on Caroline. She'd been on her way to the ladies' room when the little girl had popped out from under a display booth and latched onto her, clutching the hem of her skirt and looking up at Caroline with disarming blue eyes that could have melted stone.

"Hi!" the squeaky-voiced moppet said brightly.

Caroline summoned a nervous smile. "Hello, there. Are you lost?"

The moppet shook her head, making her silky blond hair swirl around her shoulders. "Do you know my daddy?"

"Uh, no, honey. I don't."

"He's a p'liceman."

"How nice." Caroline looked around helplessly. One would think that in a roomful of adults she could have found at least one person to bail her out, but everyone was making such a self-conscious effort to avoid looking at the judge that no one seemed to notice she had a problem. "Do you know where your daddy is?" she asked, a trifle desperately.

The moppet shook her head again. "No. Can you take me to him?"

Knowing she couldn't very well refuse, she managed an encouraging smile. "Uh... I'll try. What's your daddy's name?"

"Daddy."

"Ask a foolish question," Caroline muttered under her breath, then tried another tack. "What's *your* name, honey?"

"Ruthann." The little girl held up her free hand, fingers spread. "I'm four."

Funny, Caroline would have guessed the child was younger, but what did she know? At least they were making progress. "Ruthann, what does your daddy look like?"

Those beautiful blue eyes rolled up as the little girl thought it over. "He's big and he has a gun," she said finally.

Oh, great. That helped a lot. What was she supposed to do, wander around the room looking for Paul Bunyan with a bulge under his coat? "What about your mother?"

"My mommy went to heaven."

"Oh. I'm sorry." Caroline felt thoroughly helpless and stupid—two things that she tried to avoid as assiduously as she avoided children. Obviously, she was going to have to apply a little logic to this situation. "Ruthann, where was your daddy when you saw him last?"

She shrugged. "I dunno."

So much for logic.

"What chore name?" Ruthann asked.

"Dr. Hun—Caroline," she amended quickly.

"You're pretty, Car'line."

"Thank you." Now why on earth would such a simple pronouncement make her feel like smiling? Caroline wondered. The little girl really was a charmer, so sweet and innocent...

But this was getting her nowhere. Caroline had to do something. She looked around again and finally spotted Gloria Stafford. Caroline waved to her, but the fair's coordinator was preoccupied with a chemical combustion project that seemed about ready to burst into flames.

Wonderful. Just what she needed. A five-alarm fire and a lost four-year-old. The next time Caroline saw Bob, she was going to give him merry hell for roping her into this.

"Excuse me, but do know this little girl?" she asked a woman who was hurrying by.

"No, sorry."

"Well, could you—" But the woman was already gone. Caroline looked down at the child. "I tell you what, Ruthann. Why don't you come with me to the judges dais and we'll make an announcement about you. How would that be?"

"What's a day-as?"

"It's that big platform on the other side of the room. Will you go over there with me? I'm sure your father will find you if we take you there."

Caroline received a nod and a wide-mouthed yawn for an answer. "Okay." She held up her arms. "Carry me, please. I'm tired."

Caroline nearly choked. She'd never carried a child before in her life. There probably weren't many thirty-four-year-old women who could make that claim, but then, not many women had been given Caroline's unusual upbringing. She had absolutely no idea what to do, but little Ruthann was looking at her expectantly, and Caroline didn't know how to refuse her plea.

"Um...uh..." Caroline rubbed her hands together. "All right." She bent over and gingerly grasped the child's waist, feeling awkward and at a loss as to how to proceed. What if she dropped her? What if Ruthann changed her mind and started crying?

There didn't seem much chance of that, though. The child's arms snaked around her neck, and when Caroline lifted her, Ruthann automatically lowered her head onto Caroline's shoulder in a gesture of trust so complete that it nearly broke her heart.

When she found the child's father, she was going to give him a piece of her mind about parental responsibility. Even Caroline knew that it was impossible to watch a child every second, but the very least a policeman could do was teach his daughter about the danger of talking to strangers.

Caroline tightened her arms around Ruthann, making sure she had a secure hold, but before she could take two steps toward the judging booth, Ruthann threw her another curve.

"Car'line."

"Yes, Ruthann."

"I have to go potty."

Caroline groaned aloud. This wasn't happening. It was something out of a Salvador Dali nightmare. In a few minutes, she would wake up.

"Car'line, I have go potty, now!" Ruthann repeated firmly.

"Uh...let's find your daddy and he can take you to...uh, potty, okay, Ruthann?"

The little girl raised her head from Caroline's shoulder and shook it adamantly. "*Now*, Car'line."

This was a real problem. She certainly didn't want the child to have an accident, but neither did she want to be accused of kidnapping. The rest rooms were down the hall outside and Caroline had no right to remove the child from the gym.

She looked around in desperation and finally saw one of the teenage competitors she'd judged earlier. "Miss Crane, come here," she ordered, raising her voice sharply.

The girl looked scared to death, but she came. "Yes, Dr. Hunter?"

"I want you to find Mrs. Stafford immediately," she said sternly. "Tell her I'm taking a lost child to the ladies' room and she should join me immediately. Do you understand?"

"Yes, ma'am."

"Go."

The girl took off through the crowd, and Caroline didn't waste any time heading for the nearest exit. The hall outside was virtually deserted, and Caroline hurried down it and around the corner.

"All right, Ruthann. We'll have you to the ladies' room in just a second," she said, forcing a bright tone, but what she was really thinking was, "What do I do when I get her there?" Could four-year-olds go to the bathroom by themselves? Would Ruthann need help with the snaps on her pink overalls? And what else would Caroline need to do for the child?

Her head was swimming with dread and questions as she approached the rest-room door, but she didn't make it that far. A few feet short of her destination, a voice boomed like thunder and rumbled down the hall.

"FREEZE!"

Her heart hammering in her throat, Caroline whirled around.

"Daddy!" Ruthann squealed.

"I said freeze!"

Caroline froze. In fact, she couldn't have moved if her life depended on it, because Ruthann's father—the cop—was standing at the other end of the hall looking like the wrath of God; his feet spread, the tail of his coat drawn aside and his hand firmly in the small of his back.

There wasn't a doubt in Caroline's mind that his hand was on his gun.

Several fleeting impressions passed through Caroline's mind. The first was that she wasn't in any real danger, despite the air of menace that oozed out of the cop. If he was prudent enough not to draw a gun on his own child, he was a man who could be reasoned with. Probably.

The second impression was that he was huge. Not exactly Paul Bunyan, but not far from it. He was the epitome of the tough, macho cop, with broad shoulders, a rugged face and a mane of blond hair that looked several weeks overdue for the barbershop. Caroline thought the tough-guy image had gone out of style in the mid-eighties. Either she was wrong or someone had forgotten to tell Ruthann's father.

"All right, put her down and step away," the cop ordered in a deep voice that sounded like gravel rolling around in a barrel. "And don't make any sudden moves."

Caroline decided to comply before she offered any kind of explanation. It seemed like the most judicious thing to do since the cop was still in his quick-draw shooting stance with his hand on his gun.

"I'm putting her down now," she said, summoning her calmest tone. She bent over slowly, but Ruthann wasn't quite as cooperative. The child kept her arms firmly around Caroline's neck. "Please let me go, Ruthann," she whispered urgently, trying to keep her balance in the awkward position. "Your father wants you to go with him."

"But I have to go potty," Ruthann whispered with equal urgency, as though they were sharing a secret.

"Lady, I said let her go!"

"I'm trying!" Caroline shouted, attempting to pry the child's hands loose. "Tell that to your daughter!"

"Lieutenant Grogan!"

Caroline glanced up with relief as Gloria Stafford and one of the competitors, Janis Grogan, joined the tableau. "Daddy! What are you doing? That's Dr. Hunter!"

"I know who she is," the cop growled. "But that doesn't explain what she's doing with Ruthann."

"She's taking her to the ladies' room," Mrs. Stafford said huffily, skirting carefully around Grogan. "Caroline, I'm so sorry. Janis and her grandfather had just reported little Ruthann was missing when I got your message." She threw a disgusted look over her shoulder. "I had no idea you would be subjected to a scene like this."

Caroline finally succeeded in freeing herself from Ruthann's grasp and the child was forced to stand or fall. She chose to stand—with her legs crossed and tears swimming in her eyes.

"Car'line's taking me to potty, Daddy," she whined.

Caroline looked at Lieutenant Grogan, who finally relaxed and let his coat fall back in place. He, in turn, looked from Caroline to Ruthann, and the emotions that played across his face were almost comical: relief, followed by an understanding of the situation, followed by a flush of embarrassment.

"Janis, take your sister to the ladies' room," he ordered gruffly.

The teenager stalked past her father and threw him a sour look. "Don't forget to frisk Dr. Hunter before you slap the cuffs on her."

"Just get Ruthann to the bathroom."

Janis hurried to her sister and took her hand, casting an embarrassed glance at Caroline before hustling off.

"Bye, Car'line," Ruthann called out as she was dragged away.

Now that her heart had stopped pounding, it was everything Caroline could do to keep from laughing as Grogan came toward her. "Am I under arrest?" she asked lightly.

Gloria Stafford's hand flew to her heart. "Oh, good heavens, no! Lieutenant Grogan, this is just a horrible misunderstanding. You can't believe—"

"Relax, Mrs. Stafford," Grogan said. "I think I've got the picture now. You can go back to the gym."

She hesitated. "Well... all right. I guess everything is under control here." She looked at Caroline. "We'll be making the presentations in a few minutes."

"I'll be along shortly, Gloria," Caroline promised.

Mrs. Stafford fluttered off, albeit reluctantly, leaving Caroline alone with the cop, who was now towering over her like a medium-size mountain. She looked up and found herself staring into the bluest, most riveting eyes she'd ever seen. They weren't soft like his daughter's. They were deep and piercing, with a determined sensuality. He really was a gorgeous man—if one liked the brawny, macho type which, of course, Caroline didn't. Not at all.

But when a hint of a smile began tugging at the corners of his lips, as though he, too, was finally giving in to the humor of the situation, Caroline felt her heart flutter just a little.

She couldn't resist the impulse to hold out her hands, wrists together. "Any time you're ready, Officer."

He turned the smile up several notches, and Caroline's heart fluttered again—more insistently this time.

"You're being an awfully good sport about this, Dr. Hunter," Mitch said sheepishly, grateful that she hadn't gotten hysterical. She was a very composed lady and—as

Janis had said earlier—a gorgeous one, too, with perfect features set in an oval face. Full lips, nice cheekbones, dark silky hair... Her figure was willowy, not curvaceous, but despite what his daughter thought, that didn't make much difference to Mitch. Dr. Hunter was a very pretty package, indeed.

"It was just an unfortunate misunderstanding," she replied graciously, lowering her hands. "Although I must admit you did have me scared witless for a moment."

"I'm sorry about that, but I learned a long time ago that it's better to be an embarrassed cop than a dead one. You had my daughter and I didn't know why."

"She latched onto my skirt and wouldn't let go," Caroline explained. "All she could tell me was that her father was a big policeman named Daddy who had a gun."

His chuckle was a deep, rumbling sound that was very pleasing to the ears. "I'm sure that was comforting to you."

"Oh, it was. Unfortunately, before I could take her to the judging dais to report a missing child, she told me she had to go...to the ladies' room."

"Well, thank you for taking care of her," he said, then gave his head a little shake. "It's a sad comment on the state of our world when a nice lady plays Good Samaritan and gets accused of kidnapping as payment."

Caroline knew what he meant. "And a father can't afford to assume anything but the worst."

A look of understanding passed between them, betraying the depth of his concern for his daughter—and something else, too. It was a jolt of electricity so strong and startling that it made Caroline take a self-conscious step backward. "Did you really know who I was?"

Mitch felt the same potent jolt of awareness and took a little step back, too. "My other daughter, Janis, pointed you out to me a few minutes ago. You judged her computer project earlier."

"Yes, I remember," she said. She had an excellent memory, and Janis Grogan's project would have been hard to forget under any circumstances, but that wasn't what was on her mind at the moment. "Are you telling me that you knew who I was and still thought I might be a kidnapper?" she asked, unable to squelch a hint of indignation.

Mitch didn't blame her for being offended. "I'm sorry, Dr. Hunter, but I've known some very respectable people who committed hideous crimes. I don't take chances, particularly where my children are concerned."

A sober shadow clouded his eyes, and Caroline realized that this was a man who lived in the real world. She, on the other hand, lived in the rarified atmosphere of academia. Like her climate-controlled, biofiltered laboratory, very little touched her life that wasn't carefully screened and processed.

She preferred it her way, even if it meant that something as basic as child care was beyond her understanding. At least she didn't have to carry a gun and worry about lunatics who kidnapped children.

"There was no harm done, Lieutenant Grogan," she assured him.

"Mitch," he corrected her, holding out his hand.

Caroline accepted his hand, but she didn't prolong the contact because his hand swallowed hers and she felt a delicious tingling sensation all the way up her arm.

"Frankly, Mitch, I'm glad Janis showed up to take over," she said, clasping her hands together to make the tingling stop. "I wasn't sure what I was supposed to do with Ruthann once I got her to the ladies' room. Children aren't exactly my strong suit," she admitted.

"You don't have any of your own?"

Caroline thought fleetingly of the computer she'd created, nursed and educated, but it wasn't the same thing at all. "No. If I did, I might have handled this situation better. I've never been around children before."

"You're kidding. No brothers or sisters?"

"None."

"No friends with kids?"

"None that they bring to work." Caroline realized how sterile that made her life sound, so she quickly shifted the subject. "Look, obviously I'm the last person anyone would look to for advice on child rearing, but don't you think you should teach Ruthann not to talk to strangers?"

He chuckled. "Oh, she knows all about that—she just hasn't learned selectivity. If you had approached her and tried to carry her away, she probably would have screamed her head off and kicked you in the shins. She thinks that if she makes contact, though, it's all right. We're working on it, but it's hard when they're that age."

"I'm sure you're right," Caroline said lamely because she wasn't qualified to venture an opinion.

"Car'line! Car'line!"

The door to the ladies' room opened and Ruthann burst out, tugging on her sister's arm as she tried to reach her new friend.

Mitch squatted and held out his arms. "Come here, Ruthann. You've caused enough trouble for one day."

Janis let go and Ruthann flew to her father. "Hi, Daddy." She jumped onto his knee and gave him a sloppy kiss.

"You had quite an adventure, didn't you, young lady?"

She nodded. "I was playing hide-and-seek with Pop, but he didn't come find me."

"That's because you forgot to tell him you were playing," Mitch said patiently. "Don't ever do that again, okay?"

The little girl nodded gravely and got a hug that nearly swallowed her whole.

Caroline had never seen anything quite as incongruous. The broad-shouldered cop with the rugged face, gravelly voice, big hands and a gun neatly tucked at his spine was incredibly gentle. There was a softness about him when he looked at his daughter that Caroline found strangely touching.

"Now, say thank-you to Dr. Hunter for helping you," Mitch instructed.

Ruthann frowned. "Who's Dr. Hunter?"

Caroline found herself bending on one knee to reach the little girl's level. "I'm Dr. Hunter."

"No, you're Car'line," she replied with a shake of her blond curls. She looked at her father. "Car'line's nice, Daddy."

Mitch met Caroline's eyes. "Yeah, I think so, too," he said quietly.

Maybe it was a combination of that deep voice and those melting eyes, or maybe it was just an aberration, but an unexpected flush of heat washed through Caroline when he looked at her. She felt her face growing red and she stood up quickly, backing away from the family and the strange emotions she was experiencing. It simply wasn't logical that a Neanderthal cop with a couple of kids could make her feel so unsettled.

"If you'll excuse me, I was on my way to freshen up before all this happened. I'd better hurry or I'll miss the presentation. It's been—" She hesitated. She couldn't exactly say it had been nice meeting them, but it hadn't really been unpleasant, either. "—an experience I certainly won't forget."

"Thank you, Dr. Hunter," Mitch said, rising with Ruthann in his arms.

"Yes, thank you," Janis said, stepping forward nervously. "I'm really sorry my dad pulled a gun on you and all."

Caroline read the embarrassment oozing from every pore of the girl's body and felt sorry for her. "It's all right, Miss Grogan. He didn't pull his weapon—he was just protecting Ruthann. Now, you'd better get back inside, too. You wouldn't want to miss the judging. I'll see you later." She cast a quick, nervous glance at Mitch, then disappeared into the ladies' room.

Janis turned and glared at her father. "Thanks a lot, Dad. There goes any chance I had of winning."

Mitch was still watching Caroline Hunter and feeling as if he'd just been hit by a friendly truck. "Lighten up, Angelface. The judging results have already been tabulated. Dr. Hunter can't possibly hold this against you."

"You hope," Janis snapped as she trudged past him. "Come on. Let's go back before you decide to play Dirty Harry again."

Mitch shook his head as he followed his daughter, but he was still thinking about Caroline Hunter. She was something else, indeed; a soft-spoken, poised beauty with the most incredible whiskey-colored eyes Mitch had ever seen. And what she could do with those eyes!

They sparkled with humor and intelligence in a way that Mitch would never have expected from a computer genius. Most of the ones he'd come across were a lot like Janis— they took themselves and the world so seriously that there wasn't room for things like warmth and humor. Yet Caroline Hunter had been able to laugh at herself and at Mitch without making him feel like a fool.

And the way she'd flushed with embarrassment and retreated so quickly when he'd looked at her . . . but not before he'd seen her reaction to his compliment. Mitch hadn't generated that kind of response in a woman in longer than he cared to remember. It felt good to know that he wasn't completely over the hill where the opposite sex was concerned.

What would it take, he wondered, to engineer another meeting with the fascinating Dr. Hunter? She worked in the computer industry and Mitch investigated computer crimes. If he put his mind to it, he could probably come up with something. A couple of tantalizing possibilities danced through his imagination before he came to his senses.

The very idea was ridiculous, Mitch told himself. He didn't have time to pursue a woman and it had been so long that he'd probably forgotten how it was done, anyway. And besides that, he had three kids to think about. There wasn't room for anyone else in his life right now, no matter how beautiful, intelligent or sensitive that woman might be.

Then he remembered the way she'd blushed, and he wondered what it would take to adjust his schedule.

CHAPTER THREE

"ALL RIGHT, Dad, she won. Can we go home now?" Sam asked, shuffling restlessly from one foot to the other.

Mitch gave his son a wilting look. "After the stunt you pulled this afternoon, I wouldn't be too anxious to get home if I were you. Just be patient and let your sister relish her victory. She's earned it."

They were standing back from the display table, where a radiant Janis was putting IVAR through his paces for a ring of spectators crowded around the table. The judging was over; Janis had a blue ribbon pinned to the lapel of her dress and Mitch had a one-thousand-dollar scholarship certificate in his coat pocket. First thing tomorrow it would go into his safe-deposit box at the bank.

"She looks like she's about to bust, doesn't she?" Pop asked, grinning proudly.

"Yeah, she does," Mitch replied, absently running his hand over Ruthann's back as she slept with her head on his shoulder. "But I don't know what pleased her more—winning or having Caroline Hunter present her with the ribbon."

"That was just the icing on the cake. You know, son, it's a good thing for you that she won," Pop said. He knew all about the incident in the hall because Janis had moaned and fretted about it right up until the moment she'd been awarded first prize. "You'd have been dead meat if she'd lost."

"She couldn't lose, Pop. That little contraption of hers is just too amazing."

"I couldn't agree more, Lieutenant Grogan."

The woman's voice startled Mitch and he looked around to find Caroline Hunter standing right behind him. He moved a little to allow her room beside him.

"Hello again," he said, wondering why he was so pleased to see her. He'd wanted a chance to thank her for awarding Janis first prize, but that didn't have anything to do with the sudden jolt of excitement that leaped through him.

"Hello." Caroline smiled at him, hoping she didn't look quite as nervous as she felt. Grogan's eyes really were quite disturbing. She found it much easier to look at the little girl who was sound asleep in Mitch's arms with her head lolling against his shoulder. "I see that Ruthann is fascinated by her sister's victory."

"Too much excitement," he said, wondering how it was possible for a thirty-eight-year-old man to feel like a tongue-tied teenager. All during the presentation ceremony Mitch had divided his time between soothing Janis and watching Dr. Hunter on the dais. He'd spent fifteen intriguing minutes trying to imagine what the legs beneath her long skirt looked like, and now he felt slightly embarrassed by the tantalizing conclusions he'd drawn. "Um, Dr. Hunter, this is my father, Mitchell Grogan, and my son, Sam."

Caroline held out her hand to the elder Grogan and offered Sam a reserved smile. "It's nice to meet you both. You must be very proud of Janis."

"Oh, we are," Pop said, grinning from ear to ear. "She's a hard worker, that girl. And too smart for her own good sometimes."

Caroline understood completely. "Being different isn't always easy."

She glanced at Mitch as she said it, and he realized she was speaking from experience. When she was a girl, she had undoubtedly been at the top of her class, too, separated from the other kids by an intellect that others found intimidating. For Janis, that meant a certain degree of loneliness. He wondered if it had been the same for Dr. Hunter.

"I'm glad you're still here," he told her. "I know Janis wants to thank you and the other judges."

"No thanks are necessary. She deserved to win." Caroline hesitated. She had a very specific reason for seeking out Janis Grogan and her father, but she wasn't entirely comfortable with it. "Lieutenant Grogan—"

"Mitch," he reminded her.

His warm smile made Caroline wish they could keep things on a more formal footing, but she couldn't bring herself to be rude. "Mitch, if you and Janis have the time after the crowd clears, I'd like to speak with you for a moment."

Mitch frowned, puzzled. "Sure. There's not a problem with the judging, is there? I mean, this wasn't a mistake or—"

"No, of course not! All three judges were in complete agreement on the winner. It's an extraordinary piece of work."

A man standing near them at the end of the table heard her comment and frowned at her. "I don't get it," he said grumpily. "What's the big deal? It's just a little mechanical robot."

Mitch glanced at Janis, hoping she hadn't heard the man, but when her face fell, Mitch had to fight the urge to flatten him. How could anyone be so insensitive to the feelings of a child?

Caroline saw how the comment affected Janis, too, and she realized that the girl wasn't going to speak up to defend herself. "Oh, but you're wrong, sir. IVAR is much more than that," she said.

But the man wasn't going to let go. "Why? We got robots at the plant where I work that do a helluva lot more than that contraption."

"Do they respond to spoken commands?" Caroline asked. "Can they make decisions? IVAR does."

"What decisions? It picks up a bunch of kiddy toys. Big deal."

A murmur went through the crowd and Caroline couldn't tell whether the general sentiment supported the man's position or not. Beside her, she felt the mounting tension in Mitch Grogan, and when he suddenly passed little Ruthann to his father, Caroline suspected he was about to jump into the argument to defend his daughter—probably with his fists.

Caroline detested violence, but she really couldn't blame Grogan for wanting to punch the man. He was being offensive and rude. There was a better way to handle the situation, though.

Caroline looked at Janis. "Would you mind if I joined you back there, Miss Grogan?" she asked, stepping out of the ranks of the spectators to join Janis behind the display table. "Perhaps we can show this gentleman what makes your Integrated Voice Activated Robot so special."

"Of course, Dr. Hunter," Janis said, her eyes shining with surprise and gratitude. She moved aside to make room for her.

"What do you see on this table?" Caroline asked the man.

"Like I said, it's a bunch of kiddy toys."

"Specifically, what do you see?" she asked, picking up a bright yellow plastic pyramid from the ring of six objects that surrounded the funny-looking box on wheels that Janis called IVAR. "What is this?"

"It's a pyramid," the man said smugly.

Caroline picked up another object. "And this?"

"A cylinder."

She held both in front of her. "How do you know the difference between the two?"

He looked at her as though she were monumentally stupid. "One is shaped like a triangle and the other is round."

Caroline put the pyramid down and picked up a third object that looked like a small soccer ball. "But this is round, too, isn't it?"

The man was growing nervous. "Yeah."

"How do you know the difference between a round cylinder and a round ball?"

"One is...long and the other is...round," he said grumpily. "Hell, everybody knows the difference."

"How?"

The man shifted from one foot to the other, and Mitch couldn't keep from smiling. He wasn't sure where Caroline was going, but he knew instinctively that she was getting ready to dissect this big oaf with a razor-sharp instrument—her mind. The oaf knew it, too. Mitch folded his arms and watched. He was going to enjoy this.

"Hell, I don't know how we know the difference," the man snapped. "We just know."

Caroline was serenity personified as she held out the cylinder to bring it to the crowd's attention. "Perhaps we know the difference because a cylinder is the standard shape of a baby bottle—one of the first objects we come into contact with as infants. Later, as we develop language, we put a name to it, just as we put a name to the ball and the pyramid, the square and all the other shapes you see on this table."

"That's right," the man said as though he'd expressed the idea himself.

"It's a matter of visual perception," Caroline went on. "Our eyes see the shapes and our brain interprets the shapes, allowing us to call them by the appropriate names. It seems so simple to us, but imagine if you will, a box—not a human being, not a baby that nursed with a bottle or played with a ball—but a simple box. No eyes, no ears, no brain synapses, no experience, nothing. Just a box."

Caroline returned the objects to their original places in the circle and placed her hand on IVAR. "How do you teach a box the difference between a cylinder and a ball? In fact, how do you teach it *what* those objects are in the first place? A computer has no frame of reference. It's a blank slate. You can put it on wheels and give it a movable claw capable of picking up objects, but how do you give it eyes? How do you make it hear you? How do you teach it the meaning of words that we take for granted?"

Caroline's gaze took in the entire crowd. "That's what Janis Grogan has done, ladies and gentlemen. She has taught a box to see, listen, comprehend, obey, and most importantly, to learn. IVAR doesn't perform by rote, it interprets commands and makes decisions."

To emphasize that, she asked Janis to put her robot through its paces one more time. Janis issued a command for IVAR to retrieve the cylinder and the little box rolled across the table with a groan and a clatter. It retrieved the object and dropped it in the center of the circle. Caroline nodded at Janis and the girl issued a few more commands: Return the cylinder; retrieve the triangle; retrieve the square. Then Caroline shuffled all the objects, placing them in different positions and had Janis give IVAR the same commands. The little robot jerked and whined gracelessly, but it did everything Janis told it to.

But the crowd didn't seem terribly impressed. It was just a clumsy black box playing fetch. Obviously these people had seen too many science-fiction movies. They were so accustomed to talking androids and sophisticated computers that to them, IVAR seemed prehistoric by comparison.

But Caroline lived on the cutting edge of existing technology, not science fiction, and she knew for a fact that nothing like Janis Grogan's project existed in the real world—with one possible exception that was very close to Caroline's heart.

"Ladies and gentlemen, let me interpret what you've just seen," she said, striving for patience. It wasn't too hard to achieve, since she'd been trying for years to make laymen understand her own scientific achievements. "IVAR may seem outlandishly simple, but believe me when I tell you that I personally know a number of scientists around the world who have been attempting—with limited success—to do what this high school student has accomplished."

That brought an approving murmur from the crowd. Caroline scanned their faces and found a broad, proud smile on Mitch Grogan's face. Good, she thought. He had a remarkable daughter, and he *should* be proud of her.

Caroline looked at the disgruntled man who had started this whole thing. "Sir, the industrial robots where you work perform by rote. They do exactly what they are told, their movements predetermined by a fixed set of commands. They move ten centimeters left and six millimeters forward because they are told to do so by manual computer input. They don't move independently and they don't make decisions. IVAR does, and that's why this project won first place."

The crowd clapped enthusiastically, and Janis accepted the applause with a beaming smile. When Caroline added her own applause to it, Mitch noticed that tears sprang into his daughter's eyes. This was a moment she would never forget as long as she lived—this high praise from a woman she worshiped. Mitch didn't know whether Dr. Hunter had stepped forward to defend Janis or her own decision as one of the judges, but it really didn't matter what motivated her. The results were the same, and Mitch could have kissed her for the incredible gift she'd just given his daughter.

By the time the crowd dispersed, Janis had control of her emotions, but she seemed too tongue-tied to speak to the eminent scientist who had leaped to her defense. Mitch understood what she was feeling, because Caroline Hunter left him a little at a loss for words, too.

"That was very gracious of you, Doctor," he said, stepping up to the table.

"Yes, thank you," Janis said.

Caroline smiled at her. "I was only trying to help. You couldn't say all of that without sounding conceited, so someone had to say it for you."

Janis blushed. "I appreciate it."

Caroline looked at Mitch and got down to the reason she'd come over here in the first place. "You know, Lieutenant Grogan, I wasn't exaggerating when I said that a number of robotics experts are attempting to do what Janis has done. In fact, I have a team at MediaTech that would love the opportunity to talk to your daughter and examine IVAR."

Mitch knew how extraordinary IVAR was, but this surprised him. "Really?"

Caroline nodded. "If Janis is willing."

Janis seemed even more stunned than her father, but she managed a nod. "I'd like that."

"Good. If you'd like to bring IVAR out to the lab sometime, I'll arrange a meeting with my robotics team." As an afterthought, she added, "And if you're interested, I'd be happy to give you a tour of MediaTech and introduce you to my computer project."

Janis's mouth opened, closed, then opened again. "The OHARA?" she finally gasped. "I could see the OHARA?"

The expression on the girl's face made Caroline glad she'd offered. "If you want to."

"When?"

"Any time it's convenient for you."

Janis looked at her father eagerly. "Tomorrow, Daddy? Could you drive me out tomorrow after school? Please? It's your day off," she reminded him.

Mitch couldn't have refused a plea like that if his life had depended on it, and he really didn't want to. An experience like this could be invaluable to his daughter. "Of course, Angelface. We could be there about four if that's all right with Dr. Hunter."

He looked at Caroline for verification and she nodded. "That would be fine. I'll leave your names at the security desk and tell the head of robotics to expect you."

He grinned. "Considering the way we met, this is very generous of you, Dr. Hunter."

"Oh, don't give that a second thought. That was the most excitement I've had in ages." It took a considerable effort to drag her gaze away from those incredible eyes of his, but she did it. "Well, Janis, congratulations again," she said, shaking hands with the girl, who seemed stunned by the gesture. "I'll see you tomorrow."

"I'll see you tomorrow, too, I guess," Mitch said warmly, holding out his hand.

Caroline hesitated just a second, remembering what it had felt like the last time, and when she touched him again, it was exactly the same. It seemed that her professional calm had abandoned her just when she needed it most. "I suppose so, Lieutenant."

"I thought you were going to call me Mitch," he said softly.

Caroline didn't know how anyone could make such a simple statement sound so sexy, but Grogan did. "See you tomorrow...Mitch." She knew her voice sounded as shaky as she felt, but there was nothing she could do about it. She said a hasty farewell to the rest of the Grogan family and moved off, blending into the crowd at the exit.

"That's quite a lady," Pop said, watching her go.

"Uh, yeah," Mitch replied, so absorbed in watching Caroline Hunter that he didn't notice the speculative look his father gave him.

"A letter of recommendation from somebody like that would look good to a college scholarship committee, wouldn't it?" Pop asked.

"Very good," Mitch said absently.

"I guess that's a real good reason to take Janis out to MediaTech."

Mitch just nodded.

"You know, son, if you've got things to do, I'd be happy to drive Janis out there."

That brought Mitch out of his stupor. "Oh, no, Pop. Thanks, but I'll handle it," he said quickly.

Pop Grogan chuckled. "Yeah, I'll just bet you will."

Mitch looked at his father and found a mischievous twinkle in the older man's eyes. He'd forgotten what a mind reader Pop was. "She can help Janis," he said defensively.

Pop patted his son's arm and nodded soberly. "Whatever you say, son. I know there's nothing you wouldn't do for your kids."

Pop was right. He'd do anything for the kids. He had made sacrifices for them and was prepared to make more. He had devoted every spare minute to them for four years now, because kids had to come first, no matter what.

But as Mitch glanced again at Caroline Hunter's retreating form, he realized that maybe it was time he did something for himself, too.

The way this was shaping up, tomorrow could be the best day off Mitch had had in years.

CAROLINE'S UPBRINGING hadn't been what anyone would call orthodox. Her parents were two of the world's foremost genetics researchers and neither one of them had made much time for their daughter. A succession of tutors had taken care of her education, and the loneliness of that sterile environment had instilled self-sufficiency in her.

Her parents had expected her to excel and had very generously allowed her to choose any field of endeavor—so long as it was worthwhile and scientific in nature, of course. The creative arts were to be shunned at all costs, and sports were discouraged, save for a vigorous daily regimen of calisthenics because a healthy body was essential to a healthy, active mind.

In short, anything serious was encouraged; anything frivolous or fun was to be avoided like the plague.

Fortunately, two things had sustained Caroline through an otherwise dismal childhood. The first was her own keen intellect that had given her an unquenchable thirst to learn how the universe worked. The second was her Aunt Liddy—Lydia Tomlinson McMartin Birch Geary Van-Horn, to be exact.

"I sound more like a law firm every day, don't I?" Liddy used to joke whenever she added a new husband's name to her own. She'd had four of them at the time of her death, and had bragged shamelessly of the countless "offers" she had received in between marriages.

Caroline's mother, Dr. Justine Tomlinson-Hunter, had viewed her own sister as a disgraceful bohemian, but Caroline had adored her colorful, free-spirited aunt because Liddy had been responsible for every ounce of pure unadulterated fun Caroline had ever had. She had never known when Liddy was going to blow into town and whisk her off on an adventure.

Of course, Caroline had always protested because Liddy was taking her away from her studies, and her parents would be furious if they learned about it, but she had secretly treasured every moment she spent with her capricious aunt. Caroline had worshiped her, and Liddy's death seven years ago had been a devastating loss.

For some strange reason, Caroline couldn't stop thinking about Liddy that next morning. In fact, she felt almost as though her aunt were sitting on her shoulder whispering in her ear.

The strange sensation had started as she was dressing for work. She had pulled a conservative, long-skirted brown suit out of her closet and Liddy had exclaimed, "Oh, for Pete's sake, Sunshine. Lighten up! You're too pretty to hide behind those ugly colors. Be daring. Be bold!"

In response, Caroline had chewed thoughtfully on her lower lip and pulled out a colorful scarf to wear with the suit.

Liddy had just laughed. "That's your idea of daring? Didn't you learn anything from me, Sunshine?"

The sensation of having Aunt Liddy in the room with her had been so strong and wonderful that Caroline had succumbed. She returned the dull outfit to the closet and pulled out the white and navy pinstriped double-breasted jacket and the short navy skirt she'd bought the last time her aunt had popped into Caroline's head for a visit.

By Liddy's bohemian standards, the suit was conservative, but it was about as daring as Caroline could manage and still be suitably dressed for the workplace. She had applied her makeup—in more moderate amounts than Liddy had taught her to use years ago—and added a bit more curl to her short wavy hair. She put on comfortable navy shoes with sensibly low heels, slipped a red handkerchief into her jacket pocket, and was ready for work.

Not once that morning did she allow herself to wonder why the seldom-acknowledged Aunt Liddy part of her personality had surfaced today of all days, but she knew deep down that it had a lot to do with the visitor she was expecting at four that afternoon.

Caroline couldn't make any sense out of her reaction to Mitch Grogan. Last night she had devoted so much time to figuring it out, she *should* have come up with a logical explanation, but it still eluded her. She had never found the muscular, more-brawn-than-brains type appealing, but she couldn't deny that she was attracted to the man whose tenderness with his children was at complete odds with his rough-hewn appearance.

Of course, the fact that he had seemed attracted to her had no bearing on the equation she had chewed on all night long. Blond, blue-eyed, earthy men like Grogan were undoubtedly accustomed to having women fawn over them, and Caroline was embarrassed that she had become so flustered by a simple sexy look and a handshake. He was probably as conceited as he was handsome, and he was raising three children to boot. Since Caroline had no desire to complicate her life with romantic entanglements, excising such a man from her thoughts should have been a simple matter.

But it wasn't. And now, as if thinking about him all night wasn't enough, she was having a hard time concentrating on her work this morning, too.

The outfit she had worn didn't make working any easier, either, because everyone from the janitor to Bob Stafford had noticed the change in her appearance—and had commented on it.

Bob, not the most observant of men, asked her if she had done something different with her hair, but every other person she had seen that morning had commented on her short skirt or her suit in general—and in one instance, her anatomy. Caroline had flushed with chagrin when she ran into Tony Beecroft in the hall and he exclaimed, "My God, Dr. Hunter, you've got legs!"

She finally became so self-conscious that she donned a long white lab coat—something she rarely did unless she was working in the high-security area. The protective garment put an end to the comments and Caroline was finally able to get some work done without feeling that everyone was staring at her. In fact, she was totally unaware that the afternoon was nearly gone until security buzzed her at four to inform her that Mitchell and Janis Grogan were waiting for her in the lobby.

Trying to convince herself she wasn't the least bit nervous, Caroline hurried downstairs, stopping along the way just long enough to make certain that every button of her lab coat was securely fastened.

Aunt Liddy scolded her for being chicken but Caroline convinced herself she simply didn't want to feed Grogan's ego by giving him the impression she had done anything special with her appearance just because of him. It didn't occur to her that the issue was irrelevant since Grogan had no way of knowing how she normally dressed for work, and Aunt Liddy didn't point out that comforting bit of logic to her.

Grogan was dressed much as he had been the day before, in a sports jacket and casual slacks, but today he had added a tie. Even so, he still looked more like a physical education teacher than a police lieutenant. He was chatting with Ed Newton, MediaTech's chief of security, as Caroline came into the lobby, and Janis was standing beside him looking excited and just a little nervous.

Caroline knew the feeling.

"Hello, Janis. Mitch." She mustered a friendly smile, but as she moved toward them, she slipped her hands into her pockets just to be on the safe side. She didn't want to shake hands with Grogan and risk a repeat of that childish tingling sensation she had experienced yesterday.

The father and daughter turned to greet her, and Mitch's welcoming smile was every bit as devastating as Caroline remembered. "Hello, Dr. Hunter," they said in unison.

"Hi, Doc," Ed chimed in.

Caroline glanced at the security chief because it was safer than looking into Grogan's alarming blue eyes. "I hope you're not giving our guests a hard time, Ed," she commented lightly, then explained, "He gets paid to be suspicious of everybody."

"Oh, I'd say we're pretty safe with these two," Ed replied. "I doubt that anyone would accuse the head of the Hilliard PD Computer Crimes Division of industrial espionage."

That bit of information left Caroline dumbfounded and she looked at Mitch in disbelief. "You're a computer cop?" When he laughed at her reaction, Caroline blushed. "I'm sorry. I didn't mean that the way it sounded. You just don't seem like—I mean, you're not—"

Mitch bailed her out. "It's okay, Dr. Hunter. I know I look like someone who would be more at home busting drug dealers in dark alleys. Just goes to prove that appearances can be deceiving."

That was the understatement of the year, Caroline thought, feeling foolish. But she was also impressed. "I suppose you must have considerable expertise with computers, then."

Mitch shrugged. "A crime is a crime, whether it's the theft of a diamond tiara or a silicon computer chip." He grinned. "But I do play a mean game of Super Mario Brothers."

He was teasing her, and Caroline didn't blame him. "Well, this tour should be right up your alley, then," she replied, regaining her composure. She glanced at the two boxes at Mitch's feet. "Is that IVAR?"

"Yes, ma'am," Janis replied.

Caroline turned to her security chief. "Ed, would you get someone to take these up to robotics for us? And make sure they're careful. This is precious cargo."

"I'll handle it myself," he promised.

"Good." She turned back to her guests. "Shall we get started?"

"Yes, please," Janis answered.

Mitch saluted Ed Newton and joined Caroline and Janis as they started out of the lobby.

"I take it you and Ed already know each other," Caroline commented.

"Yeah, we've met," Mitch replied. "He attended a seminar I conducted last year on internal security and industrial espionage. And I try to keep up with who's who within my jurisdiction—the good guys as well as the bad guys."

Mitch was walking beside Caroline, and she realized with some surprise that he really wasn't a great deal taller than she was. It was just his sheer bulk that made her feel dwarfed by his size. "Any bad guys you'd care to warn me about, or have you got them all tucked safely behind bars?"

"I wish," he said with a chuckle. "Unfortunately, there are a lot of people out there looking to make a quick buck. It seems like every time we catch one, two more take his place."

"Or hers," Caroline commented lightly.

Mitch chuckled. "Naturally. Believe me, Dr. Hunter, my team has an equal-opportunity arrest record."

"Why don't you call me Caroline," she said, then glanced at his daughter. "You, too, Janis."

The girl looked at her shyly, then her eyes darted away. "All right...Caroline."

They turned a corner and Caroline started their tour in

earnest, guiding them through a rabbit warren of offices and labs on the ground floor.

"I'm afraid I won't be able to show you too much down here," she told them. "MediaTech does a lot of research for the government—everything from communications networks to weather satellites—and most of it is done under strict security. The cold war may be over, but Uncle Sam is still paranoid about security."

"MediaTech specializes in fiber-optics research, doesn't it?" Janis asked.

"That's right. We've found some remarkable uses that go way beyond telephone communications."

"Like the OHARA?"

Caroline was impressed by the extent of the girl's knowledge. "That's right. The OHARA uses light waves instead of electronic chips, making it faster and more efficient than standard computers. It also gives us an unlimited storage capacity."

"Will I really get to see your computer?" Janis asked hopefully.

"Of course. I'll introduce you after you've met with my staff," she promised. "I told them all about IVAR, and they're very anxious to ask you a few questions. In fact, you'll probably have to slap their hands once or twice to keep them from dismantling IVAR to see how it works."

"I brought all of my schematics," Janis told her.

"Good."

"But Dr. Hunter..."

Caroline heard the hesitancy in the girl's voice and stopped. "What is it, Janis?"

"Will they really be interested in what I have to say?"

She nodded. "Of course they will. I wouldn't have invited you here if I didn't think so. Now, come on. Let's go upstairs and give my team a lesson in robotics."

CHAPTER FOUR

AN HOUR LATER, every hint of Janis's nervousness had disappeared. Caroline's robotics team had seemed a bit aloof and skeptical at first, but that attitude had vanished very quickly. Within minutes, they were asking questions so complex that Mitch became totally lost, but he didn't care because he could see Janis was holding her own. They seemed to forget that she was only fifteen years old and treated her like a colleague.

Even Mitch was impressed by his daughter's performance. But as proud as he was, he also felt a little sad, too. His brilliant little girl was growing up right before his eyes, and it made him realize that he would soon be losing her to college and a career. It wouldn't be long before she didn't need her daddy anymore.

To escape that depressing thought, Mitch focused on Caroline Hunter. She was in her element here and there wasn't a trace of the shy hesitancy he had noticed in her meeting with him yesterday. She had a reserved charm with just a hint of aloofness that attracted more than it repelled; and all of it was underlaid with an unstudied, probably unconscious, sensuality.

Mitch liked her a lot. And why shouldn't he? Caroline had gone out of her way to give his daughter a day she would never forget. That alone was reason enough for him to feel kindly disposed toward her. The fact that she increased his adrenaline was just icing on the cake.

He would have liked her a lot more, though, if she hadn't been wearing that damned long lab coat. He still didn't have a clue whether or not her legs were as sexy as his instincts told him they were.

He straightened abruptly as Caroline spoke quietly with one of the team members, then turned toward him. The radiant smile she was wearing as she crossed the room made Mitch forget he was an old man of nearly forty with three kids.

"How are you doing over here?" she asked him.

"*What* am I doing here would be a better question," he replied with a grin. "You guys left me behind about half an hour ago."

Caroline turned and looked at his daughter. "She's really something, Mitch."

"I know that, but it's always nice to have an expert opinion," he told her, keeping his voice low. "You're probably getting tired of hearing me say thank-you, but I want you to know how much this means to me. Janis is never going to forget this experience."

"Thank *you* for bringing her," Caroline countered. "My people are getting as much out of this as she is."

"That's hard to believe."

"But it's true. She's a very gifted young lady." She hesitated a moment as though wrestling with a decision, then gestured toward the door. "Can we talk privately for a few minutes?"

"Uh, sure." He glanced at Janis, but Caroline read his thoughts.

"Don't worry about her. Dr. Brewster will call down to my office as soon as they're finished."

"Okay." Mitch followed her into the corridor, wondering what was on her mind.

She didn't waste any time getting down to business. "Mitch, how old is Janis?" she asked as she guided them down the hall toward the main programming lab.

"Fifteen."

"Her IQ is in the one sixty range?"

Mitch smiled. "That's a good guess. One sixty-six."

"And she's about to complete her junior year in high school?"

"That's right," Mitch replied, unable to imagine where this was leading. "She skipped the third grade and would have been promoted even further if my wife and I would have permitted it."

Caroline looked up at him. "Why didn't you? It must have been obvious quite early that she was gifted."

"We held her back because we wanted her childhood to be as normal as possible," he explained. "Kids who advance too far too quickly sometimes have socialization problems. We didn't want that to happen to Janis."

"That was probably wise of you," she replied.

Mitch heard something in her voice that made him curious. "What about you, Caroline? When did you graduate from high school?"

"I didn't. My parents never entrusted me to the public school system. I had tutors at home until I was twelve, then I started college."

"At twelve? You're kidding?"

Caroline smiled. "I assure you, I'm not. It wasn't as outlandish as you might think, though. My parents were teaching and doing research at Duke University at the time, so it was a simple matter to enroll me in classes there."

Mitch couldn't imagine it. "That must have been pretty scary for a twelve-year-old."

"Scary?" Caroline thought it over. "No, I don't recall being scared." *Just lonely,* she almost added.

They entered the main programming lab, which was nearly deserted, since it was well after five o'clock. "Janis told me you had your first doctorate before you were nineteen," Mitch commented.

"That's right." He had neatly turned the tables on her, asking questions instead of answering them, and Caroline was uncomfortable. "My office is right there," she said, picking up the pace.

Mitch recognized evasion when he heard it. Either he had struck a nerve or Caroline just didn't like talking about herself. One of these days he would find out which.

They reached her office and Caroline preceded him into the empty room. As she moved around the desk, Mitch took a quick glance at his surroundings and was a little disappointed to find the room so ordinary. It hardly seemed like the inner sanctum of a designer of high-tech computers. Like Janis, he had really been hoping to get a glimpse of the OHARA system, but the computer on her desk looked a lot like the ordinary PC he had at home.

"Hello, Caroline."

The woman's voice startled Mitch. Years of training himself to be prepared for any dangerous situation made him tense up, but Caroline didn't seem at all surprised. "Hello, Scarlett," she answered.

"You have a guest with you. I don't believe we have been introduced yet."

Mitch looked around, puzzled. The room was empty, no doubt about it. The voice was slightly tinny, but it didn't have the hollow sound of something coming over an intercom. In fact, it sounded startlingly human. He looked at Caroline, who was smiling broadly at his reaction.

"Scarlett, this is Lieutenant Mitch Grogan."

"Hello, Lieutenant Grogan. Welcome to MediaTech."

Mitch finally looked at the computer. "Well, I'll be damned," he muttered. "Um...hello...Scarlett."

"Caroline, what security designation should I assign to Lieutenant Grogan?"

"Level One," she replied. "Would you care to explain what that means to our guest?"

"Certainly," the computer responded placidly. "Lieutenant, Level One is a limited security clearance that entitles you to converse with me in general areas of information only. You are not permitted access to any of my base programming and I am prohibited from storing any input from you without Caroline's permission. Do you have any questions you'd like to ask me?"

Mitch felt as though he had slipped into a Star Trek episode. "Uh, no thank you, Scarlett. No questions."

"In that case, may I ask you one, Lieutenant?"

This was astonishing! A curious computer! "Of course," he replied as a broad grin spread across his face. If this was on the level, it was the most remarkable thing he had ever seen in his life.

"With what branch of the military are you affiliated, sir?" Scarlett asked.

Mitch looked at Caroline, but she didn't seem upset that her computer had made an erroneous assumption. She took a seat and gestured for Mitch to do likewise, wearing a smile that seemed to say, "You're on your own."

Mitch sat. "I'm not with the military, Scarlett. I'm a ranking officer with the Hilliard Police Department."

"Then you are in the field of law enforcement."

"That's right."

"I see." The computer paused. "I was not aware that law enforcement employed a system of military ranks," Scarlett confessed. "Caroline, this indicates that there is a gap in my education. Will that be rectified soon?"

"Yes, Scarlett. You will eventually be programmed with a comprehensive law enforcement data base."

"Good. May I file this new information, in the meantime?"

"Yes."

"Thank you. Will Lieutenant Grogan be participating in my education?"

Caroline shot Mitch an apologetic glance. "No decision has been made on who will create that data base, Scarlett."

"If he is not employed at MediaTech and he is not here as a data base consultant, why is he here? Is he a friend of yours?"

Mitch knew an opportunity when he saw one. "Yes," he replied, shooting a devilish grin at Caroline.

"A boyfriend?" Scarlett asked.

"No!" Caroline sat up in her chair very straight. "He is a recent acquaintance."

"I see. I do not recall that you have ever brought a friend to work, Caroline," the computer commented mildly. "It is nice to meet another one."

Mitch frowned as he tried to follow Scarlett's logic, but it didn't make sense. "Scarlett, if you've never met any of Caroline's friends, why would you describe me as *another* one?"

"I am Caroline's friend, too."

This was unbelievable. "How do you define the word 'friend,' Scarlett?" he asked cautiously, looking at Caroline to be sure she wasn't going to register a protest. Now that the computer understood that he wasn't her boyfriend, she showed no signs of objecting.

"A friend is one attached to another by affection or esteem. It also means a favored companion," Scarlett replied.

"Thank you, Scarlett," Caroline said. "Now, if you don't mind, I'd like to have a few minutes alone with my guest."

"Very well. Good afternoon, Lieutenant Grogan. It was a pleasure meeting you."

Mitch grinned. "It was nice meeting you, too, Scarlett."

Three lights went out on the computer and Mitch looked at Caroline, stunned. "That's amazing."

"Thank you."

He shook his head. He had a million questions and didn't know where to begin. "How did you do it? How on earth did you manage to create something so lifelike? I thought we were at least ten years away from an advance like this."

"Ten years? No," Caroline replied. "We're hoping to launch the system within the next six months. As for the rest, well . . . those are closely guarded secrets."

"How did she know we were here?" he asked.

"There's a video imaging camera, a motion detector and a thermal scanning device implanted in the wall behind my desk."

"How did she know I was a stranger?"

"She has imaging files on everyone who comes in contact with her. She simply compared you with the people she knows and determined that you were someone new."

Mitch shook his head. "Amazing. A computer capable of understanding the concept of friendship. It's unbelievable, Caroline," he said again, then he started chuckling as it hit him. "Scarlett OHARA?"

Caroline blushed. "The OHARA acronym was something of a fluke—she's an *optical* fiber-based unit with *heuristic algorithmic reasoning architecture.* Once I put that acronym together for the entire system, Scarlett seemed like a logical nickname."

"I like it," he told her with a grin. "It indicates that her creator has a certain degree of originality and a romantic streak a mile wide."

No one had ever accused Caroline of being a romantic before and she wasn't entirely comfortable with the label—particularly coming from this man, who had such an odd ability to set her senses stirring. She decided it was time to get down to business. "Why don't we get back to the subject of Janis," she suggested.

"All right," Mitch replied, though he couldn't help being disappointed. There was something he liked very much about the way Caroline blushed whenever he got the least bit personal. "What about Janis? Why all the questions and why did you want to speak to me privately?"

"As I was watching Janis interact with my staff, an idea came to me. In fact, it may even have been in my head on a subconscious level when I decided to invite her to come to MediaTech. I thought I should discuss it with you, though, before mentioning it to Janis."

"I'm intrigued. Go on," he said.

"School will be out in a few weeks, won't it?"

"Yes."

"How does Janis normally spend her summers?"

The question caught him off guard. "Doing normal kid stuff, mostly. Though last year, she did take a couple of classes at the junior college and she mentioned doing it again this summer. Why?"

"MediaTech has a summer intern program for college students," Caroline informed him. "The jobs have a very low security clearance, of course, and as a rule, the students don't interact with my department at all. In Janis's case, though, I might be willing to make an exception if she would be interested in working with my robotics staff—say, ten to fifteen hours a week?"

Mitch was stunned. This was the opportunity of a lifetime. "Are you serious?"

Caroline nodded. "Yes. Naturally, I would have to discuss it with Dr. Brewster, the head of the department, but I think he'll be agreeable now that he's seen what Janis is capable of accomplishing. She wouldn't have much responsibility, of course, but this could be an excellent learning experience for her, Mitch. And it would also give her a chance to continue her work on IVAR, perfecting and refining the system she has already created. If she plans to enter any of the national science competitions like the Westinghouse, this would certainly be a big help to her."

"Of course it would." Mitch was having trouble taking it all in. "This is an amazing offer, Caroline."

"Do you think she could handle it? She's very young, but she seems responsible and mature for her age."

"Oh, she is," he replied hastily. "I think Janis was born old and serious."

Caroline smiled. "I know what that feels like."

His answering smile made her flush inside. "Anyone who would name a computer Scarlett OHARA can't be *too* serious," he said with a shake of his head.

Caroline picked up a pen and began toying with it nervously. This was supposed to be a simple, straightforward business arrangement, but Mitch was making it hard for her to remember that. "Do you think Janis would be interested, then?" she asked, avoiding his eyes.

"Janis will be ecstatic. Surely you must realize that she worships you, Caroline."

That brought her startled gaze to his. "Worships me?"

"She's followed your career for years," he explained. "Just meeting you was the biggest thrill of her life. The chance to work with you will send her into orbit."

Caroline cleared her throat. "She wouldn't actually be working with me, Mitch. Let's be clear about this. If we decide to proceed, I would probably team her up with Andrea Norris, one of Dr. Brewster's senior assistants. Andrea is very patient and she has two teenagers of her own, so Janis should be quite comfortable with her. I'll look in on her regularly, but she wouldn't actually be working *with* me."

Mitch wondered why she found it necessary to repeat that, and why she seemed so tense all of a sudden. "I wouldn't expect you to take her under your wing personally, Caroline. I know how demanding your job must be."

"I'm glad you understand," she said with a nervous smile. Mitch was looking at her curiously, and when he didn't respond, Caroline felt obliged to explain, "It's just that I'm not comfortable around children, Mitch. I think I explained that to you yesterday."

"Yes, you did."

"Well, good. Janis is a remarkable young lady and I'd like very much to encourage and support her, but I don't feel qualified to take on a role as her personal mentor."

Her nervousness set off an alarm bell in Mitch's head. For some reason, children were Caroline Hunter's Achilles' heel. But why? Surely it wasn't just because she'd never been around them very much. "I don't think it makes a lot of difference whether you mentor her or not, Caroline. This would still be a valuable experience."

"Would transportation to and from MediaTech be a problem?" she asked.

"No. We'll work something out. My father is used to shuttling the kids here, there and everywhere. The women in our neighborhood call him the King of the Car Pool."

Caroline smiled politely. "I'm afraid the pay would be only five dollars an hour, but the work hours could be flexible. Two or three afternoons a week, perhaps?"

"That's fine." Mitch couldn't help but notice that their discussion had suddenly become very formal. "I won't mention this to Janis until after you've spoken with Dr. Brewster, but if you decide to proceed, I'll let Janis pick which afternoons would be most convenient for her."

"Good." Caroline stood. "Then I'll be in touch with you. I assume I can reach you through the police department."

"Precinct One," he said, puzzled by the distance Caroline had placed between them. One thing was sure, though. He was being dismissed. "If this works out, I don't know how I'll ever be able to thank you, Caroline," he said as he stood.

"No thanks are necessary. I'm sure Janis will prove to be a valuable member of the team."

"I hope so." Mitch knew he should return to Robotics and check on his daughter, but he didn't want to leave just yet. Caroline Hunter was no longer just a brilliant, beautiful woman who attracted him. She had become something of a mystery, too, and there was nothing Mitch liked more than a good puzzle. He had to find a way to unravel that puzzle, and in order to do that, he had to prolong his contact with her.

Instinct told him that asking her out on a date would be the wrong thing to do, so he had to think quick to come up with an alternative. "Um, listen. This may be presumptuous of me, but what you said earlier to Scarlett about a law enforcement data base—were you serious?"

"Yes. We want to give the OHARA system as many practical applications as possible. Given the computer's unlimited storage capacity, it will eventually become invaluable to the criminal justice system."

"How do you go about creating a data base for something like that?"

"We hire one or more professionals in various fields who work out a systematic progression of information, starting with the basics first and building on it, like an inverted pyramid. Then, we begin feeding Scarlett a little at a time," she explained, wondering why he had asked. "It's a very delicate procedure in the beginning because it's important that we not overload her."

"She could crash?"

"That's always a possibility," Caroline admitted reluctantly, "though at this point it's not likely. Her general information and logic data bases are very stable."

Mitch heard another warning bell in his head, but this time it didn't have anything to do with children or the attraction between them that seemed to make Caroline blush. This was something else entirely. Mitch would have staked his life that Scarlett's data base wasn't quite as stable as she claimed.

He stored that information without commenting on it. "So you're going to hire someone to teach Scarlett about police work. Tell me, Caroline, do you ever accept volunteers?"

Her eyes lit up. "Are you offering?"

"Maybe. I could certainly be tempted," he replied. "I have a pretty good working knowledge of computers. Nothing on this level, of course, but I know a little more than most and I certainly owe you for what you're offering Janis."

"Janis will be paid for her work," she reminded him.

Mitch shook his head. "Who are you kidding? She should be paying *you* for this kind of experience. My daughter is going to need big-money scholarships to go to a good college, and a work credit like MediaTech will look mighty impressive."

"True, but that still wouldn't mean you or Janis owe me anything. Creating a data base requires a great deal of work. Are you sure you'd want to take on something that requires so much of your time?"

Spare time was something Mitch didn't have a lot of, but this might be worth the extra effort—and not just as an excuse to get to know Caroline Hunter better. The OHARA system was going to create a worldwide high-tech revolution, and the thought of being involved with such an extraordinary event was irresistible.

"I think I could make the time," he replied.

Caroline thought over Mitch's offer. Dr. Caldwell was almost finished with the astronomy data base and a meteorologist was ready to begin his programming on weather as soon as Caldwell was done. She had planned to go into medicine following that, but the Harvard professor who was preparing the data base was moving very slowly. There was really no reason to delay construction of law enforcement files.

Of course, a lot would depend on whether or not Mitch Grogan was the right man for the job. It took a special kind of person; someone capable of thinking logically and condensing difficult concepts into their smallest components. Grogan certainly didn't *look* like that type of person, but then, he hadn't looked like a gentle, loving father yesterday until he'd held his little girl in his arms.

It was an idea worth exploring. "All right, Mitch. I know you won't want to commit to anything until you know exactly what's involved, but we could certainly discuss this further sometime."

"How about over dinner tomorrow night?"

Caroline couldn't hide her surprise. "Dinner? Tomorrow?"

He nodded. "The sooner we get started, the sooner we'll know if I'm the man for the job."

"But—"

Mitch frowned. "You do eat, don't you?"

"Of course I eat," she said, trying not to smile.

"Then what's wrong with dinner?"

There was nothing wrong with it, except that the term *dinner* sometimes went hand in hand with the word *date,* and Caroline didn't want to introduce that kind of familiarity into what should be a simple business transaction.

"I don't think dinner is really necessary, Mitch," she told him. "Why don't you come by here tomorrow after work, instead?"

"That doesn't sound like nearly as much fun."

Caroline sighed and steeled herself against the playful light in his eyes. "Creating a data base isn't fun, Mitch. It's work. *Hard* work."

He cocked his head to one side. "You don't enjoy your work?"

"Of course I do!"

"Then what's wrong with a pleasant dinner to accompany our discussion? It wouldn't be like a date, or anything," he said with exaggerated innocence.

The words were reassuring, but the teasing tone of his voice wasn't. He was practically daring her to go out with him.

And why shouldn't she? He was an attractive man in his own rough way, and he was obviously intelligent. He was funny and interesting. But he also had three children and he made Caroline feel totally off balance.

She mentally put the pluses and minuses in separate columns and compared them. There were four reasons to go out with him and four not to—if she counted each of the children as a single unit.

"Well?" he prompted when she didn't answer him right away. Caroline had the feeling he was enjoying watching the wheels turning in her head.

"It wouldn't be a date?" she asked for clarification.

He grinned. "Not unless you want it to be."

"I don't," she said firmly.

Mitch erased the grin from his face. "Then it won't be a date." He paused. "We can save that for the next time."

He was too damned charming for his own good. "Lieutenant Grogan, my work consumes one hundred percent of my life at the moment. I simply don't have time for social-izing."

"Neither do I," he replied.

"Then why are you—" there seemed only one accurate word for it "—flirting with me?"

"Because you're the most intriguing woman I've met in a very long time and I like the way you blush."

Caroline felt a humiliating warmth creeping across her cheeks. "The curse of the fair complected," she muttered.

"Come on, Dr. Hunter. What's the harm? We'll have dinner and discuss the data base. How much more innoc-uous could an evening be?"

Caroline finally realized she was making much too much of his invitation. Protesting so much was tantamount to admitting that he scared the living daylights out of her. Which he did. "All right," she said finally, reasoning that prolonged exposure to him might be just the thing to rid her of this absurd attraction she felt.

Mitch smiled broadly. "Wonderful! Should I pick you up about seven?"

"No, why don't I meet you somewhere at seven? After all, this isn't a date," she reminded him.

He nodded gravely. "Right. How about Ernesto's on Valley Boulevard?"

Caroline had never been there, but she was certain she could find it. "Very well. I'll bring our data base guideline instructions with me. That should give you a clue as to the work involved," she said as she moved toward the door.

Mitch followed her out. "That sounds reasonable."

"And you might want to be thinking about how you would teach a layperson about your job. Explaining it to me in its simplest terms will allow me to determine how effec-tive you would be with Scarlett."

"Fair enough."

Caroline wouldn't have felt quite so uncomfortable if Mitch had participated a little more in their conversation, but he suddenly seemed inclined to let her carry the load. It was as though he knew he made her nervous and was enjoying it. "I should know by tomorrow whether we can proceed with Janis's employment this summer."

"Good."

"Any questions?"

"None."

"Good."

She fell silent, and Mitch had to work to hide a smile. He was beginning to find Caroline's formality almost as endearing as her blushes. It was like a cloak she retreated behind whenever she was uncomfortable with her emotions; which meant, of course, that she *had* emotions. For him.

He filed that information for future reference, too, because he had a feeling it was going to come in very handy.

CHAPTER FIVE

CAROLINE DRESSED very carefully for the meeting with Mitch. Aunt Liddy tried to coax her into wearing something provocative, but it was easy to ignore the voice since there was nothing in Caroline's closet that fit the description. Determined to project a professional image, she chose a pair of black slacks and a white blouse with long, full sleeves. It buttoned all the way up to her throat, where she placed an antique cameo that had belonged to her aunt.

The ensemble was certainly plain. As she looked in the mirror, she decided that there wasn't a single thing about her appearance that Mitch could possibly find enticing.

Unfortunately, that didn't keep him from looking at her as though he would love to devour her when she showed up at Ernesto's. He was waiting for her at a corner table, and he stood as the hostess escorted her across the room. He looked her over from head to toe with such appreciation that Caroline felt another insidious blush creeping up her cheeks.

"Hello, Mitch."

"Hello, Caroline." He came around the table to hold out her chair. "You look lovely."

She glanced at him over her shoulder as she sat, and regretted it because his rugged, square-jawed face was too close to hers. Her breath hitched sharply and she looked away. "Thank you. That wasn't my intention, though."

Mitch was grinning devilishly when he returned to his seat. "What's wrong? Couldn't you find a lab coat to hide behind?"

Caroline's face felt as though it were on fire, which made it impossible to deny his assessment without looking even more foolish than she already felt. "Am I really that transparent?"

"Only when you blush."

If he had been making fun of her, she would have been irritated, but it was clear that he was just teasing. "I'll work on controlling it."

"Not on my account, I hope."

"No, on my own. I consider it self-defense."

Mitch chuckled. "Caroline, you don't need to protect yourself from me."

"But apparently I do need protection from myself," she quipped before she could censor the thought.

"Why?"

Caroline muttered an inward curse. They were off to a very bad start just because she couldn't control her body chemistry or her tongue when she was around this man. Looking at him was like drinking a truth serum—and an aphrodisiac.

"Why don't we get down to business, Mitch," she suggested, pulling her briefcase onto her lap.

"Could we order first?" he asked innocently.

"Oh. Certainly." She put the case back on the floor and picked up a menu. A waitress appeared a moment later and by the time they finished placing their orders, Caroline's complexion had returned to normal. Then she dug into her briefcase and got down to business.

"I suppose I should tell you first that I spoke with Dr. Brewster after you and Janis left yesterday. He was very enthusiastic about taking her on as a summer intern, and

Andrea Norris said she'd be happy to act as her immediate supervisor. If Janis is interested, the job is hers."

"Interested? She'll be ecstatic. She hasn't stopped talking about getting to meet Scarlett. In fact, Sam is about to throttle her and Pop is threatening to buy a pair of earplugs."

Caroline was fascinated by the way his face softened when he talked about his children. His enthusiasm must have been contagious, because it made her forget that she wanted to keep the conversation strictly business. "What about Ruthann?" she asked.

"Oh, Ruthann is more than willing to listen because she already thinks you're wonderful. She keeps asking when she's going to see Car'line again."

"Really?"

"Yes. You made quite an impression."

She found that hard to believe. "You have a nice family, Mitch."

"I think so. Most of the time," he added ruefully.

"When is it not nice?" she couldn't keep herself from asking.

"Whenever I do something stupid like losing my youngest daughter at a science fair or have to miss one of Sam's baseball games because of work."

"It's not possible to be perfect all the time, or to be in two places at once," she said sympathetically.

"Didn't you know? That's the definition of a parent."

Caroline glanced down. "No, I didn't know," she said quietly.

Mitch was pretty sure he'd just struck a nerve, and he was determined to find out why. Since she seemed to be in the mood to talk about something other than business for a change, now was as good a time as any. "You're divorced, aren't you, Caroline?"

"Yes."

"Would you mind if I asked why you and your husband never had kids?"

"Neither Evan nor I would have made good parents," she replied somewhat stiffly.

"Why not?"

"Because we were too focused on our careers. When parents are too obsessed with what they do, children tend to get left out."

"Is that what happened to you as a child?"

Caroline couldn't believe she had allowed the conversation to go so far astray. "I thought this was supposed to be a business dinner, Mitch," she said, squaring her shoulders.

"Answer my question and then we'll get down to work, I promise." For emphasis, he raised his right hand in a Scout's Honor pledge, but Caroline refused to find it amusing.

"I'd rather not, if you don't mind."

"Caroline, it's okay. None of us had a perfect childhood."

She sighed. She really was making too much of such simple questions. "I'm sorry. I don't mean to be mysterious. I wasn't an abused child, or anything. My parents didn't lock me in closets. They were just very busy, and they had very structured ideas of how a child should be raised."

"Even a gifted child like you?"

Caroline laughed. "Oh, most especially. I don't think they ever entertained the notion that they would have any other kind. If I had been of only average intelligence, I think they would have taken me back to the hospital and demanded a refund."

Mitch chuckled. "You're exaggerating."

"You don't know my parents," she replied.

"Are they still living?"

"Yes. They're doing research at the Le Vesque Institute in France."

"I'm sure they're very proud of you now."

She thought it over. "I guess they would be if I ever won the Nobel Prize. Unless that happens, I don't expect them to pay much attention to what I'm up to."

Mitch didn't detect any rancor, just a kind of amused resignation. "That doesn't bother you?"

"Not really. They have their lives on one side of the world, and I have mine on the other. Occasionally we come up for air long enough to acknowledge one another at Christmas, and—" she smiled at a memory "—and three years ago I did get a birthday card. It took me a week to recover from the shock."

Mitch was glad she could laugh about it because it indicated that the scars of her unorthodox childhood didn't run too terribly deep. "I don't think I could handle that," he told her. "My father is such a fixture in my life that I can't imagine being without him."

"You're lucky to have him so close and so involved in your life. But I don't miss my parents, Mitch," she assured him. "They were never around long enough for me to really become accustomed to their presence in my life. They were more like stern, authoritarian ghosts that sort of wandered in, made pronouncements, then wandered out again."

"Who raised you?" he asked.

"A housekeeper and a succession of tutors."

"It sounds lonely."

"It was." Caroline straightened abruptly. She hadn't meant to make that confession. It sounded too much like self-pity.

Mitch read her embarrassment and gave her an encouraging smile. "It's okay, Caroline. I haven't met an only child yet who didn't have a lonely childhood. If you ever

want a dose of insanity from the other side of the coin,
drop by the Grogan house sometime.''

"Thank you, I'll bear that in mind," she said formally
as she began shuffling some of the papers she had re-
moved from her briefcase.

Mitch knew he'd gone too far. But still, they were making progress. He knew more about her, now, and she'd
made it through an entire personal conversation without a
blush. He'd have to remedy that before the evening was
over, but in the meantime, he felt it would be judicious to
follow her lead and keep the conversation focused on business.

"Here's the data base guideline booklet I told you
about," she said, thrusting a thick bound document in
front of him. "It's a formulaic structure that increases
geometrically as..." She launched into a technical discussion that kept Mitch absorbed all through dinner. It was
fascinating, but he quickly realized that creating a data base
would be an even bigger challenge than he had imagined.

As the evening progressed, Caroline quizzed Mitch
closely on the topic of law enforcement, and as he broke his
work down into its basic components, she realized that he
was exactly the kind of logical thinker she needed for this
job. He had a quick, incisive mind that allowed him to
grasp concepts that most laypersons found incomprehensible. She found that talking with him was a pleasure once
she learned to ignore the effect his gravelly voice and stun-
ning eyes had on her senses.

"No, no, you have to stay away from the psychological
motivations of criminals," she corrected him when he
strayed from the factual pyramid of information he was
building. They had finished eating, their dishes had been
cleared and papers were strewn across the table. "Scarlett
will never be able to comprehend *why* people commit

crimes. It's important only that she understand what things are illegal.''

"Hmm." Mitch thought that over. "Do I explain to her why those things are against the law?"

"Yes. In fact, that's probably where you will have to begin. For example, she will have to understand that it's wrong to take a life before you introduce her to the concept of murder."

"But what if she asks about motivations?"

"You tell her to talk to me," Caroline replied with a smile.

Mitch shook his head as the enormity of what he was contemplating took hold. "I don't know, Caroline. Based on what you've told me, it seems as though it would be awfully easy to say the wrong thing to Scarlett—with disastrous consequences."

"Don't worry about that, Mitch. Believe me, it's going to be a long time before you actually have direct contact with Scarlett. Every piece of information goes on paper first, and it will be reviewed and restructured a dozen times before you start feeding it to her."

Mitch grinned. "It sounds as though I've got a job."

The devilish twinkle in his eyes jolted Caroline out of her computer-designer mode, and she became aware of him as a man all over again. Damn. She thought she had gotten past that.

"The job is yours, if you want it," she replied as she began gathering together some of the papers. "We'll have to discuss the terms of your contract, but I'm sure—"

"Oops, hold it. I think we just hit murky waters," he told her. "I can't accept payment for this work, Caroline. The department takes a dim view of cops who moonlight. I can act as a volunteer consultant, but that's all."

Caroline frowned. "Mitch, I can't ask you to do this work without reimbursement."

"You didn't ask, I offered, remember? It's the least I can do to thank you for giving Janis a job at MediaTech."

"I've told you before, no thanks are necessary." A discouraging thought occurred to her. "Mitch, is this going to be a conflict of interest for you? You do investigate computer crimes, after all, and you'd be working with a computer company."

He shook his head. "No. I checked with the chief this morning. He thinks it would be good public relations. You'll have to go through the formality of requesting my services officially through the department, but that's all."

"All right."

"Good," he said with a grin. "This is going to be fun."

Caroline tried not to be moved by his smile. "I'm glad you think so. There is one more thing, though..." She rummaged through the papers until she came up with the form she needed. "I'll have to ask you to sign this before we go any further."

Mitch took the paper and looked it over. It was a nondisclosure agreement that held him liable for any information he came into contact with. According to the terms outlined, he could be sued for leaking information about the OHARA system to the press, and it warned him that criminal action would be taken if he divulged technical secrets to any of MediaTech's competitors.

It wasn't a matter of trust, it was just good business, and Mitch had no problem with signing the form. In fact, he was glad to do so because there were huge gaps in his understanding of how the OHARA worked. Caroline wouldn't be able to fill in those gaps until he was officially a member of the team, so Mitch took a pen out of his jacket pocket and signed the agreement.

"Thank you, Mitch. Welcome aboard," she said as she folded the paper and placed it in her briefcase.

"Okay, it's my turn to ask some questions now," he told her.

She tilted her head. "Such as?"

He decided it was time to test out a theory he'd formed yesterday. "What's wrong with Scarlett?" he asked bluntly.

Caroline stiffened. "In what sense?"

"Yesterday you told me there was an instability in her logic programming and general information data base," he replied.

"I did no such thing," she said indignantly.

"Not in so many words, but I've learned that what people *don't* say is sometimes more important than what they do say."

Caroline began gathering up papers again. "I have no idea what you're talking about."

Mitch shook his head. "Caroline, you'd have a dismal career as a spy because you haven't quite got the knack of lying. There's something wrong with Scarlett."

"No, there isn't."

"Then why is the product launch six months away?"

"It may not be six months," she said defensively. "We plan to launch sooner if at all possible."

"Why isn't it possible? From what I've seen and what you've told me, Scarlett would create a major splash in the market as she is right now. Unless, of course, there's a critical flaw in her programming or her hardware."

"There are no critical flaws," she replied firmly, then relented. "Just a few bugs to be worked out."

"Such as?" When she didn't answer him right away, he reminded her, "Caroline, I've already signed the nondisclosure agreement. I'm not going to spread rumors about the OHARA or sell secrets to your competitors. Now tell me what the problem is."

Caroline finally stopped fighting the truth. If he spent any amount of time at MediaTech at all, he would find out eventually, anyway. It was just hard for her to admit that there was a problem with the system. "Scarlett loses pieces of information for no reason that we can determine," she told him finally. "We've run multiple diagnostics and I've gone through the root commands in her memory core with a fine-tooth comb, but we can't find a reason for it. She just...forgets things."

"Critical information?" Mitch asked.

"Not so far, but I refuse to allow her to be marketed until I find the problem."

"Why not? The OHARA wouldn't be the first computer to be sold with a bug or two."

Caroline couldn't believe he would even suggest such a thing. "Mitch, Scarlett isn't a little home computer to be used for balancing checkbooks or playing games. She was designed to control major systems in the government and private industry. Can you imagine what would happen if NASA installed an OHARA and it just happened to forget a space shuttle launch code?"

"I see your point."

He looked a little too serious, and Caroline finally realized she'd been had. "Of course you do. You were just playing devil's advocate, weren't you?" she asked, exasperated.

He nodded. "Something like that. I wanted to find out if you have a code of ethics."

"Why?" she challenged.

"Because things like honesty and integrity are important to me."

"Well, you can stop worrying," she told him. "MediaTech is a very ethical company."

Mitch leaned forward. "I wasn't talking about the company, Caroline."

She shifted uncomfortably in her chair. "I'm very ethical, too, Mitch."

"Good. I like working with people who set high standards for themselves and those around them."

"Well, I do." The look on his face was entirely too personal, and Caroline suddenly felt off balance again. "Speaking of work, I should tell you that you'll be able to do most of the early planning on the data base at home. It won't require a lot of time at MediaTech until you actually start inputting the information."

She had retreated behind her cloak again, and Mitch had to hide a smile. "Will you be supervising what I do?" he asked her.

"I'll check on you from time to time to make sure you're on the right track, and I'll always be available if you have questions, but you'll report directly to my chief programmer, Henry Bergman."

Mitch was disappointed. "Really? I was hoping I'd be working with you."

Caroline looked at him sharply. "Why?"

She had him there. He couldn't very well tell her it was because discovering what her legs looked like was becoming something of an obsession. She probably wouldn't want to hear that he was dying to kiss her, either. "Well, because...we seem to think alike in many ways, and we work well together. Scarlett is your baby, after all. I like the idea of working directly with the boss."

Caroline couldn't believe it, but Mitch seemed to be the one who was flustered now. Unfortunately, she was pretty sure she knew why. "And you like the way I blush," she added, trying not to smile.

He grinned. "Am I that transparent?"

He was back to flirting again, and it suddenly made her wonder... "Mitch, I hope you're on the level about constructing this data base," she said sternly. "If you're not— if you're just using it as an excuse to—"

He didn't let her complete the thought. "I'm not," he assured her. "I'm doing the data base for me, Caroline. Please believe that. It's been a long time since I took on an intellectual challenge." He grinned again. "Though I will admit that the thought of seeing you blush from time to time holds a certain allure."

She couldn't help being moved by the devilry in his eyes. "It's not my fault that I blush so much around you," she told him. "If you wouldn't look at me that way, I probably wouldn't become so disconcerted."

"What way?"

"As though..." She stopped. It was too embarrassing to put her interpretation of his looks into words.

"As though, what?" he asked insistently.

"As though you're speculating."

"On what?"

"I don't know!" she exclaimed. She was sorry she had led them down this path, but it was important that they get this out of the way if they were going to work together. In order to do that, she had to be blunt. "Mitch, forgive me if I'm misinterpreting you, but I have a feeling that you're expecting something from me that just isn't going to happen."

He was innocence personified as he asked, "Haven't I been a perfect gentleman this evening?"

"Yes. And as a consequence, I haven't blushed in nearly—" she checked her watch "—three hours."

"I noticed. But just for the record, that doesn't mean I've stopped finding you attractive, Caroline," he informed her.

Hearing him say it outright shouldn't have made her feel so good, but it did. She tried not to let it show, though. "You're very attractive, too, Mitch, but that doesn't mean I'm interested in anything more than a professional association. I simply don't have time for a personal life right now."

"Maybe you should take the time."

"That's easier said than done."

"Why?"

Caroline found it hard to confess, "I've been working nonstop on Scarlett for so many years that I don't think I could slow down if I wanted to. Particularly not when I'm so close to the successful completion of my life's dream."

"Is that all you've ever dreamed of, Caroline?" he asked softly. "A talking computer?"

"Yes, it is. Isn't that enough?"

"I suppose it depends on what you want out of life. To me, it seems very gratifying professionally, but a little on the lonely side personally."

Caroline stiffened. "Some people weren't meant to distinguish between the two."

"That's nonsense," he replied. "Apparently you made a choice a long time ago...or maybe your parents made the choice for you. They left you alone so much that now you think it's the only option you have, but you're wrong."

He was bringing up a subject Caroline normally avoided like the plague. "I don't agree. Now, could we terminate this discussion permanently, please."

"Permanently, no," he replied. "But we can table it for the time being."

"Mitch, we are not going to have a relationship," she said firmly. "Is that clear?"

"No."

This was exasperating! "If you think I'm going to find your persistence flattering, you're very wrong," she told him forcefully as she began shoving papers into her briefcase.

Mitch knew he'd gone too far. Damn! He was really out of practice. "Caroline, I'm sorry."

When she didn't stop loading the briefcase, he put one hand on hers and stilled it. She stiffened, but didn't pull away. "I said I'm sorry."

It took a lot of courage, but she managed to look him in the eyes. "What, exactly, do you want from me, Mitch? Why are you pushing so hard?"

"Because it's been a long time since I've met a woman who attracts me as much as you do."

He was either a very smooth liar or he was telling the truth. Though it created cracks in the defense system she was trying to build against him, she chose to believe the latter. "I would be lying if I said I wasn't flattered, Mitch," she admitted reluctantly. "Though what you could possibly find attractive about me, I can't imagine."

Mitch cocked his head to one side and looked at her intently. Was it possible she had no idea how gorgeous she was? "You mean other than the fact that you're brilliant and you have an incredible smile—whenever you're not trying to hide it. You're warm, compassionate, beautiful, and just shy enough to make a man wonder if you've ever been properly kissed."

Caroline couldn't have felt more out of breath if she'd just completed a 10K marathon. "I *have* been kissed," she managed to tell him. "I was married, remember?"

"Ah, but did he know how to do it right?"

She straightened her spine. "And you think you do?" she challenged.

"Why don't we experiment sometime soon and find out?"

"No, thanks. I don't believe in living dangerously."

"What's dangerous about a kiss?" he asked innocently.

That was exactly the problem. She didn't know what could possibly be dangerous about a kiss, and she didn't want to find out. After all, her ex-husband had never made her stammer and blush, not even on their wedding night; it only stood to reason that if Mitch Grogan could unnerve her with a simple look, kissing him would be close to suicidal.

Of course, even though her logical, rational self was screaming for her to avoid Mitch, something very strong and primal inside her was making just as much racket, pulling her in the opposite direction.

A lifetime of being rational made it a little easier to tell him, "I'm sorry, Mitch, but you are just not my type." It wasn't a lie, after all. It just felt like one.

He didn't seem the least bit daunted. "What type do you favor, Doctor?"

"Intellectuals."

Mitch thought it over. "I've read Nietzsche and Proust. Does that count?"

"That depends. Did you understand them?"

"I caught a few words here and there."

She shook her head. "Not good enough."

It was everything Mitch could do to keep from laughing with delight. It had been years since he had sparred with a woman like this. Best of all, he could tell by the sparkle in Caroline's eyes that she was enjoying it every bit as much as he was. "In that case, would it help if I could explain Isaac Newton's fourth law of mechanics?"

Caroline raised one eyebrow. "Newton didn't formulate *four* laws."

"I could make one up," he offered.

Caroline couldn't help it. She had to laugh. "Mitch, please," she begged. "You're a very nice man, but I don't have time for nice men right now."

Mitch wasn't about to give up, because no matter how much Caroline protested to the contrary, she really did like him. It would just be a matter of time before she realized that their attraction to each other was too potent to fight.

But for now, a strategic retreat was the best course to follow.

"All right. I quit. But if you do get an opening in your schedule for a nice man, you will let me know, won't you?"

"You'll be the first one I'll call," she promised.

Now that that was settled, she finished packing her briefcase, laying aside one folder of papers for Mitch to take home to study. That left only the dinner check on the table, and they both reached for it at the same time. Caroline was quicker. "MediaTech can pick up the tab. This was a business dinner, remember?"

"The way you keep reminding me, how could I forget?"

He was teasing and she didn't mind. "It seems that I *have* to keep reminding you in self-defense," she joked back as she placed the appropriate amount of money on the tray with the check.

A waiter appeared almost instantly to take it away and Mitch chuckled. "I think that's their way of telling us we've overstayed our welcome."

"Don't worry about it. MediaTech is a big tipper. Mitch, thank you for volunteering to help with this project."

"It's my pleasure." He held out his hand to seal their business deal, and Caroline hesitated.

You're being stupid, she told herself crossly and reached for his hand.

The instant they touched, the insistent birdlike peep of a beeper went off, and Caroline nearly jumped out of her skin. She withdrew her hand quickly and fished into her purse while Mitch reached into his coat pocket.

"It's mine," she told him as she thumbed a button and checked the phone number displayed on a tiny read-out panel. "It's the lab. I wonder what they could want at this hour," she said, frowning. "Excuse me, Mitch."

With her purse and briefcase in hand, she headed off to find a telephone. Mitch waited a moment, then followed her. When he found her in the foyer off the lobby, she was just finishing, and from the look on her face, he could tell that the news wasn't good.

"What's wrong?" he asked.

"I'm sorry, Mitch. I have to go. There's been a break-in at the lab."

Without asking for details, Mitch took her arm and headed for the exit. "Come on, let's go."

"Mitch, you don't have to—"

"I'm a cop, remember? This is what I do for a living." Caroline didn't protest as he led her out.

CHAPTER SIX

IT TOOK less than ten minutes to reach MediaTech. Caroline had insisted on driving her own car and Mitch hadn't argued with her. Since he wasn't in an official department vehicle tonight, he didn't have lights and sirens to speed their arrival, anyway. He followed her to the sprawling complex, expecting to find at least one squad car in front of the building when they arrived, but except for a few civilian vehicles scattered here and there, the lot was quiet and deserted.

"Caroline, didn't security report the break-in?" he asked as soon as they were out of their cars, hurrying toward the building.

"I doubt it," she replied, taking a card key out of her purse.

He frowned. "Why not?"

"For one thing, I don't know what the hacker tried to access or if he was successful in getting through the security system."

Mitch stopped. "Wait a minute. You mean this wasn't an actual, *physical* break-in? No bad guys with guns charged in to storm the fortress?"

Caroline turned to him. "You don't have to sound so disappointed, Mitch. We may have had a serious security breach here."

"I know that," he replied. "I was just hoping to get the chance to impress you with my sleuthing skills—maybe even get to draw my gun and protect you from a gang of villains, thereby earning your undying gratitude. It's something of a letdown to realize that all I have to protect you from is some midnight computer hacker with a modem and a big telephone bill."

Caroline was upset, but not so much that she wasn't amused by his comment. "Sorry. I tried to tell you it wasn't necessary to come out here with me. You don't have to stay."

"No, I'll stay. As long as I'm here, I might as well find out what's going on in case you do need to file an official report."

Caroline used her card key to open the door and hurried to the security desk. The night man who had called her at the restaurant was behind the desk and Ed Newton was there, as well. The guard had called him even before he had notified Caroline.

Ed looked up. "Hi, Doc." He shot a curious glance at Mitch. "I see you brought in the big guns."

"I'm just along for the ride," Mitch told the security chief. "What's going on?"

"That's what I'm trying to figure out," Ed replied. "Apparently, someone tried to access the OHARA core."

"What?" Caroline demanded in alarm as she moved around the desk. "How did they get past perimeter security?"

"I have no evidence that they did," Ed replied. "Apparently, Scarlett just sounded an alarm when someone fed her an inaccurate security access code."

The guard moved aside to make room for Caroline and Ed at the console. Mitch leaned over the counter and got an upside-down view of three video monitors and a computer screen. "Would you care to explain what that means?" Mitch asked.

Caroline sat down and began feeding commands into the computer keypad as she answered him. "The OHARA is completely independent of the electronic-based computer that controls the bulk of MediaTech's normal operating functions. In order to get to Scarlett from outside the building, you first have to get through a very intense layer of computer security.''

"You mean it's possible to access Scarlett by modem?''

"Yes. I work at home sometimes and I have a computer linkup with her.''

"Isn't that dangerous?'' he asked.

"I didn't think so until now,'' she replied tightly. "MediaTech's perimeter security is impenetrable. We've had hackers try to get through it before, but they've never gotten very far.''

"Until now.''

Caroline shook her head as she looked at the computer screen. "This doesn't make any sense.''

Mitch came around the desk and looked, too. She had apparently asked for a list of all commands the computer had been given in the last hour. As near as Mitch could tell, there was no indication that anyone had accessed the computer from outside the building.

"Ask for a complete activity list,'' he suggested, but Caroline was already punching that command into the keyboard.

One screen at a time, the computer displayed a complex message system. He saw a section on building maintenance that obviously controlled the lights, temperature and air filtering devices. Another segment logged the personnel who had entered or left the building. Screen after screen scrolled past.

Everything looked normal to Mitch, and to Caroline, too. "I don't understand,'' she said, leaning back in the chair. "There's nothing here. According to this, no one tried to access Scarlett from outside the building.''

"What about from inside?" Mitch asked. He reached over Caroline's shoulder and keyed the list in reverse until they were at the personnel log again.

"Hmm." Ed looked over the list. "There were three employees in the building at the time. Only one of them is from Caroline's department, though."

"Brad Lattimore," she said. "He's in data base management. He wouldn't have any reason to try to access the core."

Mitch was a born skeptic. "According to this, he's still here. Why don't we ask him about it."

"All right," Caroline said as she rose. "I need to go upstairs and check with Scarlett, anyway. I can't find out from here what access code the hacker tried to use. Only Scarlett can tell me that." She turned to her security chief. "Ed, I want you to add a new clearance code to the security system right now. If someone has found a way to bypass the system, he or she has access to all of MediaTech's operations."

"I'll get right on it," he promised.

"And talk to those other two employees, too," she instructed, then hurried off with Mitch at her side.

"Are you sure nothing like this has ever happened before, Caroline?" he asked her.

"Absolutely. Ed Newton is very good at his job. We've never even had anyone gain access to the perimeter computer, let alone reach Scarlett."

Mitch heard the concern in her voice. It bordered on panic, despite the fact that it was very controlled. Since she was responsible for the million-dollar computer, he could understand her concern, but what he was sensing from Caroline was more than that. It reminded him very much of the panic he had felt two days ago when Ruthann had disappeared at the science fair.

Interesting.

When they got upstairs, Brad Lattimore was at his desk in the far corner of the programming lab. He looked too young to be out of high school, let alone have a position of responsibility in a major research company, but that didn't surprise Mitch. The computer industry was young in more ways than one. What did surprise Mitch was that the employee wasn't hunched over the keyboard with his eyes glued to a monitor. His computer terminal that provided a link with Scarlett was dark and he was poring over a thick sheaf of printouts, instead.

Mitch cleared his throat as they approached, and Brad looked up in surprise. "Dr. Hunter. What brings you back? I thought you were gone for the day."

"We had a little problem," she replied. "Brad, you haven't tried to access the OHARA core tonight, have you?"

He seemed genuinely puzzled that she would even ask. "No, ma'am. I've been going over the revisions Dr. Caldwell turned in today for the astrophysics data base. Is there a problem with the core?" he asked.

"No. Nothing for you to worry about," she assured him. "Go back to work. Or better yet, go on home. It's nearly eleven o'clock."

Without waiting for him to respond, Caroline turned and headed for her office. When they were well away from the young programmer, Mitch asked, "Does he work late often?"

"Quite a bit."

"Even on Friday nights?"

Caroline had never stopped to analyze Brad's work habits. And since she didn't have a personal life to take her away from the office, she rarely questioned why any of her staff worked late, either. "Apparently so."

"I'm surprised you allow that sort of thing."

She caught his implication and looked at him in surprise. "Mitch, I trust all my employees. And that's not just blind faith in human nature. Everyone who works here has to undergo a very rigorous security check. I suppose I should have warned you about that."

He grinned. "You mean Ed is going to be poking around in my closets looking for skeletons?"

"Yes."

"Hmm. I guess I'd better do a little housecleaning before he arrives. I wouldn't want him to choke on the dust bunnies."

Caroline sighed. It was amazing that despite the serious circumstances, Mitch could make her smile. "I'll warn him to wear a filter mask."

They reached her office and the lights came on automatically, as did Scarlett.

"Hello, Caroline. Hello, Lieutenant Grogan. Are you here about the attempted core breach?"

"Yes, Scarlett, I am," she replied as she moved behind the desk. "Please show me a complete visual display of the access code that was used and all subsequent communication."

Caroline sat and Mitch looked over her shoulder as Scarlett displayed a conversation that began with a sequence of letter and symbol codes.

> . > .68092.if? > . > .yimrestp.894 > . > .interface

In response, Scarlett had informed the user:

I AM SORRY, BUT THAT IS NOT A VALID ACCESS CODE. SECURITY HAS BEEN NOTIFIED OF AN UNAUTHORIZED ACCESS ATTEMPT. PLEASE IDENTIFY YOURSELF.

The hacker had then changed the letters and symbols, but kept the pattern.

When Scarlett had refused access and demanded identification again, a third sequence was fed to her.

At that point, Scarlett had replied:

YOUR FAILURE TO PROVIDE A VALID ACCESS CODE LEADS ME TO BELIEVE THAT YOU ARE NOT CLEARED FOR ENTRY INTO THIS SYSTEM. THIS INTERFACE IS BEING TERMINATED.

Scarlett had then disconnected the link.

Mitch was fluent in a number of computer languages, but the lines of code the hacker had used were just gibberish to him. "What do you make of it?" he asked Caroline.

"I have no idea," she replied.

"Is it similar to the actual code that you use to get into the memory core?"

"Not even remotely."

"Would those codes do anything at all?"

"No." Caroline was genuinely mystified. "I used strings of command codes similar to this years ago when I first started constructing Scarlett, but I haven't used them in years. Not since I downloaded the data base into the OHARA."

Mitch frowned. "Are you saying you began constructing the Scarlett data base before you began work on the OHARA system?" he asked.

"That's right. I started the initial data base on an ordinary personal computer while I was still in college. Once the OHARA went on-line, I was able to transfer all those data files into the new system."

Mitch was confused. "Wait a minute. Maybe you'd better clarify some things for me, Caroline," he suggested. "I think I need a more complete picture of how this computer is put together. I realize there was a lot you couldn't tell me before I signed that nondisclosure agreement."

"All right. What don't you understand?"

"Well, first of all, I don't understand why you use the names OHARA and Scarlett as though they were two different entities."

"Because they are," Caroline told him. "OHARA is the optical hardware unit that houses all the programming. Scarlett is a software program. Several, in fact. She is a collection of information and logic data bases that enable her to 'think' and reason."

"Where are those data bases stored?"

"In the protected core," she replied. "And there are only two ways to reach that—by using the OHARA access code or by a retina scan."

"Could any other computer use the Scarlett software program?" he asked.

She looked very uncomfortable. "Yes, if the user also had a copy of the Translator."

"What's that?"

"It's a program that allows Scarlett to communicate with other computers. As you know, different types of computers speak different languages. I built a program into the OHARA to translate all languages so that every program in the world will work on Scarlett."

Mitch whistled softly. Now he had the full picture of how valuable the OHARA really was. Government, businesses and even private individuals tended to resist the introduction of new computer technology because it generally took years for programmers to write software that would make the computer do more than hum and take up desk space.

Caroline had eliminated that drawback and in so doing, she had created a veritable gold mine.

Now he knew why she seemed so worried by the attempted break-in. People had been known to kill for less than what Scarlett OHARA represented.

"How many access terminals do you have in the building?" he asked.

"There are six in the programming lab that allow us to do manual keystroke input."

Mitch gestured to the computer on Caroline's desk. "How many voice input terminals are there?"

"Just two. Mine and Henry Bergman's."

"What about the computer you have at home?"

"That's manual input only. No voice interaction."

Her answers clarified several things that Mitch hadn't understood before, but none of it helped in figuring out who had attempted to access the OHARA computer tonight. He went back to studying the screen and so did she.

"You know what I find most puzzling about this?" Caroline said.

"What?"

"Why were these particular access commands chosen. What gave anyone the idea that they might work?"

"Maybe I was right earlier. It could have been some eager-beaver midnight hacker who had nothing better to do than play a harmless game of trying to break into a high-security computer."

"That would certainly be a comforting thought," she said, though she didn't really believe it. MediaTech had several competitors who stood to benefit greatly if Caroline failed. Whoever launched the first optical computer stood the greatest chance of success. As far as Caroline knew, no one was as close to completion as she was, and that made her a prime target for sabotage.

She addressed her computer again. "Scarlett, do you show any record of a previous access of this nature?"

"No, Caroline. I have been given incorrect access codes before, but it was always a matter of human error."

"Thank you, Scarlett. End session," she instructed, shutting the computer down. She swiveled her chair around to face Mitch. "This is scary, Mitch."

She wasn't kidding. She really was scared. "No harm was done, Caroline," he said gently. "You need to keep that in mind."

"But whoever did this managed to breach every layer of our perimeter security network, and he or she knew enough about the system to cover it up. That implies a certain degree of inside knowledge."

"Unless the access came from inside in the first place," he reminded her.

"You mean Brad Lattimore?" she asked. "No, I can't accept that. If Brad had a legitimate reason to access the core, all he would have to do is ask for permission."

"But his work would be supervised, wouldn't it?"

"Of course."

"Then maybe he was trying to do something that required privacy—like copying the data base programs or the Translator to sell to the highest bidder. I assume you do have some new form of floppy disk that is optical fiber instead of the old-fashioned magnetic tape."

"Of course. Data from an optical computer couldn't be stored on a magnetic floppy. But Mitch, even if Brad made copies of the programs, he couldn't smuggle them out of the building. You've seen what our security is like. All briefcases and purses are searched thoroughly."

"Do you do strip searches, too?" he asked.

"No, but they're not necessary. I invented a special security device that is installed at every exit. It's an electronic pulse wave that automatically destroys any data stored on a disk," she informed him. "Any disk that was smuggled out would be useless."

That was a compelling argument, but Mitch knew that there were always ways of getting around security measures. He didn't press the point, though, because Caroline didn't seem to want to consider the possibility that one of her employees was involved in industrial espionage.

"Well, there is one other alternative we're overlooking," he told her.

"What's that?"

"Maybe this is a figment of Scarlett's imagination."

Caroline frowned. "You're kidding, right? Mitch, she's just a computer. She doesn't have an imagination."

"She has curiosity and an obvious attachment to you. Didn't you tell me earlier tonight that she runs programs on her own when no one is providing her with any input?"

"Yes, but that's nothing more than a review and analysis of what she has learned. She takes new data, compares it with old information and draws analogies."

"Like when she compared the military ranking system with my rank in the police department?"

"Exactly."

"So you don't think it's possible that she came across one of those old code strings you used to use and didn't know what to do with it?"

Caroline considered the possibility. "I don't see how that could be, Mitch. But then, I don't know what's making her lose pieces of data, either," she admitted wearily.

"Could the two events be related?"

"Only if there's a bigger problem with the system than I've been willing to face."

Mitch could tell how much it cost her to make such an admission. The haunted expression in her eyes said it all. Caroline might call Scarlett "just a computer," but she was much, much more to her creator.

"How are you going to proceed?" he asked her.

Caroline shook her head. "I don't know. I guess I'll go back into the OHARA core and search the codes line by line for anything that would have caused this. And I'll dig into MediaTech's computer, too, and see if I can find out how our hacker got through the security perimeter."

"Will you have Ed do a check on Lattimore?"

She nodded and even managed a smile. "If it will make you happy. I can guarantee that he won't find anything, though. Brad is one of my best programmers."

"Sometimes they're the most dangerous."

Caroline didn't want to believe that, but she knew better than to discount Mitch's opinion. He dealt with crimes like this every day. "Should I prohibit my staff from working overtime when I'm not here?"

"That's up to you, but it would be a precaution. If you limit unsupervised access to the computer, you'll cut down on the risk of espionage."

"All right."

She looked so disheartened that Mitch would have given anything to be able to take her into his arms. He didn't dare do that, though. "It will be all right, Caroline," he assured her, instead. "As far as we can tell, no harm has been done."

"I hope you're right, Mitch."

"Do you want to file a report with my department?"

She thought it over. "Nothing has been damaged. Apparently, nothing was stolen. I can't even prove that an illegal access occurred since there's no evidence that the perimeter security was breached. What would be the point?"

She was right. There was really nothing he could do officially. "Okay. But you'll let me know if this happens again, won't you?"

"Sure." She rose. "Come on. I'll walk you out."

When she started for the door, Mitch noticed that she had left her purse and briefcase behind. "You're not going home now?"

"No. I've got a lot of work to do tonight."

Mitch didn't see any point in trying to argue her out of it. She'd already made it clear that her work was her life. And he really couldn't blame her. Right now, Scarlett was threatened and Scarlett was everything to Caroline. His children were everything to him, and he knew that if someone had threatened one of them, nothing would have stopped him from standing guard the rest of the night, either.

CHAPTER SEVEN

CAROLINE PULLED UP in front of the Grogan house wondering if she'd taken leave of her senses. Somehow, she had allowed Mitch to talk her into a Saturday-afternoon visit to his home.

As she had escorted him out of the building last night, he had thanked her for an intriguing evening and had once again expressed his gratitude for the interest she was taking in his daughter. He had told her how much the news of Janis's employment was going to mean to the girl, and before Caroline realized what she was saying, she had agreed to tell her personally rather than letting Mitch do it.

There was a certain logic to speaking with Janis, of course. Duties and responsibilities would have to be laid out eventually. A work schedule had to be drafted. Those things might as well be defined from the very beginning.

But going to the Grogan home to do it? *That* was crazy. She'd spent most of the night and a good portion of the morning digging into the OHARA core with nothing to show for it. A search of the MediaTech computer had been just as unproductive. Caroline was tired. She was frustrated. She was still scared because it had been so easy for someone to make contact with Scarlett, even though no damage had been done that she could detect. And on top of all that, she still felt off balance emotionally because of Mitch Grogan.

Having contact with him again so soon wasn't the smartest thing she had ever done, but she had made a commitment and she would live up to it.

She got out of the car and started up the driveway. The house was a modest two-story frame structure that looked a lot like the other houses around it. The neighborhood was well-kept and very active—kids were riding bicycles along the sidewalk; two doors down, a man was mowing his lawn while his wife pulled weeds from a flower bed. Across the street, an elderly couple were sitting in chairs under a small shade tree, studying Caroline. It was all very suburban and peaceful.

She might as well have been on another planet.

Caroline headed toward the front door, but before she got halfway up the walk, she heard a high-pitched squeal of laughter and the rumble of Mitch's voice coming from the backyard. She changed direction and headed around the house, stopping at the corner where she was partially hidden by a huge azalea bush.

"Burn it in, Babe! Burn it in here!" Dressed in shorts and a cutoff T-shirt that bared a stretch of his midsection, Mitch was squatting with his back to Caroline as Sam hurled a baseball at him. A sleek black Labrador retriever was racing back and forth between them, trying to catch the ball, and off to one side, Ruthann was going in big circles on a tricycle, squealing with delight because she was effectively eluding Pop Grogan, who was making a good show of trying to catch her. Janis was lying on a blanket in the middle of Ruthann's racecourse with her nose in a book, completely oblivious to the furor around her.

It was the most perfect picture of family life Caroline had ever seen. The only thing missing from the tableau was a mom in an apron.

As near as she could tell, though, they seemed to be doing fine without one.

Sam's baseball hit Mitch's gloved hand with a resounding thwack and he lobbed it back to him. "Good one, Sam. But you're still a little out of the strike zone."

"Oh, yeah? I want a second opinion. Pop, get over here and ump. Dad's gone nearsighted."

"Leave me out of it!" the elder Grogan shouted back. "I got my hands full with Evil Knievel, here."

"Faster, Pop!" Ruthann shrieked. She turned too sharply and ran over the blanket, finally eliciting a reaction from her sister.

"Hey, Short Stuff! Watch where you're going."

"Catch me, Jannie! Catch me!"

"Forget it," the teenager replied and went back to her book.

"Hey, Dad, we got company!" Sam called out when he finally spotted Caroline. "It's that computer jock."

Mitch stood and turned, kicking the kinks out of his knees as a broad smile spread across his face. "Hello, Caroline. Welcome to Candlestick Park."

Caroline was relieved that she knew Candlestick Park was a baseball stadium in nearby San Francisco. Unfortunately, that was the extent of her knowledge about the sport. "I don't know, Mitch, this looks more like the Indianapolis Speedway to me," she said as she walked around the azaleas.

Mitch started toward her. His arms, legs and thighs were well-muscled and his cutoff T-shirt exposed a tantalizing V of light, baby-fine hair on his abdomen. He looked exactly like the macho jock Caroline had at first assumed him to be, which made the sudden lurch of her heart and the quickening of her pulse all the more incomprehensible. But at least she wasn't blushing which, considering the direction of her thoughts, was a miracle.

"Car'line!" Ruthann's tricycle tipped to one side, upper wheels still spinning as she abandoned it and sprinted across the yard. The four-year-old darted past her father, but he reached out and snagged her, propelling her onto his hip before she could throw herself at their guest.

"Hello, Ruthann," Caroline said as she reached the two of them.

"Hi!" The little girl leaned forward precariously, trusting her father not to drop her, and he didn't. She planted a sloppy kiss on Caroline's cheek. "Are you here for the bobbycue?"

"Bobbycue? Oh. Barbecue. Uh, no," she replied. "I came to talk to Janis."

Ruthann's face fell. "Make her stay, Daddy."

Mitch looked at his guest and grinned. "I'll work on her, Short Stuff," he promised. "Thanks for coming, Caroline. Janis has no idea," he added in a whisper.

Pop joined them with a friendly greeting and latched onto the dog's collar when the Lab tried to throw himself at their visitor, too. Sam was still at the back of the yard throwing his baseball into the air, looking put-out that his practice session had been interrupted. Janis was scrambling off the blanket, shrugging into a beach cover-up.

"I'm sorry it's so late," Caroline said. "I spent most of the day at MediaTech."

"I figured as much," Mitch replied. "Did you come up with any answers?"

"Not a one."

Mitch looked at Pop and gave him a brief rundown of the break-in.

"Don't worry, Dr. Hunter. Mitch will figure it out," Pop told her.

Caroline gave him a grateful smile, but replied, "It really isn't a matter for the police."

"Hello, Dr.—Caroline. What isn't a police matter?" Janis asked as she joined them. Mitch explained again.

"Is Scarlett all right?" the teenager asked with alarm.

"She's fine," Caroline reassured her.

"That's a relief. I still can't believe I got to meet her," she said, beaming. "She's the most amazing thing I've ever seen."

"I'm glad you think so," Caroline replied. "My staff was pretty impressed with IVAR. In fact, that's why I'm here. I need to ask you something."

Janis looked surprised. "You're here to see me?"

Caroline nodded and Mitch suggested, "Why don't we sit down? That way the drop will be shorter when Janis faints."

"Da-ad. I've never fainted in my life." She rolled her eyes, but headed for the back porch where five chairs were clustered around a patio table.

"I'll go keep Sam occupied," Pop said, and Caroline could tell from the twinkle in his eyes that Mitch had already shared the news with him. "You want me to take her?" he offered, reaching for Ruthann, but the little girl shook her head and shied away from her grandfather.

"No," she said petulantly. "I wanna stay with Car'line."

"It's okay, Pop," Mitch told him, and gestured toward the dog. "I'd appreciate it if you could keep Grover out of our hair, though."

"Sure." The elder Grogan drifted off with the big dog.

Caroline joined Janis at the table and Mitch sat on the top step of the porch only a few feet from Caroline's chair. Ruthann tried to wiggle out of his lap so that she could reach their guest, but he held her firmly.

Janis looked suspiciously from her father to Caroline. "What's going on?"

"I have a proposition for you, Janis," Caroline began. "I discussed it with your father over dinner last night—"

Janis's head swiveled toward Mitch. "Is that where you went last night? You had a date with Caroline?" she exclaimed, her eyes shining with excitement.

Mitch felt compelled to respond, "It wasn't actually a date." He shot an amused glance at Caroline, though. "We were discussing business. I'm going to be doing some work on the OHARA."

"Dad, that's great!"

"And you will be working on it, too," Caroline told her. "If you'd like to, that is."

"You're kidding, right?"

"No, I'm not." She explained the summer intern program and the position she was offering Janis in the robotics department. She outlined what her responsibilities would be, and told her that time would be allocated for her to advance her research on IVAR.

Janis was stunned. "You're kidding?" she said again.

Caroline was very glad she had let Mitch talk her into doing this herself. She wouldn't have wanted to miss this reaction for the world. "I swear, I'm not. The offer is legitimate and your father has given his approval."

"Oh, Caroline. Thank you!" Before either of them realized what was happening, Janis was out of her chair, throwing her arms around Caroline's neck.

"Um...you're welcome," she stammered, completely at a loss. Instinctively, though, she patted the girl's back before Janis finally pulled away, her face flushed with embarrassment.

"I'm sorry," she apologized as she straightened and tried to look dignified. "I guess that wasn't very professional, was it? I promise I'll do a good job, though. Really, I will."

"I know you will, Janis."

The hug was more than Ruthann could handle. "Me, too!" she squealed, wiggling out of Mitch's arms before he could catch her. She scurried across the porch and hurled herself at Caroline. "I get a hug!"

Caroline froze for a second, but the little girl crawled into her lap, wrapping her arms around her neck, and Caroline really didn't have any choice but to comply. It felt strange, but she couldn't bear the thought of rejecting the child. There had been too many times when she was small that she had begged for a hug from her parents and been sternly told to behave herself. She had finally learned that it was easier not to ask for—or even crave—a hug unless she was with Aunt Liddy.

Now she knew why her aunt had never pushed her away. There was something warm and sweet about having something so small and trusting in her arms. She squeezed the little girl tightly.

"You give good hugs, Car'line," Ruthann told her with a giggle as she squirmed around until she was sitting comfortably on Caroline's lap.

"Ruthann, you're making a pest of yourself," Mitch said mildly. "Come here."

Caroline looked at Mitch and shook her head. "It's okay, Mitch. She's not bothering me."

"But she's getting grass stains on your white slacks," Mitch cautioned her.

Caroline looked down at the big green splotch on her knee. "It will come out, I'm sure."

Ruthann crinkled her nose at her father. "See. Car'line likes me." She looked up. "Don't you, Car'line?"

"How could anyone not like you?" she replied, smiling down into those beautiful blue eyes. "You're like a warm, wiggly puppy I fell in love with when I was a little girl."

Ruthann's eyes lit up. "You had a puppy, too? Was he like Grover?"

"No, the puppy wasn't mine. I got to see him when I visited my aunt. I do have a cat now, though."

"What's his name?"

"Einstein."

Ruthann frowned. "That's a dumb name. If I had a kitty, I'd name it Fluffy."

Janis crinkled her nose at her sister. "If you had a kitty, you'd squash it and pull out its hair. That's why Grover won't come near you."

"That's not so!" Ruthann argued. "Grover loves me. Doesn't he, Car'line?"

Mitch chuckled and moved from the porch step to the table. "Pipe down, Short Stuff," he said as he sat beside Caroline. "We still have some business to talk over."

Ruthann fell silent, content to snuggle in Caroline's arms and listen as they returned to the discussion of Janis's summer employment. Caroline laid out the girl's duties, and Mitch called for Pop to join them when it came time to decide what afternoons Janis would work. Sam came along and put his two cents in, reminding his grandfather that he was already committed to transportation duty on Tuesday and Thursday afternoons because of baseball practice. Keeping that in mind, Janis decided on Wednesdays and Fridays from one to five.

Once the practicalities were out of the way, Janis and Caroline began to discuss robotics, Ruthann still on Caroline's lap. Pop began making noises about getting the charcoal for the barbecue grill going, but it was nearly half an hour before he finally matched action to words. Sam tried to entice his father into resuming pitching practice and when that failed, he settled for playing Frisbee with Grover on the lawn. Mitch sat and watched Caroline interact with his daughters.

It was really remarkable, he thought. For the first time he could remember, Janis had someone to talk to who actually had something to teach her. Though Janis rarely made a big deal of it, she was usually one or two steps ahead of everyone she conversed with. It was fun to watch her sharing ideas and complex scientific theories with a woman who could challenge her.

And Ruthann. He'd seldom seen his rambunctious little girl be quiet for this long, or be this patient with not being the center of attention. Yet despite the fact that the conversation didn't include her, she really wasn't being left out, he realized. Whenever Ruthann piped up with a question, Caroline always answered her patiently, taking her seriously and never treating her as an intrusion. She stroked Ruthann's hair almost without being aware that she was doing it, or so it seemed to Mitch.

Whether she realized it or not, Caroline Hunter had great instincts.

Eventually, though, even her patient answers and soothing touches weren't enough for Ruthann. As soon as her eyes started drooping and a nap seemed imminent, the little girl started fighting sleep. She became increasingly squirmy and demanding, until it was impossible for Caroline and Janis to carry on an intelligent conversation. She finally crawled out of the snug cradle of Caroline's arms, grabbed her hand and demanded that she come see the new tricycle she had just received for her birthday.

"Why don't you go play with Sam and Grover, instead?" Mitch suggested, but Ruthann kept tugging at her new friend.

"No!" she said petulantly. "I want Car'line to see."

Caroline shot Mitch a bewildered glance, but she rose, anyway.

"You'll spoil her," Mitch warned.

Caroline frowned with indecision. She knew nothing about child rearing and discipline, after all. "Would it be better if I didn't go with her?"

He grinned and shook his head. "It's strictly up to you. Just be aware that the more you give her, the more she'll want."

Caroline wondered if that was why her parents had given her so little of themselves. Had they been afraid she'd want too much? Or that they didn't have enough to give? "I'd like to see her tricycle," she said, and allowed herself to be dragged away.

Mitch didn't believe that for a moment, of course. Caroline just didn't want to disappoint his daughter. A man who loved his children as much as Mitch did could very easily fall in love with a woman like that.

"She's wonderful, isn't she, Daddy?" Janis said quietly as she came around the table and eased into the chair beside his.

"Yeah, she is."

"I told you she would be."

Mitch smiled at the memory of Janis playing matchmaker at the science fair. "Yes, you did. I'll have to pay attention to your instincts more often."

"Do you really like her?"

"Yes."

"I think she likes you, too. She gets kinda...well...*shy* when she looks at you."

There was a note of disbelief in her voice that made Mitch chuckle. "Don't make it sound so abnormal, Angelface. Your old man isn't over the hill, yet."

"Oh, I know that. All my friends think you're a real hunk."

Mitch laughed. "Really?"

"Sure. Tory thinks you look just like Nick Nolte."

"Nick Nolte, huh?" He squared his shoulders and jutted out his chin. "I could handle that comparison."

"Oh, Dad. What does Tory know? She's only fifteen and she's blind as a bat."

"Gee, thanks a lot," Mitch said, then he noticed the twinkle in his daughter's eyes.

She grinned. "Gotcha."

"Janis! You made a joke! I'm impressed."

She leaned over and gave him a hug. "See if you can get her to stay for dinner, okay? Pop and I will keep Ruthann out of your hair if you want to sit in the backyard and make out later."

"Janis!"

"Come on, Dad. Wise up! She's the best thing that ever happened to this family."

"You're just prejudiced because she gave you a job," he replied, though he really didn't feel like arguing with her assessment.

"Just don't let her get away, okay?" Janis advised him, then went into the house muttering something about wanting to call her friend Tory to tell her the exciting news about her job at MediaTech.

Well, now Mitch knew that he had the permission of one child to court Caroline and he was positive Ruthann wouldn't object, either. Sam hadn't shown much interest in her, but these days he didn't care much about anything that wasn't related to baseball or his other passion, camping. Pop would be thrilled if Mitch found someone special, and Mitch himself was beginning to think he'd go crazy if he didn't get to kiss Caroline soon.

Now, if he could only convince the lovely but reluctant Dr. Hunter...

Out in the yard, Ruthann had dragged Caroline out to the swing set near the back fence, and was generally making a nuisance of herself, sliding down the slide and demanding that Caroline catch her each time. Caroline was gamely doing her best to keep up, but from the increasing amount of noise Ruthann was making and her frenetic pace, Mitch could tell that his youngest child had about reached her limit.

He decided it was time to rescue his guest.

"Okay, Short Stuff, that's enough. I think you're over-due for a nap," Mitch said as he joined them at the swing set. "Caroline's had about all the fun she can handle for a while."

He reached for his daughter, but Ruthann deftly eluded him.

"No!"

"Ruthann..."

She dashed under the slide and wrapped her arms around Caroline's legs. "Car'line wants me to stay." She turned her trusting blue eyes up to her protector, looking for support. "Don't you, Car'line?"

Caroline shot a perplexed, what-do-I-do glance at Mitch, but he just shrugged. "Um... I think you should do what-ever your father thinks is in your best interest," she an-swered.

The little girl frowned. "Uh?"

She's four years old, Caroline reminded herself. *Keep it simple.* "I think it's time for a nap, too."

"Oh."

Mitch moved toward her. "Come on, Short Stuff. I'll put you down."

"No! I want Car'line to take me."

"Ruthann," Mitch said sternly.

"It's all right, Mitch," Caroline said. Ruthann lifted her arms and Caroline picked her up.

He grinned. "You're a real soft touch, you know that?"

"Sorry," she said with a hint of color creeping into her cheeks. "I haven't had any practice saying no."

"You haven't had any practice saying yes, either, but you seem to be doing fine. Come on. I'll show you where the pest sleeps."

"Nap time?" Pop asked as they passed by the charcoal grill he was still trying to get to stay lit.

"Long overdue, wouldn't you say?" Mitch answered with a nod.

"But I'll miss the bobbycue!" Ruthann protested.

"No, you won't. We'll be sure and wake you in time to eat," Pop promised, then smiled at Caroline. "You are staying for dinner, aren't you?"

"Oh, no. I really couldn't. I've stayed much too long as it is."

"Please, Car'line? Please stay."

"You haven't lived until you've tasted Pop Grogan's famous barbecue burgers," Mitch told her.

"The secret's in the sauce," Pop said.

"Please, Car'line. Please, please."

Ruthann's arms tightened around her neck. Caroline knew she should refuse. Staying was absurd. She didn't have time for family picnics or chasing toddlers. And if she did stay, she might be sending a completely wrong message to Mitch.

She had a lot of good reasons for refusing, and only one for staying. She was having fun.

Didn't she deserve that, from time to time?

"All right," she said finally. "Thank you, I'll stay."

"Goodie, goodie!" Ruthann shouted right in her ear.

"Yeah," Mitch said as a slow grin spread across his face. "Goodie, goodie. Come on. Let's get the munchkin to bed." They started for the house again. "You want me to take her? Is she too heavy?"

"No, she's as light as a feather," Caroline said. "She's so tiny."

"I was a preemie," Ruthann informed her.

Without warning, Caroline's heart lurched treacherously as a flood of memories came rushing to her; memories of another little girl that had been born prematurely.

"Oh," she said, laying her cheek against the girl's silky hair as she fought down the feelings and shoved them back into oblivion where they belonged.

She followed Mitch into the house through a cozy kitchen and the dining room. As they moved into the hall, she could hear Janis, apparently talking on the phone, and she caught a glimpse of her in the living room. It was a pretty house—that much she could tell—and it was as tidy as any place inhabited by three kids could be.

Ruthann had stopped babbling by the time they reached the stairs, and her head was lolling sleepily against Caroline's shoulder when Mitch led them into the bedroom.

The small room was decorated with stuffed toys and frilly ballerinas dressed in pink. Mitch threw back a ballerina-patterned comforter and stepped aside to let Caroline lower the little girl onto the bed. It seemed perfectly natural for her to sit beside Ruthann as she placed the blanket over her.

"There you go...Short Stuff," she said, hesitating for just a second before using Mitch's name for his daughter. "You get some sleep, now, and I'll see you after your nap." She gently brushed a tangle of curls off the child's forehead, and Ruthann took her hand, looking at her gravely.

"Car'line, do you have a mommy?"

The question came out of nowhere and took her completely by surprise. "Yes, I do. She lives in France."

"Is that near San Fra'cisco?"

Caroline smiled and glanced at Mitch, who had just pulled the drapes, throwing the room into heavy shadow.

"Geography isn't her strong suit," he said softly as he moved across the room to the door.

"No, Ruthann. France is across the Atlantic Ocean, a long way away," she answered the little girl.

"Is your mommy nice?"

That question was harder to answer than it should have been, but there was no point in confessing that to Ruthann. "Yes, she is."

"Judy has a nice mommy, too," Ruthann told her.

"Who's Judy?"

"My friend. Her mommy makes cookies, but Larry's mommy doesn't like to do that. She buys cookies."

"Well, maybe Larry's mother doesn't have time to bake."

"If I had a mommy, she wouldn't have to bake cookies if she didn't want to."

Caroline felt a tug at her heart. "But I'll bet you'd like it if she did, wouldn't you?"

Ruthann nodded. "Choc'lat chip."

"Does Pop make cookies for you?"

She shook her head and scrunched her face in disgust. "He burns them. Only mommies make good cookies. Are you a mommy, Car'line?"

Those feelings that Caroline was certain she had buried long ago washed through again, compounding the poignancy of Ruthann's sweet sad questions, and Caroline suddenly felt tears stinging her eyes. It was absurd, but they were there. And so was a very old pain.

"No, I'm not a mommy, Ruthann," she said, then hastily pressed a kiss to the baby-soft cheek. "You go to sleep, now, sweetie," she said, then she stood and hurried into the hall, turning her head away as she brushed past Mitch.

CHAPTER EIGHT

MITCH HAD no idea that Caroline was upset as he quietly closed Ruthann's door and followed her into the hall. "I'm sorry about that," he said softly. "We put Ruthann in day care a few months ago so she'd have contact with kids her own age, and she's finally figured out that she's the only one there who doesn't have a mother."

"It's okay," Caroline said, but her heart was so choked with emotion that she had to stop and lean against the wall.

"Caroline?" Mitch moved around her and realized she was crying. "Caroline? What's wrong?"

She put her hand over her mouth, and then brushed at the moisture on her cheeks. "I'm sorry. This is silly. I don't cry."

"You couldn't prove it by me," he said in a soft, wry voice as he placed a comforting hand on her arm and ran it lightly up and down.

For a split second, he thought she was going to lean against him so that he could wrap her in his arms. He could see that she wanted to, and he was more than willing to do whatever it took to ease the pain he saw in her eyes, but the moment passed. She didn't reach for him, and Mitch knew better than to challenge her desire to handle this pain, whatever it was, alone.

"I'm sorry," she said again.

"Stop apologizing and tell me what's wrong," he urged gently.

Caroline took a deep breath that hitched in the middle. "I almost had a baby once," she whispered. "I didn't plan it. My husband and I certainly didn't *want* it. It should never have happened."

So that was it. Mitch understood a lot of things now about her reactions to children. Strangely, though, he had a feeling Caroline didn't understand it at all. "Did you have an abortion?" he asked quietly.

Caroline shook her head. "No. My husband wanted me to, but I couldn't, even though I knew it was the right thing to do."

He frowned. "Why was it the right thing?"

"Look at me," she said disparagingly. "Look at my life. I have no maternal instincts. I resent anything that takes me away from my work. I'm as self-centered and self-absorbed as my parents were, and I made up my mind when I was very young that I would never have a child just to use as a procreation trophy." She dashed at the tears on her cheeks again.

He could have argued with some of her assertions, but he didn't. "If that's the way you really felt, why didn't you have an abortion?" he asked, instead.

She looked genuinely bewildered. "I don't know. I just couldn't go through with it. It was stupid and illogical, but—" her voice broke "—I discovered I really wanted that baby."

Mitch brushed her cheek gently and she didn't flinch from his touch. "What happened?"

"I decorated a nursery, bought baby clothes and read a dozen books on prenatal care." She paused. "Then I had a miscarriage in my sixth month. It was a girl, but she was too small to survive." Caroline took a deep breath and straightened her shoulders, pulling herself together. "I'm sorry, Mitch. This is ridiculous. That was nine years ago, and I haven't even thought about the incident in ages. I knew it was for the best even then, and I put it behind me."

"Without allowing yourself time to grieve, I'll bet," he said.

"Maybe so," she said with a little shrug. She looked at him. "But it's too late for that now. And I really don't regret losing the baby anymore."

"Of course you do," he replied. "That pain you're feeling wouldn't have come back if you didn't still feel the loss."

She shook her head. "No. It was just that when Ruthann asked if I was a mommy..." She didn't bother completing her argument because it sounded illogical even to her own ears. Mitch certainly wasn't buying it, and Caroline didn't want to examine her resurgent emotions too closely. "Was Ruthann really born prematurely?"

Mitch let her shift the subject, even though this new direction was painful for him. "Yes. She was born eight weeks too soon...and my wife died because of it."

Caroline was stunned. "Oh, Mitch. I had no idea. I had wondered what happened to her, but I didn't know. I didn't want to ask..." She shook her head. "How can something like that happen in this day and age?"

His eyes took on a shadowed sadness. "She had a very difficult pregnancy from the beginning, but she refused to abort. Like you," he told her. "She spent nearly five months in bed. I know that's the only reason Ruthann is here today, but I think that was one of the things that killed Becky. She went into labor at the end of the seventh month and she just wasn't strong enough to handle it."

"Didn't the doctors do a cesarean section?"

"Not soon enough," he replied tightly. "They tried to stop the labor because Becky was adamant about giving the baby every possible chance to go to full term."

Caroline reached out and gently stroked his arm. "Tha must have been a painful decision for both of you."

"For me, it was, but not for Becky. This was the way sh wanted it." He shook his head bleakly. "You can't imag ine how many times I've asked myself whether I shoul have refused to support her decision."

The darkness in the hall did nothing to conceal the sad ness on his face. Caroline's heart went out to him. "I' sorry, Mitch. I can't even imagine what you must have gon through."

He gave her a very small, sad smile. "It's okay, now. still miss her, but I have Ruthann, and that's more consc lation than you can imagine. I could have lost them both." He paused a moment, studying Caroline's solemn, beauti ful face. He knew he should have felt a stab of disloyalty fo wanting to take her into his arms here, just a few feet awa from the bedroom he and his wife had shared, but the fee ing didn't come. He had done his grieving for Becky. H cherished her memory, but he believed with all his hear that she would want him to be happy again.

His heart also told him that Caroline Hunter could mak him happy if only she'd give herself half a chance to fall i love. He was tempted to ask her about her ex-husband be cause he wanted to know what kind of wounds her divorc had left, but now wasn't the time. It seemed to him tha they had come a long way in just a few minutes, and it wa time to look forward, not back.

He turned his smile up a notch. "Well, have we de pressed each other enough or should we have another go a it?"

Caroline managed a smile, too. If he could do it, so coul she. "Why don't we forgo depression and see if your fa ther needs any help with dinner."

They let the past go and tried to shake off the lingering effects of their separate sorrows. "You cook?" he asked with surprise as they started down the stairs.

"Of course. Even self-absorbed computer designers have to eat sometimes."

"Great. Maybe you can give Pop some lessons."

"Wait a minute." Caroline stopped one step below Mitch and turned. "You told me he made great hamburgers."

Mitch grinned. "I lied."

"Why, you rat," she said, grinning.

"Hey, I would have told you anything to get you to stay."

Her smile faded. "Mitch...I'm only staying for dinner. Nothing more."

He shrugged. "That's a start," he said, then jogged past her down the stairs before she could formulate a response.

POP'S HAMBURGERS weren't bad at all, but on the whole, Caroline found dinner with the Grogans to be a very strange experience. There was none of the formality she had grown up with. When her parents had been home to eat, they had used the evening meal as a time for quiet contemplation, refueling themselves mentally and physically after a long day in their research lab. Conversation had been discouraged.

The Grogans, on the other hand, treated dinner as a free-for-all. They laughed and teased one another. They shared their plans for the coming week. Sam talked about baseball and the camping trip the family always took to Big Sur every July. Janis gave voice to the nervousness she felt about the upcoming prom because she was going with three girlfriends, none of whom had a date. Ruthann had awakened from her nap as cranky as a grizzly bear roused prematurely from hibernation.

Mitch spent most of the meal reassuring his oldest daughter and trying to placate his youngest. Pop did his best to include Caroline in the conversation whenever he could, but mostly they listened to the kids, and in that department, Caroline was completely out of her depth. They spoke a language of pop culture that went right over her head.

They ate on the back porch as the evening shadows lengthened across the yard, and by the time they finished, it was nearly dark. Caroline offered to help with the dishes, but Janis and Pop wouldn't let her lift a finger. They cleared the table, corralled Ruthann, who was taken away against her will, and Janis practically dragged a bewildered Sam into the house, telling him it was time to watch TV.

Within seconds, it seemed, Mitch and Caroline had the backyard all to themselves, and the sudden quiet was almost a shock to the system.

"Do you get the feeling there's a conspiracy afoot?" Mitch asked, shooting Caroline a crooked grin.

"Is there?" she asked.

He nodded. "Yes."

Caroline frowned. "Do they think there's something going on between us?"

"Isn't there?" He speared her with a look that was so warm and piercing, Caroline felt a little breathless. Looking at Mitch and thinking rational thoughts were incompatible events. This had been one of the strangest days of her life and she had never been more off balance than she was at this moment.

Instead of responding to his question, she edged her chair away from the table and ambled down the steps into the yard. Mitch followed her, as she knew he would. She wasn't running away, she just needed some time to take it all in.

She went all the way to the swing set before she stopped. "I didn't have one of these when I was a child," she told him, running her hand lightly up the sturdy steel posts that supported the structure.

"Wanna give it a try? I'll push," he offered.

Caroline shook her head as she turned to him. "No, thanks. I'm too old to relive my first childhood and too young to slip into my second."

"You don't have to be a child to enjoy a little foolish fun," he told her.

"No, but you have to understand the basic precepts behind the concept." She sat in one of the swings and Mitch took the one beside her. It was a moment before she spoke again. "Mitch, for me, watching your family is like viewing life on another planet. It's a nice, friendly family, but I wouldn't even begin to know how to fit in." She finally looked at him. "Do you understand what I'm trying to tell you?"

Mitch looped his elbows around the swing chains and locked his hands in front of him. "I think so. But I also think you could be a fast learner if you wanted to be."

She shook her head. "No, Mitch. This territory is just too unfamiliar."

Her pronouncement didn't seem to faze him in the least. In fact, he seemed almost amused. "Didn't you ever watch 'Leave it to Beaver' and 'Father Knows Best' when you were a kid?"

Caroline shot him a sidelong glance. "Surely you jest. My parents considered television to be the cruelest curse ever perpetrated on mankind."

"Well, you're not living under your parents' jurisdiction now. You don't watch *any* TV?"

"Only the news and some documentaries occasionally."

"PBS must love you at pledge-drive time."

She chuckled, relieved that he wasn't pressing her about family and dating. But she knew he hadn't abandoned the issue permanently. "I've been known to contribute."

"What about movies?"

"I've seen *Gone With the Wind,*" she said with a mi chievous grin.

"Come on. That's all? Don't you have *any* vices?" H kicked the ground and set his swing in motion, swayin gently up and back.

"When I was married, my husband tried to get me inte ested in 'Star Trek,' his favorite TV program, but I neve got hooked." She looked embarrassed. "I do like countr music, though," she admitted reluctantly.

Mitch hooted with laughter. "That's a start, I guess Anyone who enjoys achy-breaky hearts and lonesome trai whistles can't be totally beyond redemption."

"You're making fun of me."

"No, I'm not," he said gently. "It's just hard for me t imagine your life-style."

"My work is my life-style, Mitch."

"And you don't have time for anything else." He didn phrase it as a question. He was just quoting.

"That's right."

He stopped swinging. "Then why did you stay here t night?"

It was a good question that deserved an answer. "I don know. Because it seemed like fun, I guess. And Aunt Lidd would have approved."

"Who's Aunt Liddy?"

Caroline's smile melted into something so soft and swee that it took Mitch's breath away. "She was my mother' bohemian sister. She was married four times, travele around the world more times than I could count, and sinc she didn't have any children of her own, she took her ma ternal instincts out on me whenever the spirit moved he She took great delight in infuriating my mother by kidnap ping me at least once a year."

"You loved her a lot," Mitch said.

Caroline nodded. "It nearly killed me when she died, but I have some very strange and wonderful memories of the times we spent together. She dragged me into some of the most outlandish escapades you could imagine."

"Ah, so you did have some fun as a child," he said in a "gotcha" tone of voice.

"Of course I did," she replied defensively, embarrassed by the picture of a lonely, deprived childhood she had obviously painted for him. "Studying was fun for me, Mitch. Learning and challenging myself were my greatest joys."

"Next to your Aunt Liddy," he said wisely, and Caroline nodded.

"Yes."

"I think I would have liked her."

"I know she'd have liked you."

"Really? What would she say about us dating?"

Caroline fixed him with a stern gaze. "Mitch, we are not going to date. You and I are oil and water."

He shrugged, conceding her point. "Maybe so, but what would Aunt Liddy say about us?"

She thought it over and finally confessed, "She'd probably tell me to add a little lemon, a clove of garlic, and make a salad dressing."

"Your aunt was a very wise lady," Mitch said softly as he wound his hand around Caroline's swing chain and slowly pulled her toward him.

Caroline could have dug in her heels and resisted, but she didn't. She held her breath as Mitch edged their swings together, dipped his head and kissed her. His mouth slanted across hers with his lips parted ever so slightly, and Caroline's world tilted on its axis.

She closed her eyes, her hands tightened on the chains she was clutching, and when Mitch deepened the kiss, Caroline lost herself in the warm, sweet sensations he evoked. His tongue traced her lips, then gently touched hers before plunging deeper into her mouth, demanding more than passive acceptance. She gave him more, mating her mouth to his until an incredible, jolting wave of heat coursed through her.

And then the kiss ended, leaving Caroline wide-eyed and breathless. Mitch released her swing and it settled back into place, but the hunger on his face was every bit as arousing as his kiss had been.

"I was right. You're dangerous," Caroline murmured.

"That which does not kill us makes us stronger."

This was insane. She couldn't be falling in love with this man. It just wasn't possible. But if it wasn't possible, why was she aching and breathless? Why did she want to throw herself into his arms and stay there? Sex had never been terribly important to her, but Mitch Grogan was making it seem more tantalizing than she had ever imagined it could be.

But sex wasn't love, and Caroline had never allowed her body to rule her mind. "No, Mitch," she said firmly. "It wouldn't work. We are not going to have a relationship."

"Why not?"

She straightened and tried to muster a little dignity and logic. "I believe in being practical," she said in a thoroughly practical voice. "I know that a few dates wouldn't necessarily constitute a relationship. Certainly not a commitment. But what's the point of even starting something that would end disastrously?"

He frowned. "What makes you so certain of that?"

She met his gaze steadily. "I'll give you three reasons."

He was disappointed but not surprised by her response. "You mean my kids?"

She nodded. "If you're going to spend time with a woman, it should at least be someone who knows the rules of baseball. Sam thinks I'm a space alien because I didn't know who Alejandro Peña is."

"Sam's a hard case," Mitch said. "He doesn't like anything but sports and camping. You do okay with Janis, though," he reminded her.

Caroline was too restless to sit still any longer. She stood and moved to the end of the swing set. "That's because Janis and I have some common ground. I know what it's like to be different from other kids, but that's where the connection ends, Mitch. I've never even been to a prom. I had no friends to talk on the phone with for hours at a time. In fact, I don't think I was ever a teenager. I went straight from infancy to adulthood. I'm not equipped to deal with children."

Mitch stood and moved to her. "Tell that to Ruthann."

"She's too young to know any better," Caroline replied, moving around the post she was holding on to, placing it between them for protection.

"You're right. You really don't know kids. They're the most honest, discriminating judges of character in the world. All they care about is whether or not you've got any love to give them."

She raised her chin defiantly and looked him squarely in the eye. "I don't, Mitch."

"Then you don't know yourself, either."

"Mitch—"

"Come here, Caroline," he ordered, stepping around the post and pulling her into his arms. He sealed their bodies together and Caroline had never imagined that any man could be so strong, feel so incredible, and yet be so gentle. It was terrifying because it was so wonderful.

His head dipped toward hers, but Caroline averted her face. "Mitch, don't. Please," she begged.

He froze for an instant, then obediently dropped his arms to his sides so that nothing was holding her against him except the warmth of his body and the aura of strength that drew her like a magnet. "All right, Caroline," he said, his

voice harsher than she had ever heard it. "Walk away. B
if you do, bear in mind that you're running from the wro
things."

She shook her head, but was so captivated by the inte
sity of his eyes that she couldn't move. "It would nev
work."

"Don't tell *me*," he replied gruffly. "You're the o
you're trying to convince."

Caroline swallowed hard and finally stepped back. S
suddenly felt so cold that she shivered. "I'm sorry, Mitc
Tell your father and the kids good-night for me."

She hurried away and disappeared around the house.

"Damn it!" Mitch cursed, lashing out at the chains
Caroline's swing. The seat swayed crazily, then settled in
a gentle rocking motion.

"Damn it," he said again, softer this time.

It was a long time before he returned to the house.

CHAPTER NINE

"COULD IT be a virus?" Brad Lattimore asked.

Caroline looked at him across the conference table where she and her OHARA programmers were meeting. "We ask that question every time there's a memory lapse, Brad, and we still haven't come up with an answer. If it's a virus, it's like none I've ever seen. Dr. Bergman and I have been through every line of code in the OHARA command core and we've found nothing that could be causing the losses. At this point, I don't think we have any choice but to do a line-by-line inspection of every data base."

Everyone in the room groaned, and Caroline didn't blame them. The course of action she had outlined was a time-consuming, excruciatingly tedious process. Nearly three weeks had passed since the attempted break-in and while there had been no further repeats of that event, late yesterday afternoon, Dr. Caldwell's entire astronomy data base had crashed because a large block of information had simply vanished from Scarlett's memory.

Such a massive failure, the first of its kind, had sent everyone into a panic. Since each data base was self-contained, Caroline had been able to separate astronomy from the main core before it caused a collapse of the whole system, but it had been a close call. Much too close. Work would now be suspended on every other data base, since there was no point in risking a repeat of the incident.

"Could we try replacing all the seeds on the mother

board?'' someone asked, referring to the small optical-fiber units that were the OHARA equivalent of computer chips.

Caroline shook her head. "We tried that once with no effect, remember? The problem isn't in the hardware, it's in the programming."

"Could it be the result of sabotage?" Brad asked. "Is it possible that this isn't a systems problem at all? Maybe someone is getting into the core and wiping out information one piece at a time."

Caroline was startled and a bit relieved that Lattimore was the one who'd broached the subject. Surely it was one more indication of his innocence. After the attempted break-in, Ed Newton had run another background check on the young programmer, but hadn't come up with anything to indicate that he might be involved in industrial espionage.

"We can't rule out the possibility of sabotage," she told him. "But it seems highly unlikely that someone is accessing the core on a regular basis since Dr. Bergman and I are the only ones with the required clearance." Despite the strain she was under, Caroline shot her chief programmer a mischievous smile. "Are you sabotaging Scarlett, Henry?"

Bergman, the oldest member of the team, grinned back. "No. Are you?"

"Not unless I'm doing it in my sleep." She stopped smiling and looked at her staff. "I know I'm asking for a tremendous amount of effort, people, but it's got to be done. At this point, we don't have a choice. Sarah, I want your team to start with—"

"Dr. Hunter?" The door to the conference room opened and Caroline's secretary poked her head in.

Caroline turned. "Yes, Lorraine?"

"Security just called. They need you downstairs for an entry authorization."

"For whom?"

"Janis and Mitchell Grogan are here."

She stiffened. "So? Janis is supposed to start work in robotics today, and Mitch Grogan already has clearance. What's the problem?"

Lorraine Wasserman shook her head. "Security says Mr. Grogan *doesn't* have clearance."

"Damn," Caroline muttered. Ed Newton was on vacation and apparently his staff had been negligent in his absence. "All right. I'll handle it." The secretary slipped out and Caroline turned to her chief programmer. "Henry, will you make the assignments we discussed earlier, please. I'll meet with each team later."

As she hurried out of the room, Caroline realized that her stomach had just tied itself into a few more knots. She didn't need this today. It had been three weeks since the Grogan barbecue...since Mitch had kissed her in the backyard on the swing set in the moonlight. She had walked away that night and had spent at least a small portion of every day since telling herself that she had made the right decision.

She had managed to convince herself of that, but only because she hadn't been forced to come face-to-face with Mitch. At her insistence, Bob Stafford had handled the official requests for Mitch's services with the Hilliard Police Department. Henry Bergman had taken charge of helping him get the data base started, and Mitch had directed all his questions to the chief programmer. He had visited MediaTech several times to bring his work in for approval and revisions, but Caroline hadn't made any effort to see him—or vice versa.

She studied his data base, of course; everything concerning Scarlett had to have her approval. But she made her suggestions and corrections on paper, then returned it to Henry.

It wasn't an unusual situation. She normally had very little contact with any of the data base consultants when they began their work, but with Mitch it was different. No matter how hard she tried to deny it, she had a relationship with him. It was a purely *hormonal* relationship, but it existed nonetheless. That was one thing she couldn't deny. Seeing him today would probably undo every bit of progress she had made in excising him from her thoughts.

Yet despite that grim possibility, Caroline found her heart racing as she went downstairs. She steeled herself for the meeting, and swore that she would resist any temptation to touch him. She did not want to see Mitch. She was not looking forward to this, she told herself sternly.

But when she entered the lobby and discovered that the man being detained by security was Mitchell Grogan, *Sr.*, instead of his son, her disappointment was as strong as her relief.

She covered both emotions as best she could. "Janis. Mr. Grogan. It's nice to see you again." She found a welcoming smile for Mitch's daughter, whose eyes were shining with excitement. "Are you ready to start work?"

"Yes, ma'am," she said with a beaming smile. "That's all I've been able to think about for weeks now."

Caroline didn't bother asking how the girl's final exams at school had gone. It was a foregone conclusion that Janis had aced them. Instead, she inquired, "How was the prom?"

"Fun, I guess," Janis replied. "My friend Tory had a sleep-over at her house afterward, and I enjoyed that a lot more."

"Did you find a nice dress?"

Janis chuckled. "Yes, but you should have seen daddy trying to help me pick it out. He knows nothing about fashion."

"But he did a better job of it than I would have," Pop commented.

Janis nodded in agreement and confided to Caroline, "Pop wanted me to wear a crinoline and a hoop skirt."

The elder Grogan shrugged. "That's what they wore back in my day."

Caroline had to smile. "You went to high school during the Civil War?"

"I've aged well," he said gravely, then grinned. Caroline noticed for the first time that his eyes were nearly as blue as Mitch's, and just as mischievous. "I hope you don't mind, Caroline, but I decided to take you up on that offer of a tour you made at the barbecue. From what Mitch and Janis tell me, this is quite a place. I'd like to see where my granddaughter will be spending her Wednesday and Friday afternoons."

Caroline had completely forgotten about the polite invitation she had made to him, but she couldn't very well renege. "Of course. I'll be glad to take you on a quick tour."

Apparently, Pop sensed her hesitancy. "Is this a bad time?"

"No, of course not." A fifteen minute tour wasn't going to hurt anything. "Just let me get Janis squared away, all right? She has some employment forms to fill out."

Caroline led them down to the personnel office in the administration wing and left Janis there, then she placed a quick call to Andrea Norris to tell her to come down and take charge of her new assistant.

"I'll drop by robotics later to see how you're doing," Caroline promised the girl, then left with Pop.

"You know, Janis smiles more around you than I've ever seen her smile before," Pop told her as they started the tour.

"That's just hero worship," Caroline replied, uncomfortably. "It will wear off once she realizes that I'm as human and fallible as everyone else. Now, all of these labs on the first floor are devoted to..."

She gave Pop the same tour speech she had given his son and granddaughter nearly a month ago. He seemed to find it interesting, but Caroline got the impression that there was more on his mind than viewing MediaTech.

Twenty minutes later, the tour was over and she was able to escort him back downstairs. For courtesy's sake, she felt obliged to make polite conversation. "How are Sam and Ruthann?"

"Just fine," Pop answered. "Sam won the first ball game of the season and Ruthann keeps asking when you're coming back. Janis isn't my only grandchild who's taken a shine to you."

That was a subject Caroline didn't want to address. "I understand that you were a teacher," she said mildly, hoping he'd take the hint as they entered the elevator.

He did. "Yep. I taught high school for twenty-six years."

"Mathematics?"

"Who, me? No," he said with a chuckle. "I taught English. I always figured Janis must have gotten that calculator brain of hers from Becky's side of the family because it certainly didn't come from me."

"But Mitch is very intelligent," she observed.

"That he is, but he's not a genius like Janis." The elevator doors opened and they moved into the lobby. "I guess Mitch told you about his wife."

The comment seemed casual, but Caroline sensed that Pop was finally getting down to the real reason he had come. "He told me how she died."

"Becky was a sweet girl. She loved Mitch, and God, how she adored those kids."

What was he getting at? she wondered. "Her death must have been very hard on Janis and Sam."

He nodded. "And Mitch. There for a while, I didn't know if he'd be able to hold it together, but he finally made some kind of peace with it. For the kids' sake, I guess."

"I'm sure he still misses her," Caroline said politely. She didn't want to hear about Mitch's pain or the heroic manner in which he had gotten on with his life. The less she knew about him the better off she would be.

The guard stepped forward to do an inspection, but Caroline waved him off and escorted Pop through the security station to the door.

"Of course he misses her," Pop replied. "That's only natural. But you know, I've always hoped he'd find somebody else one of these days. Not to replace Becky, of course." He stopped at the door and looked her squarely in the eye. "But he's a man with a lot of love to give, Caroline. It's been four years, and he's never shown any real interest in anyone." An unspoken "until now," hung in the air between them.

Caroline held his gaze as long as she could, then glanced away. She had absolutely no reason to feel guilty. It wasn't her fault that Mitch had become attracted to the wrong woman. "I hope you enjoyed the tour, Mr. Grogan," she said stiffly.

He seemed disappointed that she hadn't taken the bait, but he smiled, anyway. "Oh, I did. Now I guess I'd better head out. I have to pick up Ruthann at the day-care center. It's her last day and they're giving the kids a little graduation ceremony. Should I tell her you said hi?"

Caroline looked at him. "Certainly. If you think that would be . . . appropriate."

His answering nod told her that he understood what she was saying: Don't do anything that's going to mislead the child. "Maybe I'd better not say anything, then. Thanks for the tour, Caroline. Tell Janis that I'll be out here to pick her up at five."

"Stop in to see me anytime."

"Same to you. The door's always open to you at the Grogan house."

He left, and Caroline watched him go, feeling that she'd been foolish to be relieved earlier. Seeing Mitch couldn't possibly have made her feel any worse than she felt at this moment.

AT THE END of her first day on her first real job, Janis waxed positively poetic about everything at MediaTech. Her co-workers were brilliant and friendly. The equipment was state of the art. The research was fascinating and complex. Caroline Hunter was the most beautiful, intelligent, supportive, wonderful woman in the world.

That wasn't exactly what Mitch wanted or needed to hear, but he listened to his daughter with patience and enthusiasm all through supper and into the evening. Unable to get a word in edgewise, Sam went up to his room to reorganize his baseball card collection and Pop played a game of animal-alphabet flash cards with Ruthann to keep her busy.

Mitch just listened, asking questions occasionally, because this was important to his daughter. He couldn't deny that he was relieved, though, when she finally began to wind down. What with his work on the data base and his persistent memories of Caroline's shy blushes and the kiss they had shared, Caroline occupied too much of his mind as it was. It would be a long, grim summer if he had to listen to Janis rave about her on a biweekly basis.

"You know what was weird, though?" Janis asked, her face taking on a puzzled frown.

"What?" Mitch asked dutifully.

"I got the strangest vibes that something was wrong. Everyone was very tense. No one said anything outright, but they were definitely upset."

Janis wasn't always perceptive when it came to deciphering other people's moods, but Mitch didn't discount her insight. "Caroline, too?"

"Definitely. She tried to pretend that everything was fine, but I could tell she was really worried about something."

Now what was that all about? he wondered. Had Caroline been tense around Janis because of what had happened after the barbecue? She'd certainly made a point of avoiding him whenever he dropped by MediaTech to consult with Henry Bergman. In fact, he was beginning to find the impersonal little notes she wrote in the margins of his data base sheets irritating. She was treating him like a total stranger, or worse, like a criminal to be shunned at all costs. What had he done that was so terrible, after all? He had kissed her. Big deal. It hadn't meant anything...unless of course, she was finding it as impossible to forget as he was.

A slight glimmer of hope blossomed inside Mitch, but he squashed it quickly. Caroline had made it abundantly clear that she wanted nothing to do with him. More likely, something was wrong with her surrogate child, Scarlett. Another minor memory loss, perhaps. Or maybe another illegal access attempt.

Mitch decided not to express any of those possibilities to his daughter. "Caroline was probably just distracted because she has so much responsibility on her shoulders. But if there is a problem, I don't want you prying into it, young lady. If it's something you need to know about, Caroline or Mrs. Norris will clue you in."

"Oh, I wouldn't say anything," Janis swore, then paused hesitantly. "There is one thing, though. Do you think it would be inappropriate for me to ask Caroline if she'd like to come with us to the State Science Fair next month? I would really like for her to be there."

Mitch didn't think that was a good idea, at all. "Honey, Caroline is awfully busy."

"Is that why you aren't seeing her anymore?"

Mitch had known that question would surface sooner or later, and he'd been dreading it. "Janis, I was never 'seeing' Caroline. Not in the way you mean. We went out one time to discuss the data base."

"But she came here, too."

"To offer you the internship," he reminded her.

Janis frowned. "I thought you liked her."

Mitch certainly couldn't deny that, but he couldn't very well admit it, either. He didn't want to place any blame on Caroline or be forced to explain to his daughter that Caroline had vetoed a relationship because of the children. "It just didn't seem like something that would work out," he replied lamely.

"Well, you should have tried harder, Daddy."

"Janis, Caroline is very involved with her work right now."

"That's just an excuse. I'm not a child—I *know* she liked you. I could see it in her eyes. Obviously you screwed it up somehow!"

Mitch gritted his teeth and prayed for patience. His serious, logical daughter didn't get emotional very often, but when she did, she could be explosive. "Janis, I know you think a lot of Caroline, and that's fine. I approve. She's offered you an incredible opportunity and you *should* be grateful to her. What you *shouldn't* do is create some romantic fantasy about Caroline falling in love with me and becoming your mother. That's not going to happen."

It was obvious he had given voice to a very private dream, and Janis didn't react well to having it challenged. "It could happen if you wanted it to!" she said, rising to her feet.

"Janis—"

"Oh, what's the use. You don't understand at all!" She stormed out and Mitch could hear the pounding of her feet all the way up the stairs and into her room. When the door slammed, it practically shook the entire house.

Ruthann, who had abandoned the flash cards in favor of her coloring book, sat up and looked at her father. "What's wrong with Jannie?"

"She's mad at Daddy," Mitch replied.

"'Cause you made Car'line go away and not come back?"

Mitch tended to forget that, little as she was, Ruthann could be very intuitive. "I didn't make Caroline go away, Short Stuff. She just doesn't have any reason to come back and see us."

"She'd come back if you told her to."

"I'm sorry, baby, but it doesn't work that way."

Ruthann didn't want to hear that any more than Janis did. "Yes, it does. Daddies can do anything. Make her come back."

God, how frustrating! Mitch would have given anything to comply with his daughters' wishes, but he couldn't. "Baby—" He reached for her, but Ruthann sidled away and stood, facing him defiantly.

"Make her come back, Daddy! Now."

"I can't."

Her little face scrunched up in frustration as intense as her father's and she stormed out, doing the best impersonation of Janis Mitch had ever seen. Her tread on the stairs wasn't as heavy, despite her best efforts, but the slamming of her door was nearly as effective.

"Geez, what a mess," Mitch muttered, burying his head in his hands.

"Hey, what's going on?" Sam shouted from the top of the stairs.

"Women!" Mitch shouted back.

Sam had suffered with two sisters long enough to know what that meant. "Oh. Do you want me to load your gun and barricade the doors?"

Mitch shook his head wearily. "Go back to your room!"

Another door slammed.

He ran his fingers through his hair, then looked at his father. "You going to join the mutiny, too?"

"Not me. I think you're better off without her."

Mitch had been trying to convince himself of that for weeks, but it stung to hear his father say it. "Caroline is a wonderful woman."

Pop made it a habit not to interfere in his son's life, and when Mitch hadn't wanted to discuss Caroline's abrupt departure after the barbecue, Pop hadn't pushed. He'd known something was wrong, though. His son didn't have any of the sparkle or good humor it had taken him so long to reclaim after Becky's death. That was why Pop had cornered Caroline into giving him a tour today. He'd wanted to see if she'd volunteer any information. He'd been disappointed but not surprised that she'd closed up like a clam; she was a very closed woman. Not at all what his son needed.

"Tell me, son, how hard did you try with her?" he asked.

Mitch sighed wearily. "Pop, if I had pushed any harder, she could have sued me for sexual harassment."

"Then what was the problem? I could have sworn she was really attracted to you and I know you have it pretty bad for her. You've been a real bear ever since the barbecue."

"I don't want to talk about it, okay?"

"Why not?"

"Like I told Janis, it just wasn't meant to be."

"Because of her work, or your kids?"

"The kids," he replied reluctantly. "At least that's what she *said*."

"But you don't believe her?"

"No. You saw how she was with Ruthann."

Pop chuckled. "Yeah. Like a fish out of water."

"Then you weren't looking close enough. If she really didn't like kids, she could have found a dozen ways to discourage Ruthann. Instead, she held her, stroked her hair, played with her...she even tucked her into bed."

"Then what's her real problem?"

"I think she's afraid to try and fail. She had parents who were probably very well intentioned, but they didn't know how to nurture a child. They were too obsessed with their work, and she's afraid she'll be just like them. She's built her life on success and she doesn't want to risk her perfect record of achievement."

Pop heard the note of bitterness in his son's voice. "That's a shame."

Mitch looked at him, frowning. "I thought you just said it was for the best."

"Ah, but what I think doesn't count. It's what *you* feel that matters, and you're feeling an awful lot for a woman you barely know. That indicates some pretty strong chemistry."

"Well, it's beside the point, because nothing is going to come of it."

Pop reached over and squeezed Mitch's arm. "I'm sorry, son."

"Me, too," he said with a strained smile. "But I've got to think of the kids first. There's no point in wasting time on a woman who isn't even willing to try."

"That doesn't make it any easier to forget the ones that get under your skin, though, does it?"

Mitch reached for the remote control and flipped on the television, signaling the end of a discussion that was a lot more painful than it should have been. "No, it doesn't."

He and Pop fell silent as the twenty-four-hour news channel began filling them in on the day's events around the world. Neither of them noticed Janis slip away from the door and hurry back up the stairs, dashing at tears on her cheeks.

CHAPTER TEN

MITCH TOOK a late lunch hour the next day and used the time to drop by MediaTech. He had worked late the night before on some data base revisions Caroline had requested, and he wanted to make certain he had them right this time before he went any further. That was really just an excuse, though. What Janis had said about Caroline's being upset bothered him and he wanted to see for himself. He tried to rationalize that it was just his cop curiosity, but the little part of him that had started to hope she was regretting her decision wouldn't let him rest until he knew for sure.

Since he normally dealt with Dr. Bergman, Mitch didn't have any idea how he was going to finagle an audience with Caroline. But luck was with him. Bergman wasn't available, and when his assistant offered to take the data base sheets and pass them on to him, Mitch declined and headed straight for Caroline's office.

He had another piece of luck when he found that her secretary wasn't at her desk. Perfect. Caroline's door was ajar, and Mitch rapped twice, but when there was no response, he pushed the door open, expecting to find the room empty.

It wasn't. Caroline was at her desk, so deeply engrossed in studying a computer printout that she was oblivious to his presence.

Mitch could tell at a glance that Janis had been right. Caroline was pale, and lines of exhaustion indicated she hadn't slept in days.

He hated to interrupt her, but he had to know what was wrong. "Caroline?"

Her concentration was so absolute that it took a moment for her to respond. "What?" she asked, then looked up. Mitch's presence registered on her, and she took a startled breath. "Mitch. Hello."

If Mitch hadn't been so concerned about her, he might have laughed at her reaction. She looked confused, as though she had just been snapped back to earth from some distant part of the galaxy. A flush of pleasure flashed across her face, then she squelched it quickly. That was something, at least. Whatever she felt for him was still there, whether she wanted to admit it or not.

"Hello, Caroline. I'm sorry to disturb you," he said, stepping to her desk. "I brought these data base sheets for Dr. Bergman, but he's not available."

It took Caroline some time to answer, as though part of her was still back on whatever planet she'd been visiting. "Uh, no. He's working in the control room today."

"Why don't I just leave them with you, then," he suggested, placing the folder on her desk.

"Thank you. I'll have Henry get them back to you as soon as we've gone over them." She hesitated a moment as though she was trying to decide what she should say. "We've both been very impressed with your work. You're doing a good job."

"Really?" She didn't invite him to sit, but he took a chair, anyway, and smiled ruefully. "You couldn't prove it by all the little notes you keep leaving in the margins."

"I'm sorry about that, but this is very exacting work. One piece of information even slightly out of sequence could spell disaster."

Disaster? Mitch wondered at her choice of words. "Caroline, what's wrong?"

She looked startled. "Wrong? Nothing is wrong, Mitch."

"I don't believe that."

She took a deep breath. "Mitch, please don't start with me. I know that you were disappointed the night of the barbecue, but I thought I made my feelings about us clear."

"You did make yourself clear, Caroline. That's why I haven't made any attempt to see you. But as it happens, I meant what's wrong with Scarlett." He gestured toward the dormant computer. "This is the first time I've ever come in here that she didn't snap to attention and say hello."

Caroline blushed with embarrassment. "Oh. I'm sorry. I misunderstood." She glanced at the computer. "We've temporarily shut down all terminals except for the direct access ones in the control room."

"Why?"

"Scarlett suffered another memory loss."

"A bad one this time?" he asked, though he already knew the answer. Nothing short of catastrophe could be responsible for the exhaustion and worry in her eyes.

"Very bad. The astronomy data base crashed day before yesterday," she told him. "We're not making any effort to reconstruct it right now, and we won't be inputting any new information until we've isolated the problem and corrected it."

"Do you want me to stop work on the law enforcement data base?" he asked.

"No, the shutdown won't affect your work at this stage, but it may mean a delay in actually feeding the information into Scarlett."

"You're scared, aren't you, Caroline?" he asked gently.

"Yes." The answer popped out before she could censor it, but she was surprised to find that it felt good to be able to admit it to someone. She'd been putting up a front for her staff and trying to convince Bob Stafford that this was a minor setback, not the end of the world. She hadn't realized until this moment that she needed someone to reassure *her* that everything was going to be all right.

"We came within a hairbreadth of losing the entire system, Mitch," she told him as she leaned back in her chair. "If I hadn't been here to shut the command core down, everything would have crashed."

"I'm sorry, Caroline. I know this isn't what you were hoping for."

"You're right. It's not. For the last few months, I've come in here every day thinking that today is the day I'll find the problem, correct it and announce the OHARA launch. Instead, the problems keep getting more serious and the launch date looks farther away than ever."

Mitch wanted to tell her that she had too much of herself invested in the computer, but he couldn't. It was her work; and as she had told him, her work was her life. "Is there anything I can do to help?"

"I don't know what it would be," she replied wearily. "No one is going to wave a magic wand and make a miracle happen. I just have to keep going over the programming codes until I find the one that's causing the problem."

"And if you don't?"

Caroline's soft hazel eyes turned as hard as stone. "That's not an option, Mitch," she said harshly. "I know this system will work. I've staked my entire career on it. I've courted investors and made believers out of a board of directors who used to think I was living in a science fiction dreamworld. I'm one step away from making artificial intelligence a reality, and I won't accept defeat now."

"Caroline..." Mitch didn't know what to say. Did she need to be prepared to accept the possibility of failure, or did she need someone to tell her that her hard work would eventually pay off? Or did she just need a hug and a friendly shoulder to cry on? Though he knew it was a chauvinistic notion, Mitch suspected it was the latter. Caroline wasn't weak, but she *was* human and everyone needed a little comforting from time to time.

Unfortunately, her big desk was between them, and Mitch suspected that if he tried to circle it, she would clam up. "If there's nothing I can do to help, I guess I should leave you alone to get back to work," he said finally, hating the gulf between them.

Caroline stood. "Probably so." She hesitated a moment, then moved around the desk. "Thanks for bringing the revisions by. I'll get them back to you as soon as I can."

Mitch stood, too. "There's no rush. I can probably survive a few days without reading any of your irritating little notes in the margins."

"Irritating?" she said with a frown. "Why did you find them irritating?"

"Because they're so impersonal, like something a stranger would write."

Caroline looked down. "I'm sorry, Mitch. I suppose I have been ... distant."

"Only from about here to the planet Neptune."

She mustered the courage to look at him. "You know why."

"Because I pushed too hard?"

"Because you make me feel things that I—"

"Caroline, we've got to talk. Now!"

Mitch almost cursed aloud when a harsh voice at the door interrupted her. Had Caroline been on the verge of making an admission? An admission that might have led to a discussion that might have led to a crumbling of her reservations that might have led to ... what? A relationship? Or another rejection?

He'd never know now, because Bob Stafford was standing in the doorway looking as though he wanted to strangle someone.

"What's wrong?" Caroline asked, moving toward him.

Stafford cast an uncertain glance at her visitor, and Mitch said, "Would you like me to wait outside, Mr. Stafford?"

The administrator thought it over, then shook his head. "No, you're part of the team now, Grogan. You'll find out sooner or later."

"Find out what?" Caroline asked insistently.

Stafford closed the door before announcing coldly, "The Richmond Group just announced that they're launching VIC."

"What? That's not possible!"

"Oh, yeah? Tell that to the reporter from *PC Imaging* who just called to find out how MediaTech felt about the introduction of the world's first optical-based, artificially intelligent computer."

"He was just stirring up trouble," Caroline argued, but her face had turned several shades paler. "VIC can't possibly be ready."

"Then why is Richmond holding a private, by-invitation-only demonstration for the press, their investors and a few industry insiders next week?"

Caroline moved to the desk and leaned against it. "This can't be happening," she murmured. "It's just not possible."

Mitch had a pretty good idea he knew what was going on. If he was correct, he could understand why Caroline was in shock and Stafford looked about ready to erupt. The Richmond Group was MediaTech's biggest competitor; if their optical interface computer was ready to be marketed, Stafford's company was in big trouble. The millions they had invested in Caroline's work could be lost, and with the

OHARA project already in trouble, the board of directors might decide to scrap it altogether and cut their losses.

"Are you absolutely certain about this, Mr. Stafford?" Mitch asked.

Stafford nodded. "After I got the call from the reporter, I started checking around. A computer researcher at Cal-Tech and another one at Computer Labs confirmed that they had received invitations to the demonstration."

"But why haven't we heard anything about it?" Caroline asked. "You can't keep a demonstration like this secret for very long."

"From what I gather, Richmond is moving fast on this."

"A preemptive strike," she said, her anger rising.

"That would be my guess. Randall Thalberg said he just received his invitation yesterday."

"When is the demonstration?"

"Monday."

Caroline came up off the desk in an explosive flash. "This isn't possible! We've been ahead of them every step of the way!"

"Not anymore," Stafford said sarcastically. "Apparently, Howard Richmond figured out how to design *his* computer without any bugs."

The comment was a slap in the face to the designer of the OHARA computer system.

"Caroline, what is VIC?" Mitch asked, hoping to distract her before she exploded in Stafford's face.

She looked at him blankly, barely registering his presence. Her ability to concentrate and shut the rest of the world out really was a little scary, Mitch decided. "VIC stands for Verbally Interactive Computer," she answered after a moment. "The Richmond Group has been working along the same lines as MediaTech. They succeeded in bringing their optical computer on-line about a year after we got the OHARA up and running."

"Were they trying to create the same kind of software data base that Scarlett uses?"

"Yes, but again they were well behind us. Ten months ago, we heard that Vic's primary data base suffered a total collapse. They couldn't possibly have reconstructed it so soon."

"Industry rumors are notoriously unreliable," Mitch reminded her gently.

"Not this one," she argued. "Three days after the supposed collapse, Howard Richmond fired his top two programmers—the ones who were responsible for creating the data base. One of them was so furious that he went straight to the press."

"A disgruntled ex-employee?" Mitch suggested.

"No. I'm telling you, Mitch, VIC collapsed! Its base programming was faulty and it couldn't stand the weight of all the information they were feeding it. Richmond can't possibly be launching unless—" Caroline froze and her eyes turned dead cold. "Unless they acquired a working data base from another source."

"Whoa! Slow down, Caroline," Mitch said. "If you're suggesting that—"

"Let her finish," Stafford said shortly, cutting him off. "Frankly, I'm surprised that it took her this long to realize it. It was my first thought when I heard the news."

Caroline looked at Mitch. "It's the only way they could have accomplished it," she said, imploring him to believe her. "Somehow, Howard Richmond got his hands on Scarlett."

Mitch saw three possibilities in her accusation. One, she was overreacting. Two, she was a poor loser. Three, she was correct. With stakes this high, Mitch wasn't prepared to discount her accusation, but even if she was right, it wasn't particularly smart of her to voice it. "Caroline, that allegation is nothing but slander unless you can prove it," he cautioned her. "Can you?"

"Not yet, but I will."

"How? What are you going to do? Storm The Richmond Group and demand that Howard confess?"

She speared him with a wilting glare. "How stupid do you think I am, Mitch? I know how difficult industrial espionage is to prove."

"Then stop slinging accusations that could get you sued."

"Why? Are you going to run and tell him what I said?"

"I just don't want you to say or do anything you might regret later," he replied patiently.

"I will not roll over and play dead, Mitch!"

"I'm not suggesting that you should. Just watch what you say and who you say it to, all right?" he replied. "I think you're forgetting that I'm a cop."

"Then *you* do something!"

"Based on what? Your intuition that Richmond couldn't have beaten you to the draw? That's not a solid basis for a criminal investigation."

"He's right about that, Caroline," Stafford interjected. "At this stage, we have absolutely nothing to prove Richmond has done anything wrong. We can't file a formal charge with the police department until we've got more than suspicions to go on."

"Launch a full in-house investigation," Mitch advised her. "Ed Newton knows what to do and what to look for. If someone at MediaTech sold technology to Richmond, there will be evidence of it somewhere."

Caroline was obviously annoyed by Mitch's response to the situation. "Fine. Ed will be back from his vacation Monday. He'll start then. In the meantime, I have no intention of sitting around here twiddling my thumbs," she said as she moved briskly around her desk.

"What are you going to do?" Mitch asked.

Caroline reached for the phone. "I'm going to get an audience with VIC."

"How?"

She stopped with the receiver in her hand and glared at him. "I don't think you want to know that, Lieutenant Grogan."

In a few short minutes, Mitch had gone from being a member of the team to an unwelcome outsider. "Caroline, be careful," he cautioned. "Any move you make now could put you at risk of being accused of industrial espionage yourself. You can't afford that."

"I know what I'm doing," she said coldly. "And when I've got proof of what Howard Richmond has done, you'll be the first to know."

For Caroline's sake, Mitch knew he had to leave. He would have to sever his work ties to MediaTech, too, most likely. If a crime really had been committed, he couldn't risk having a charge of bias leveled against the Hilliard Police Department.

"All right, Caroline. But be careful." He looked at Stafford. "Make sure she doesn't do anything foolish, all right?"

"Goodbye, Mitch," Caroline said sharply before her boss could respond.

"Goodbye, Caroline." He turned and left.

Stafford shut the door behind him, then turned to Caroline. "What *are* you going to do?"

She began stabbing at numbers on the phone pad. "I'm calling Evan. I want a private interview with VIC, and my ex-husband is going to arrange it for me."

CAROLINE HAD MET Evan Converse about the time she finished her third doctorate degree. She had been a serious, practical, twenty-two-year-old virgin who'd never had more than a handful of dates in her life. Evan, at age twenty-five, had been finishing his doctorate in computer sciences. His dissertation on creating a verbal interface processor to enable computers to talk had dovetailed neatly with Caroline's dissertation on artificial intelligence.

Theirs was a match made in heaven. Or so it had seemed to Caroline in the beginning. Evan had been as cautious and practical as she was, yet they shared the same seemingly farfetched dream. He had convinced her that together they could create the world's first verbally interactive computer. It never dawned on Caroline that she had always had that dream and she had never questioned her faith in her ability to do it—with or without help. Having someone to share the dream with, someone who could help her over the obstacles and bolster her determination had seemed like a sound, sensible idea.

On that basis, she had convinced herself that she was in love with Evan Converse; and for that reason, the marriage had been a disaster. Evan might have shared her dream, but he hadn't been much help in overcoming obstacles or solving the thorny problems that stood between Caroline and success. As for bolstering her determination, he hadn't been much good in that department, either. In fact, as their three-year marriage deteriorated, Evan had become more of a stumbling block than a helpmate; smart as he was, he was no match for Caroline. Eventually, he began to resent her brilliance, and as his resentment grew, so did the trouble in their marriage.

Her pregnancy had been the last straw. Their research had been at a critical phase and Evan hadn't understood her unwillingness to have an abortion. Yet Caroline had been unmovable and there had been nothing Evan could do but complain.

Then she had miscarried, and when she turned to her husband for emotional support to help her through the surprising and nearly unbearable pain of that loss, all she found was a man who was happy that his partner wouldn't have anything to distract her any longer.

Caroline had filed for divorce a month later. Evan had put up a fight at first, trying to win her back, but eventually he had given up and accepted the inevitable. When the divorce became final, Caroline had accepted a position as chief designer of an optical interface computer at MediaTech. Unfortunately, it had taken Evan nearly a year to land a job as a section supervisor at The Richmond Group, where he had been put in charge of creating a verbal interface processor.

Caroline had fully expected her ex-husband to harbor resentment against her because she had a position of far more power and authority than he did, but that hadn't happened. Once the sting of the divorce passed, they had actually managed to salvage a friendship. They didn't socialize because neither of them was socially active, anyway, but Evan called her from time to time just to chat and find out how she was doing. It was all very civilized; almost antiseptically so, as a matter of fact, and Caroline was glad. She didn't resent her ex-husband or even dislike him. She just never should have married him.

Caroline knew that using her past association with Evan to gain entry to the VIC computer system would place him in a ticklish situation with his boss, Howard Richmond, but she was beyond caring. She had to see Richmond's computer—before the launch, if possible. Failing that, she had to get an invitation to the demonstration.

Unfortunately, when she called The Richmond Group she was told that Dr. Converse was unavailable. Not wanting to tip her hand too quickly, she refused to leave a message at the research lab. Instead, she called Evan's apartment and told his answering machine that she needed to speak with him immediately.

He didn't call her back. Not that night or Friday, or at any time over the weekend. When it became clear that he might well be away, Caroline began looking for another way to obtain an invitation to the demonstration. She called every friend who owed her a favor until she found one who wasn't going to be able to use her invitation.

On Monday at four p.m., she presented it to the guard who was screening visitors in The Richmond Group's spacious, ultramodern lobby. If Mitch Grogan wanted proof that someone had stolen her life's work, Caroline would give it to him. No matter what it took.

CHAPTER ELEVEN

THE GUARD at the door of The Richmond Group addressed Caroline as Dr. Leister, the name on her invitation, and needless to say, she didn't bother correcting him. She moved into the lobby, where some of the best brains in the computer industry were mingling, sipping champagne and waiting to see if the grandiose claims Howard Richmond had made in his invitation were true.

Caroline accepted a glass of champagne from a passing waiter, then moved to join her colleagues.

"Dr. Hunter. Good to see you again," Paul Bradley, a reporter from *PC Imaging* said as he intercepted her. "Are you here scoping out the competition?"

Caroline didn't want to talk to reporters. "Just curious, like everyone else," she replied, trying to skirt around him.

Bradley didn't let her go. "Bob Stafford wouldn't comment when I called him last Thursday. Do you have anything to say?"

"I'll reserve my comments until after I see Vic in action," she replied cautiously.

"Professional jealousy?" he asked.

Caroline tried not to grit her teeth. "You know better than that, Paul. I'll be the first to applaud any legitimate advances in the quest for artificial intelligence."

He grinned. "That's the most politically correct and noncommittal answer I've heard in my entire career. And totally unquotable," he added.

"That was my intention," she replied sweetly, then slipped away from him and began mingling with a group of computer designers she had known for most of her career. Caroline had called one or two of them in her search for an invitation, but she had been careful to make the conversation sound casual until she discovered if they were attending or not. As a result, none of them knew that she hadn't been invited, and certainly no one questioned her right to be here since so many of Richmond's other competitors were here, as well.

The general consensus among them was surprise that Richmond was taking this gigantic step forward, especially since everyone thought that Caroline was the front-runner in the race.

Howard Richmond had gone out of his way to create a festive party atmosphere in their high-tech lobby, which wasn't surprising. The Richmond Group had long been considered to be all flash and little substance. Howard was obviously going to take great delight in rubbing his success into the noses of those who had looked down on him for so many years.

As she listened politely to the conversations and tried to quell her nervousness, Caroline glanced around hoping for a glimpse of Evan. She wanted to talk to him, even though she didn't consider it likely that he knew anything about the theft of Scarlett—if indeed such a thing had taken place. Evan had faults, but he was an ethical man who wouldn't have associated himself with anything illegal. Since he wasn't one of the chief designers who had worked on the project, concealing the theft from him wouldn't have been difficult. In fact, it was likely that only a few people at Richmond knew anything about it.

There was a possibility, though, that Evan could get her a private interview with the VIC, and Caroline knew she would need that. She doubted she could learn anything of substance from the demonstration that was about to take place, and what she needed was hard proof. The only way she could get that was by examining VIC's data base programming and comparing it to Scarlett's. Nothing short of that would hold up in court.

Unfortunately, Evan was nowhere to be seen, but when Caroline caught a glimpse of a familiar set of broad shoulders and long shaggy hair, she nearly dropped her champagne glass.

"Excuse me, " she muttered as she elbowed her way through the growing crowd. "Mitch?" The man turned, and Caroline's heart leaped into her throat. He was here! Despite the skepticism he had voiced, he had come! "What are you doing here?" she asked.

Mitch smiled at her surprised expression. There couldn't be any doubt this time that she was glad to see him. "I told you once, I like to keep abreast of what's going on in my jurisdiction," he replied.

"How did you get an invitation?"

"I have my resources," he answered smugly. "I've been working on the edges of this business long enough to have earned a favor when I need one. Ed Newton isn't the only head of security I've had in my seminars. How about you? Should I ask how you got your invitation?"

She didn't see any reason not to tell the truth, since her only unethical act had been her failure to correctly identify herself to the guard outside.

Caroline didn't want to read too much into Mitch's presence, but she had to know one thing. "Your being here, Mitch... does that mean you believe m—"

"Shh." He touched one finger to her lips, silencing her. "I don't think you want to ask that question in the present company," he whispered, glancing around.

Caroline looked, too, and discovered she was completely surrounded by reporters. No one seemed to be paying special attention to her, but the last thing she needed was to see in bold headline print that she had accused Howard Richmond of industrial espionage and theft.

She nodded, but she was undeniably disappointed. His reaction last week had hurt her far more than it should have, and it seemed very, very important that she have Mitch's support.

Whether by design or accident she couldn't have said, but Mitch kept Caroline distracted with small talk about his kids. Sam was doing fine. Ruthann already missed her friends at the day-care center. Janis had talked nonstop after her first day on the job, but she seemed to have settled down after her second day. In fact, getting her to talk about MediaTech Friday night had been like pulling teeth, which wasn't unusual with Janis. Like Caroline, she tended to slip off into a world of her own where little intruded on the realities of her mathematical mind.

Caroline tried to listen to Mitch's chitchat, but it was hard for her to concentrate on the words. His deep, mesmerizing voice did have a calming effect, though, and she was very glad he had come, no matter what the reason.

When Howard Richmond finally showed up, gladhanding his way through the crowd like the lord of the manor, Caroline's calm deserted her. She had never liked the man, anyway, and now she was convinced she had a reason to hate him. There was something too slick about his manners and his charm. He smiled often, but it rarely seemed to reach his eyes. He was entirely too calculating for Caroline's taste, and it was everything she could do to maintain a polite mien as he worked his way toward her.

Just the expression on his face when he saw her, though, was enough to justify the trouble she had gone to to be here. For once, his phony smile faltered, and there was no mistaking the surprise in his eyes. He recovered quickly, but not before Caroline got a glimpse of something she chose to interpret as fear.

"Caroline. How nice to see you," he said, extending his hand to her.

She had to force herself to take it. "Thank you, Howard. It's nice to be here."

He looked for a moment as though he was going to ask how she had gotten in, but too many eyes were on him. Caroline had gambled on the hope that he wouldn't want to cause controversy by confronting her, and she'd been right. Instead of challenging her, then, he turned his fake smile on Mitch. "I don't believe we've met," he said, extending his hand again.

"This is Mitch Grogan," Caroline told him. "He's a good friend of mine.

"Oh. Pleasure to meet you, Mr. Grogan. Please enjoy the demonstration." He looked at Caroline. "I know you'll find it fascinating, my dear."

He moved on to the next group of guests without waiting for a response.

Mitch glanced down at Caroline curiously. "You didn't want to tell him who I am?" he asked quietly.

She looked at him innocently. "I told him you're my friend. You are, aren't you?"

"Yes, but I don't know that I'd call us *good* friends. Not yet, anyway."

He was looking at her in the way that always made Caroline blush, but she didn't this time. She didn't protest the innuendo, either. She had too many important battles to fight now; fighting Mitch, as well, was the last thing she wanted. "I decided that it wasn't wise to let Richmond know I'm suspicious just yet," she explained. "Curious, yes. But not suspicious."

"Caroline, he had to know you were going to be suspicious," Mitch told her, keeping his voice low. "Otherwise, he wouldn't have excluded you from the invitations list."

"Well, if I'm right about...you know what, I hope that's not the first mistake he's made."

Before Mitch could respond, Richmond began calling everyone to attention. He threw open the doors to a small lecture hall and his guests began pouring in. Inside, his staff of programmers and the designers of the various VIC systems were seated on either side of the stage. In the center, bathed in a bright pool of light, sat a four-foot-tall computer tower, a monitor and keyboard on a small desk.

Caroline and Mitch found seats near the center aisle farther from the front than she would have liked, but it didn't really matter. The room held only seventy-five people, and everyone had a good view.

It didn't take much encouragement to quiet the crowd when Howard Richmond took the stage, looking and sounding a great deal like a carnival barker. "Ladies and gentlemen, when Bell Laboratories succeeded in proving that it was possible to build a digital optical computer in 1990, everyone in this industry knew that the race was on to create a new wave of technology that had heretofore only been dreamed of by the likes of Isaac Asimov and Arthur C. Clarke.

"Ladies and Gentlemen, I'd like to introduce you to the finish line of that race. The world's first verbally interactive computer—Vic, for short. And I'd like to invite you to sit back and be astounded."

If he was hoping for applause, he didn't get any from his skeptical audience. He didn't seem too disappointed, though. He stepped back and turned to the beige tower in the middle of the stage. "Hello, Vic."

"Hello, Dr. Richmond."

"Vic, we have a number of guests here who would like you to tell them a little about yourself."

"What would they like to know?" the masculine voice asked, causing a considerable stir among the audience.

"How you were constructed and what your purpose is," Richmond replied, smiling smugly.

Vic complied with the request, to the astonishment of everyone in the audience, with two exceptions. Caroline was too distraught to be astonished. When Mitch reached over to lightly rub her clenched fists, she took hold of his hand and held on for dear life.

Mitch soothed his thumb across the back of her hand comfortingly, but most of his attention was focused on evaluating Vic and the answers he gave to Richmond's next series of questions. The voice was obviously masculine and it wasn't nearly as smooth as Scarlett's speech patterns. Vic spoke as though individual words had little meaning for him—they were just strung-together syllables with only marginal inflection, unlike Scarlett, whose voice and speech patterns were amazingly human.

Mitch knew that meant very little in determining whether Vic had been built on Scarlett's technology. In both computers, the voice processor was a system completely separate from the information data base. This computer spoke in a coherent, effortless fashion and, despite the lack of inflection, it gave a very effective performance.

Eventually, Richmond stopped asking questions and threw the floor open to his guests, inviting them to satisfy their curiosity. It was a necessary step to prove that Vic wasn't just reciting a series of preprogrammed responses, and it was the opportunity Caroline had been praying for.

On the other side of the room, someone asked Vic how many calculations it could make per second. Someone else rose and asked what the total memory capacity was, then a third person asked, "Vic, calculate the exact decimal value of two elevens."

A buzz of alarm went around the room, but was silenced completely when Vic responded. "Are you certain you wish me to perform that function? That calculation is a nonterminating decimal, point one eight one eight one eight into infinity. It would be more fruitful to set specific parameters for the calculation."

The answer was one that no ordinary computer could possibly have given, and the audience burst into applause and appreciative laughter, but Caroline's grip tightened convulsively on Mitch's hand. He looked at her, frowning as her face grew pale with fury. She seemed to be having a problem remaining silent.

And she didn't for very long. A few minutes later, after another set of questions, she finally came to her feet and Mitch stopped breathing because he had no idea what she was going to say.

"Vic, do you have any friends and if so, what are their names?" she called out.

Mitch took a breath. It wasn't as bad as he had feared. Howard Richmond had quite the opposite reaction, though.

"Vic, halt," he commanded before the computer could answer, then he mustered a patronizing smile. "Dr. Hunter, this is a computer, not a lonely hearts club. I'm sure you'll agree with me that no one would expect a computer to have friends—or even understand the concept of friendship."

He received a spattering of nervous laughter and Caroline got a lot of curious looks. Richmond didn't give her a chance to continue. "Now, are there any more questions? If you'll raise your hands, please..." He called on another guest, and from then on he identified each speaker so that he exercised complete control over the proceedings, which lasted for nearly an hour before he politely told them they'd seen enough. He invited everyone to sample more celebratory champagne in the lobby, and the show ended.

Howard Richmond received a rousing standing ovation, then everyone began talking at once as they filed out of the lecture hall. It sounded like the excited chatter of birds, and it was almost more than Caroline could stand. She wanted to scream. She wanted to tell these fools that they had been applauding *her* work, not Richmond's. Somehow, he had stolen Scarlett from her, and he had brazenly presented it to the world as his own! He wouldn't get away with it. No matter what it took, she would prove that Howard Richmond was a thief and a charlatan. Then she would see that he was sent to prison for as many years as the law allowed.

She was so angry that she barely realized that Mitch had taken her hand again and was guiding her out.

When she looked up at him, her eyes were blazing with fury. "Mitch—"

He shook his head. "Not here, Caroline. I know we need to talk, but we need some privacy for this."

He was right. "My place?" she suggested.

Mitch nodded. "I'll be there in half an hour."

"No, we can't leave just yet," she replied.

He leaned over to whisper in her ear. "You are not going to confront Richmond." He wasn't asking, he was ordering.

Caroline wasn't that foolish. "No. But there is someone else I have to see."

"Who?"

Instead of answering, she looked around until she spotted her ex-husband. Mustering as much goodwill as she could manage, Caroline moved through the room until she reached Evan Converse.

Mitch stayed with her the whole way, wondering what she was up to now, and what her relationship was with the tall, thin, bespectacled man she had just cornered.

"Hello, Evan."

Whatever their association, the man didn't seem unhappy to see her. In fact, his face lit up and he gave her a friendly kiss on the cheek. "Caroline! How are you?"

"Still in shock. That was quite a performance your computer gave."

"Thank you. Though you know it's not *my* computer. I'm just part of the team."

"Don't be modest, Evan. You've done a remarkable job."

"Thanks, Caroline." He took her hand and kissed her cheek again. "That means a lot coming from you. Listen...I'm sorry I couldn't get back to you. This was a crazy weekend, what with the launch coming up and this new project I'm working on. Did you know Howard has put me in charge of modifying my VIP for the new robot we're designing?"

"No, I hadn't heard."

"What's a VIP?" Mitch asked, mostly as a reminder to Caroline that he was there.

Evan looked at him blankly. "Have we met?"

Caroline jumped in. "I'm sorry, Evan. This is Mitch Grogan, a good friend of mine."

"Grogan... That name sounds familiar. Do you work at MediaTech?"

"I'm handling a short-term project there," Mitch replied cautiously. Caroline was wise not to want anyone to know she had involved the police in her suspicions, but if she wanted to keep it a secret for much longer they were going to have to make a strategic retreat soon, or else someone was bound to recognize him.

"And Mitch, this is Evan Converse," Caroline said. "My ex-husband."

Ex-husband? Mitch was surprised, but that was quickly overcome by a flash of anger. This was the man who had wanted Caroline to abort her child and who was probably at least partially responsible for her conviction that she would make a terrible mother.

Mitch managed a civil greeting and Evan answered the question he had been asked about the verbal interface processor. Caroline didn't let him go on too long about his work, though.

"Evan, I need to talk to you about something," she told him. "Would it be possible for us to meet for a cup of coffee? Tomorrow, maybe?"

Evan's thin face took on a hesitant frown. "Caroline, if this is about Vic, you know I can't answer any questions—"

"Evan, we *have* to talk," she said more forcefully, then lowered her voice. "There's something you don't understand."

He looked perplexed, but Mitch was certain Evan would have capitulated if Howard Richmond hadn't chosen that moment to intervene. "Evan! There you are." He shot a glance at Caroline and Mitch. "You folks will have to excuse us, but the press is clamoring for pictures of the design team. They're waiting for you in the auditorium," he told Evan, patting him on the back to send him on his way.

Converse shot an apologetic look at Caroline, then disappeared into the crowd.

"I hope you're not trying to wrangle any of our design secrets out of your ex-husband, Caroline," Richmond said with a condescending smile that made Mitch want to punch him in the face. If the sudden tension in Caroline's body was any indication, she was having the same reaction.

"Are you accusing me of industrial espionage, Howard?" she asked tersely.

"Of course not. That was a joke."

"It wasn't funny."

"Oh. Sorry." He didn't look apologetic at all. "I know that having us beat you to a launch date is very upsetting, Caroline, but I hope there are no hard feelings."

Mitch was proud of her. She glared at him, but she kept her mouth shut rather than shout the accusation he knew was on the tip of her tongue. That was good. It was far better to have Richmond think she was a poor loser than to have him on his guard. It was going to be hard enough to prove that he had stolen the Scarlett data base.

When Caroline didn't respond, Richmond shrugged and hurried off to join his design team.

"Good girl," Mitch muttered, releasing a long-held breath.

"Let's get out of here," she said harshly.

Caroline scrawled her address on a piece of paper, shoved it at Mitch and hurried out.

"IT WAS Scarlett. I know it was, Mitch. No one can convince me otherwise."

Caroline was pacing her living room in the same frenzy he'd found her in when he arrived five minutes ago. He hadn't really had a chance to do more than glance around this one room of her condo, but he hadn't been at all surprised to find that her computer was one of the most prominent fixtures in the room. Einstein was curled up on the chair opposite Mitch, but the aloof white Persian cat couldn't have cared less about his mistress's distress.

"Caroline, nothing Vic said today could be considered *proof* that he was constructed from stolen technology," he said patiently, hoping she would eventually calm down.

"But I still know it!"

"How?" he asked.

Caroline knelt beside him on the sofa, facing him. "Mitch, if someone cut off Ruthann's hair, dressed her in dungarees and made her look like a little boy, would you still recognize her?"

"Of course I would."

"Then trust me when I tell you that Vic has the same data base as Scarlett. I created her. I know how she thinks, and Vic answered every question today in exactly the same way Scarlett would have! No two humans would do that, and no two computers would, either, unless they had identical programming. Somehow, Howard Richmond got his hands on the Scarlett data base. You have to believe that!"

He could see how important it was to her that he believe. That alone might have been enough for Mitch Grogan, the man who was falling in love with this difficult, beautiful woman, but it wasn't enough for Mitch Grogan the detective. Fortunately, he had more than her suspicions to go on. Now that he had met Howard Richmond and seen the demonstration, he had his own.

"I do believe you, Caroline," Mitch told her.

The relief that flooded through her was so potent it took all the fury out of her. That was what she needed to hear, and she could have kissed Mitch for saying it. "You heard the similarity, too, didn't you?"

"No, I didn't. But I've had only one conversation with Scarlett. I'm not competent to judge how she would have answered those questions."

Caroline settled onto the sofa with her legs curled under her, still facing him. "Then why do you believe me? Last Thursday, you acted as though you thought I was making wild accusations because I'm a poor loser."

Mitch gave in to the temptation to touch her, gently stroking her arm as he said, "I'm sorry, but I had to accept that as a possibility."

"Yet you came to the demonstration today."

"Because I knew there was also a possibility you were right. Now, I'm pretty sure you are."

"Why?"

"Because Richmond had absolutely no reason to censor your question unless he was afraid Vic knew the answer. If the computer hadn't known what friends were, it simply would have said so and no one would have thought it the least bit unreasonable. But if Vic had answered the question, it would have raised a lot of suspicion. Particularly if it had said 'Caroline Hunter is my friend.' That is what you were hoping for, wasn't it?"

She nodded. "I'm sure they've tried to erase a lot of information like the answer to the question I asked today, but they can't have gotten it all. That's what Richmond was worried about."

"I agree."

"Then you see why I've got to talk to Vic alone."

"No, no, no," he said, shaking his head firmly. "You can't do that, Caroline. At best, you could be accused of trying to steal a rival's computer secrets. At worst, they could charge you with attempted sabotage."

"Then what am I supposed to do?" she demanded.

"Launch an in-house investigation. Look for suspicious behavior among your employees. Search for ties between MediaTech and Richmond employees, then we can start digging into bank records and big purchases—anything that would indicate someone at MediaTech has come into a large sum of money recently. If one of your people sold the data base to Richmond, he or she didn't do it for free. There's an incriminating trail of green paper somewhere, and we'll find it. It will just take time."

"I don't have time!" Caroline said, springing off the sofa in agitation. "You heard Richmond's speech today. They're gearing up for production right now. By fall, they'll be ready for full-scale marketing. Did you see how Lewis Granger headed for the stage right after the presentation?" When Mitch looked blank, she explained, "Granger is the NASA representative who has been breathing down my neck for the last year wanting to know when the OHARA would be ready. He represents a government contract worth millions—which MediaTech is about to lose to The Richmond Group! I can't let that happen."

Mitch stood and moved in front of her, forcing her to stop pacing. He put his hands on her shoulders. "Caroline, listen to me. This has to be done by the book. If we can get enough proof, we can slap an injunction on Richmond to stop production until we can take the case into court to prove that he stole the data base. Until then, you'll just have to be patient. And thorough."

That was the last thing she wanted to hear, but she accepted his judgment. "All right. We'll do it your way." It seemed like the easiest thing in the world to slip into his arms, so she did. "Thank you, Mitch."

His arms tightened around her; he pulled her close and pressed a kiss to her hair. "Aw, shucks, ma'am. I'm just doin' my job."

That wasn't all, and they both knew it. She raised her head and looked at him. "Are you hungry?"

He grinned. "Starved. Are you offering to cook, or is that a polite way of telling me to go home and eat?"

"I'm cooking."

"Good. I don't want to go home yet."

She slipped out of his arms. "I don't want you to go home yet, either," she said softly as a pale pink blush spread across her cheeks. "I'll see what's in the fridge."

She turned and hurried out of the room.

CHAPTER TWELVE

CAROLINE'S KITCHEN was a model of efficiency, and so was her method of cooking. At least once a month, she devoted an entire day to making casseroles and freezing them. Cooking dinner for Mitch was simply a matter of thawing a dish of lasagna in the microwave and throwing together a salad.

Mitch called home and left a message with Sam to tell Pop not to expect him for a while, then he offered his services as assistant chef. Working together, they had the meal on the table in less than half an hour.

There was still a great deal of tension in the air, but it had more to do with the exciting sexual chemistry between them than Caroline's distress over what had happened today. Through dinner, though, Mitch avoided the former topic and concentrated on the latter, outlining a plan for her to investigate Howard Richmond's theft of the Scarlett data base.

At first, it bothered Caroline that Mitch referred to it as "alleged" theft, but she finally realized that he was just responding to his own training as a police detective. He really did believe that she had a case, and he was prepared to help her. For the first time since her Aunt Liddy's death, Caroline didn't feel as though she was totally alone in the world. She had a connection to this man that was gradually becoming less frightening.

"Caroline, I mentioned finding connections between MediaTech and Richmond employees," Mitch said with a touch of hesitation as they cleared the table and rinsed their dishes at the sink. "There's one very obvious connection that needs to be considered, don't you think?"

She looked at him blankly. "What connection?"

"Your ex-husband."

"Evan?" The very idea of him as an industrial spy was laughable. But then, Mitch didn't know Evan Converse the way she did. "Mitch, are you suggesting that Evan paid me to sell the secrets of my own computer to Howard Richmond?" she asked with a chuckle.

"Of course not," he replied, handing her an empty salad bowl. "But is there any way he could have gotten the technology from you without your knowledge? You told me that you have a terminal here. Has Converse visited? Could he have gotten hold of the data base disks or taken a peek at your access codes? Do you talk in your sleep?"

The last question threw Caroline. She looked at him in astonishment and found a strange coolness in his eyes that told her he was fishing for more than clues to the theft. "No. To all of the above," she said tightly. "Evan calls me occasionally, but he's been here only once that I can recall—and that was before I established a link between my home computer and Scarlett." She paused a moment before adding firmly, "And I haven't slept with him since the day I found out I was pregnant, nearly ten years ago."

"Sorry. I had to ask."

"Well, now you know," Caroline said as she began loading the dishwasher. "Evan couldn't be responsible for the *alleged* theft."

Mitch let the argument go for the time being, but he would reserve judgment on Evan Converse's innocence until he had a chance to investigate the man more thoroughly. He realized that he would have to keep his own bias under control, though; hurting Caroline didn't make Converse a thief, just an idiot, and there was no law against that.

"You and Converse have obviously remained friendly," he commented mildly. "He seemed glad to see you today."

"We *are* friends," Caroline replied. "We just never should have been husband and wife."

"Did you love him?"

The question seemed to have caught her by surprise, but Caroline didn't flinch from responding to it. Instead, she closed the dishwasher and considered her answer carefully. "To tell you the truth, Mitch, I'm not sure."

"Caroline, love isn't something that's easily mistaken for the common cold or appendicitis. If you've ever been in love, you'd know it."

"Emotions aren't always easy to define."

"Were you in love with Evan Converse, or not?" he asked more insistently this time.

Caroline looked at Mitch and simultaneously conjured up an image of her ex-husband—not Evan as he was today or as she had viewed him at the time of their divorce, but the serious, intelligent man she had married twelve years ago. Even then, when Caroline should have been enraptured by the bloom of first love, Evan had never made her feel the way Mitch did now. As much as she wanted to deny it, she was beginning to understand that there was a big difference between loving someone as a friend and "being in love."

"No," she said finally. "I don't suppose I was ever in love with him."

"Then why did you marry him?"

"Because we shared a common passion for our work, I suppose. I thought we would make a good team."

"Like your parents?"

"I suppose so. My parents had the perfect marriage—a flawless meeting of the minds that has allowed them to accomplish great things together that they might never have achieved individually.''

Mitch suppressed a shudder. "That sounds very cold and sterile, Caroline. What you're describing is a business partnership, not a marriage.''

"Isn't marriage a partnership?'' she asked coolly.

"That's part of it,'' he admitted. "But there's more to it than that. Didn't you find that out with Converse?''

"Yes, I suppose so.''

Mitch didn't want to force her into a discussion of something that would be painful, but he really needed an answer to his next question. "Did you divorce him because of the baby?''

"I don't blame Evan for wanting me to have an abortion. When we got married we made a decision not to have children. *I* was the one who reneged on the agreement we made when we got married. In essence, I was forcing him to have a child he didn't want.''

"Then he was a fool.''

"Mitch, not everyone is cut out to be a parent,'' Caroline argued.

"Oh, I know that,'' he said ruefully. "I'm living proof that it takes a lot of hard work, but it's worth it, Caroline. I think you must have known that in your heart or you wouldn't have wanted your baby so much.''

Caroline obviously didn't want to talk about the child she had lost. "Why don't we get out of the kitchen?'' she suggested as she headed for the living room.

Mitch let the subject drop and followed her. He still had questions, though. Caroline was a fascinating enigma, and he knew that the only way he was ever going to get closer to her was to unravel the puzzle. At the moment, it seemed more productive to keep the conversation light, though. "Tell me, what did your parents think of Converse?'' he asked. "Did they approve of the match?''

"They never got to know him very well, but they thought he was a logical choice for a husband," she replied, taking a seat on the sofa.

Mitch grinned as he sat next to her. "That figures. What about your Aunt Liddy? Did she approve?"

Caroline laughed. "Are you kidding? She told me that if I married him, I'd become a dried-up old prune-face like my mother before I turned thirty."

Mitch laughed, too. He was sorry he'd never have the chance to get to know Caroline's aunt. He could have used her help, about now. "You thought so much of your aunt, I'm surprised that you didn't heed her warning."

"Mitch, I loved Liddy, but her life wasn't exactly appealing to me—gadding about the world, divorcing husband after husband . . . I wanted stability, not chaos."

"So you compared your parent's sterile marriage to your aunt's erratic life-style and instead of finding a happy medium, you chose to be like your parents."

"I guess I did."

"And ended up divorced like your Aunt Liddy."

Caroline chuckled at the irony. "I've never thought of it that way before, but you're right. And now, I'm married a second time—to my work."

"Another sterile union," Mitch said softly.

"Mitch—"

"Hush, Caroline," he said before she could start an argument. He cupped her jaw, rubbing his thumb over her cheek, and drew her face to his. "Stop thinking for five minutes and let yourself feel."

Caroline found it difficult to breathe. "I don't know if I can do that."

"Sure you can," he whispered as he kissed her.

It was a very soft kiss, as soft and tantalizing as the kiss he had given her on the swing set. And just like that one, it quickly evolved into something more urgent, as though sweet, simple contact between them wasn't enough. Mitch's arms encircled Caroline and hers went around his shoulders as they strained to get closer. Their tongues danced and mated with a feverish intensity that forced a tiny whimper of frustration out of Caroline's throat, and Mitch responded by running one hand up her side until her breast was cupped in his hand.

When Caroline arched her body, accepting the intimacy and begging for more, Mitch began working at the buttons of her blouse. His lips left hers to trail down her throat, and Caroline gasped when his mouth closed over the crest of one breast, lathing it through the fabric of her bra.

An explosion of heat erupted inside her so intensely that she cried out. Mitch's lips found hers again, but it was too much for Caroline. Her feelings were too passionate, too profound, too real...and entirely too frightening.

The small part of her mind that could still think grasped for a sliver of sanity, and she pulled away.

"Mitch, stop. Please..."

His eyes were dark and hooded with emotions every bit as intense as hers, his breath was just as irregular and his need was very apparent, but he didn't drag her back into his arms.

"Caroline—"

"This is ridiculous," Caroline said, gasping for air as she edged away from him—and the passion she was feeling. "I'm an adult. Adults don't get carried away like this."

Mitch frowned. "Why not, for God's sake?"

"Because..." It took her a moment to think of an answer; to *think*, period. "Because love should be sane and sensible. Two people with common interests and shared values who want the same things out of life. It's not runaway hormones and necking on the sofa like a couple of teenagers."

Mitch realized what she had said before she did. "Are you in love with me, Caroline?"

"Of course not!" she said, buttoning up her blouse and trying to steady her breathing. "I was speaking figuratively."

A slow, sexy grin spread over Mitch's face. "Leave it unbuttoned."

Her hands were trembling so much that it took considerable effort, but she kept on with what she was doing. "No. I won't."

"I'll just have to undo them again," he warned her.

The prospect made her heart leap into her throat and she knew she had to escape. "This is happening too fast, Mitch," she said as she rose from the sofa.

She moved away from him, keeping her back to him as though the feelings would disappear if she couldn't see him, but Mitch wasn't going to let her retreat this time. Caroline had a deep well of passion inside her that had never been tapped. No matter what it took, he was going to be the one to unleash it; maybe not tonight or tomorrow, but soon.

He followed her and ran his hands lightly up her arms, and when he felt her shiver, he gently turned her toward him. "Then we'll slow down, if that's what you want," he promised.

"You don't understand, Mitch!" she cried, twisting away from his caress. "I don't want it to happen at all!"

The soft, sexy light in his eyes turned hard and cold with frustration. "Damn it, Caroline, make up your mind! Do you want me to be patient and go through a long courtship or do you want to give in to what we're both feeling and let nature take its course? Or do you really prefer the third alternative?" He pointed toward the door. "I can walk out of here and never come back. Make up your mind which, because I'm not going to play this game anymore."

"I am not playing a game with you!"

"Yes, you are." He grabbed her shoulders and fought the urge to shake her. Instead, he simply held her still so that he could look into her eyes and be certain she was listening to what he had to tell her. "It's a game called 'Caroline Is Afraid to Fall in Love.' But I'm *not* afraid, Caroline. I want this. I want *you*," he said intensely. "I want to show you that love *is* necking like teenagers. That it is anything *but* sane and sensible. It's hard work. Sometimes it's painful and sometimes it's wonderful. Sometimes you want to wring your lover's neck and at other times nothing matters but being with her. It's kisses and kids and fights and compromises. Most of all, Caroline, it's being alive. Now, stop lying to yourself and make up your mind, damn it. Do you want that or not?"

Caroline's jaw quivered as a single tear coursed down her cheek. Mitch was right. She had been playing a game with herself, and it was time to stop. "Yes," she whispered. "I want that."

Finally. That was everything Mitch needed to hear. "Then for crying out loud, stop fighting yourself and let me love you," he said gently, taking her into his arms.

Caroline felt his arms close around her, felt the strength and warmth of him... It was too wonderful to be real. "This is scary, Mitch," she whispered.

"It's supposed to be, Caro," he murmured as his lips brushed hers. "Anything worth the risk is scary. Just stop thinking. Stop throwing up roadblocks and creating detours. Sit back and let yourself enjoy the ride."

As he spoke, his warm breath caressed her cheek and then her throat. When he began nibbling at her earlobe, Caroline's breath hitched in her throat. "Life isn't an amusement park, Mitch," she managed to tell him.

"How do you know?" He stopped what he was doing and looked at her. "Have you ever been to one?"

"No," she admitted softly.

He ran one hand up her back and the other traveled from her waist upward until the heel of his hand was lightly pressed against her breast. "Then you have no idea how wonderful a roller coaster can be, do you? Or a Ferris wheel? Or the tunnel of love?"

Caroline shivered, but not from cold. Mitch's voice was as mesmerizing as his touch, and Caroline knew that she was lost. "No."

His soft smile made her melt inside. "Good. Then let me introduce you to the wonders of an amusement park, Caroline."

"But Mitch, I'm not...I haven't used..."

He silenced her with a gentle kiss. "I'll take care of it, Caroline," he promised as his lips brushed hers again and he began the slow, methodical task of opening up a new world to her.

As he worked his magic, Caroline was only vaguely aware of guiding him to her bedroom. She kicked her shoes off and Mitch helped her out of her clothes, kissing and caressing her until she was naked. Her inhibitions melted away with her clothing, and she gave herself over completely to the feelings she had been fighting for weeks.

The sensations he evoked in her were incredible. Heat and light seemed to coalesce, centering low in her abdomen, making her ache for fulfillment. Every sense sprang to life and was filled by Mitch—the scent of a masculine cologne and something stronger, earthier, musky...the taste of his skin...the sound of his fevered breathing and deep short moans that came from his throat...the feel of heat and sweat as his skin slid along hers...the sight of his incredible eyes, dark with passion, as he rose above her and seemed to drink in the sight of her.

And then he pressed into her, and Caroline discovered senses she never knew she possessed. She gasped as a wave of pure sensation washed over her, and Mitch froze.

"Am I hurting you?" he asked, his voice rough and yet incredibly tender, too.

"No. No, it's wonderful," she said hoarsely, straining against him. She moved her hips rhythmically and wrapped her legs around his, straining as he began moving with her, slowly at first, then more forcefully.

Caroline moaned as the heat raged out of control and Mitch kissed her fiercely, plunging his tongue deep into her mouth in a frantic imitation of the pounding thrusts of his hips. The heat turned to fire and began to spread. It stole Caroline's breath away. It coursed through her and her cries were lost in Mitch's mouth until she wrenched her mouth away from his and cried out his name.

The wave passed, but Mitch didn't stop and another began building. She strained against him, reaching for the heat until it burst over her, searing every one of her senses. She heard her own voice calling his name and then his hoarse voice joined hers in a moan of ecstasy. He raised up on his elbows, his hands clasping her shoulders as he thrust again and again until he cried out with one final crash of pleasure.

He froze there, his eyes closed and his head thrown back, and then he slowly lowered his head and opened his eyes. They were dark, intense, and so filled with love that Caroline's eyes filled with tears.

"My sweet Caro," he whispered, kissing her gently, then he moved lower, pressing moist kisses against her breasts and back until he claimed her mouth again. Then he eased his body off of hers, wrapping her in his arms and pulling her with him until she was cradled against him, her head on his shoulder.

She stayed there, listening to his breathing return to normal, feeling his heartbeat, reveling in the nuzzling kisses he pressed into her hair until he drifted off to sleep.

CAROLINE DRIFTED in and out of consciousness, never quite asleep but not fully awake, either, but always aware of Mitch's body beneath hers. She didn't want to examine what had happened, but she had to. Mitch Grogan wasn't the type of man who would wake up, put on his clothes and say "Thanks, kid. See ya later." He wanted more than that from her. And Caroline wanted more, too. She wanted to explore this newfound thing called passion. Like any dedicated scientist, she needed to dissect it, understand it, recreate it and call it her own, as though she were the first to discover it.

But she wasn't the first. Mitch had already known what to expect; though from the way he had looked at her, Caroline wondered if perhaps he'd gotten a bit more than he'd bargained for, too. What would he want from her now? And more importantly, what could Caroline give him? How much of herself would she have to give up in order to have a relationship with this man—and what would she get in return? Mitch had already disproved her long-held belief that sex was grossly overrated. What other convictions could he shake?

"I can hear the wheels turning in that beautiful head, Caro," Mitch said sleepily.

The rumble of his voice in his chest made her cheek tickle. "Is that what woke you up?"

"Probably." He used one finger to tilt her face up to his so that he could kiss her. "Are you all right?" he asked.

She nodded. "There were a couple of dips in the roller coaster that really shook me up, but I'm fine."

"I was kinda impressed by the tunnel of love," he said in the soft, gravelly sexy voice that had always thrilled her.

She blushed and brought her head back to his shoulder to hide her face, but Mitch just chuckled. "Where are we now, Caro?" he murmured, pressing a kiss to her temple.

She smiled languidly. "You don't know? We're in bed, Mitch."

"For how much longer?"

"Until you have to get up and go home."

"And after that?"

Caroline had known this was coming, but she still wasn't prepared for it. She didn't run from it, though. Instead, she rose on one elbow and looked down at him. "Are you asking me for a commitment, Mitch?"

"Yes," he answered, brushing a damp curl off her forehead. "This is too special to let go of, Caroline. *You're* too special..."

"But you're part of a package deal, Mitch," she reminded him softly.

He didn't flinch from the truth or try to soft-pedal it. "That's right. Love me, love my kids. Can you do that?"

"I don't know," she answered honestly.

"Are you willing to try?"

Caroline closed her eyes and lowered her head to his chest, brushing her cheek lightly against the soft mat of curls. "What if I fail? What if I do or say something that hurts them? What if our relationship doesn't work out and they—"

"Caroline, you can ask questions and look for problems from now until the end of time, but you'll never know if you can do it until you try."

He was right. And the alternative to trying was to lose Mitch once and for all, right now. That would be unbearable. Caroline was alive for the first time in her life. She felt soft, warm and womanly. She felt as weak as a kitten and strong enough to move a mountain, all because she was in the arms of a strong, confident, loving, sensitive, sexy man.

She had to give herself a chance to believe in his kind of love, because there was so much to gain if he was right.

"All right, Mitch. I'll try."

She felt his chest rise and fall in a sigh of relief. With one arm tightly at her waist, he rolled over, pinning her under him and then kissed her until she was breathless. "You won't regret it, Caro," he whispered against her lips.

God, how she hoped he was right.

When he kissed her again, she stopped hoping and started feeling.

CHAPTER THIRTEEN

MITCH LEFT Caroline's shortly after midnight. He didn't want to. He wanted to stay with her until the sun came up so that he could make love with her one more time in the sleepy hour before dawn. But he had to work tomorrow, and he had three impressionable kids to consider. They would believe him if he told them that he'd had to work all night, but he didn't want to lie to them.

As he pulled into the driveway, he was surprised to see lights on. Pop usually went to bed as soon as he got the two youngest kids tucked in. Janis was his night owl, but her room was dark, thank goodness.

The lights downstairs began going out one by one as Mitch made his way inside, so he wasn't surprised when he unlocked the front door and found his father poised at the foot of the stairs, ready to ascend with a glass of milk—probably warm—in one hand.

"Hi, Pop. Couldn't sleep?" he asked quietly as he secured the door behind him.

"Nope. Sam made me watch a horror film with him tonight," he explained. "Those slimy green monsters gave me the creeps. Sam's already sleeping like a baby, of course."

Mitch grinned. "You want me to check under the bed for you?"

"Thanks, but I already did that."

"Find anything?"

"Only that it's been too long since I ran the vacuum up there." Pop took a sip of his milk and eyed his son. "You must be on a pretty big case to keep you out so late."

"Yes. Well, it wasn't a case...exactly. I mean, it *was* a case. At first. But then..."

Pop chuckled. "You don't have to explain, son. You always were about as transparent as a pane of glass when it came to women. I'm glad to see that hasn't changed."

Mitch reminded himself he was a grown-up, not an adolescent who'd been caught necking in the back seat of his father's car. "I was with Caroline, Pop. I went to The Richmond Group this afternoon to see if there was any basis for the accusations she made last week. We...ended up at her place."

Mitch didn't often go into the details of his work, but he had told Pop about this one. "I thought as much. Did you solve the case? Or is there even a case to be solved?"

"Yes and no. Or vice versa," he corrected himself. "I'm convinced someone at Richmond has stolen some very powerful technology from Caroline, but proving it is going to be tough."

"Guess that means you'll be seeing a lot more of her."

"A *whole* lot more, Pop," he said, his voice laced with a significance he knew his father would understand.

Pop nodded thoughtfully and sat on the stairs, and Mitch joined him. "Are you sure this is really what you want, son?"

"Yes."

"What about the kids?"

"What about them? They love her already," Mitch replied.

Pop shook his head. "Ruthann would love anything in skirts that she could call Mommy and Janis would like nothing better than to have another genius in the family.

But they're both romanticizing her. I don't want you to make the same mistake and get hurt."

"I'm not, Pop," Mitch said, letting the warm, incredible emotions he had felt tonight wash over him. "There's something very special about Caroline. She makes me feel the way Becky used to when I first met her—as though I'm Superman, Flash Gordon and Dick Tracy all rolled into one."

"So you wanna be Caroline Hunter's hero, too?"

Mitch leaned against the wall and looked at his father. "I want something for me, Pop," he said seriously. "I love my kids and I'd do anything in the world for them, but I deserve a life, too. Caroline has made me feel really alive again for the first time since Becky died. I don't want to give that up."

"But what about the kids?" he said again. "What affects you, affects them."

"Pop, if I didn't honestly believe that Caroline will be good for them, I wouldn't have been able to give her a second thought. That's part of what attracted me to her in the first place. She has so much love to give, and she doesn't even know it." He put his hand on his father's arm. "I'd like to have your blessing, Pop, because I'll sure as hell need your help."

A frown creased his weathered face. "What kind of help?"

"Patience and support. For Caroline. You said yourself that she's a fish out of water when it comes to kids. It's going to take her a while to adjust and figure out that she won't damage them for life if she says the wrong thing. Can you help me make her feel comfortable around here?"

"Mitch, I told her last week that the door to the Grogan house was always open to her, and I meant it," he replied. "You just be careful. I don't want you to fall too hard too fast and find out that the girls aren't the only ones who have fallen in love with an idea rather than a flesh-and-blood human being."

"I won't." He gave his father a hug, then both men rose and started up the stairs. "Listen, I've invited her for dinner here tomorrow night, but we can go out if you don't want to cook."

"No, that's okay. I'll cook. It'll be better to start her out slow," Pop said with a grin. "Restaurants can get kinda complicated with Ruthann. You don't want to scare her off too soon."

Mitch grinned. "That was my thinking, as well."

"Smart boy."

WHEN CAROLINE arrived at Mitch's house the next evening at six, she was every bit as nervous as she had been the first time she'd been there. Maybe even more so. Then, she had been fighting her feelings. Now, she had acknowledged them and had made a commitment that scared the living daylights out of her.

She had to give the relationship a chance, though, because she wanted it to work as much as Mitch seemed to. This was the worst possible time to be introducing an unfamiliar set of challenges into her life, but chances for a kind of happiness she had never known—or even believed existed—didn't come along every day. She couldn't let this one pass.

It would have helped quiet her nervous stomach if Mitch had been home when she arrived at the house, but Pop was the one who greeted her with the news that his son had just called to say he'd be late. "He had to set up a stakeout with his men, but he wasn't going to have to work it until after midnight," Pop informed her. "Come on in and make yourself at home."

"Thank you. Is there anything I can do to help you with dinner?" she asked as she placed her purse on a deacon's bench that ran along the wall at the foot of the stairs.

"Nope. Everything is under control. You're welcome to join me in the kitchen, though," he said as he started out of the foyer. "I've got to check the roast."

"All right. I'll—"

"Car'line!" Ruthann and Janis appeared at the top of the stairs, and Caroline smiled up at them.

"Hello, ladies."

Ruthann came charging down at breakneck speed, but her sister stayed where she was. Caroline's heart leaped into her throat when the little girl almost stumbled, and she reached out to steady her, but Ruthann had other plans. She threw herself into Caroline's arms, leaving her no choice but to receive and return a monster hug.

"I knew Daddy would bring you back. I knew he would. I knew it," Ruthann chanted as she placed a sloppy kiss on Caroline's cheek.

"Yes, he did," Caroline replied. "Your father is a very persuasive man." She looked up the stairs. "Hello, Janis. How are you?"

"Fine."

It wasn't the most enthusiastic welcome Caroline had ever received. "How's your work coming on IVAR? You must be getting him ready for the state competition soon."

"In three weeks," Janis said as she started down the stairs.

"Janis! Come set the table!" Pop called from the kitchen.

"I'll help, too," Ruthann squealed, wiggling out of Caroline's arms. "Car'line sits by me!"

The little girl raced off to the dining room, but Caroline waited until Janis reached the bottom of the stairs so they could walk in together. "I'll give you a hand," she offered.

"You don't have to bother," Janis said. "We're used to doing it."

The blatant rebuff surprised Caroline, but she couldn't imagine what the problem was. "Is it all right if I keep you company?" she asked.

"If you want to."

The dishes were already stacked on the table and Ruthann had climbed into a chair so that she could reach them. She was pulling a stack of plates toward her, and Janis took them out of her hands before she could do any more damage than wrinkling up the tablecloth.

Caroline didn't know what to do. Should she dive in and help or honor Janis's wishes and not invade the girl's territory?

Ruthann had no such qualms, though. She was determined to be helpful. "Which side, Car'line?" Ruthann asked holding up a knife. "I forget."

"Right side, with the blade pointed toward the plate," she responded.

Ruthann frowned as she tried to decide which was her right and which was her left. Instead of telling her, Caroline picked up one set of silverware and laid it out for the child to copy, sparing Ruthann the embarrassment of admitting that she had forgotten. As Janis silently set out the plates and folded the napkins, Caroline and Ruthann worked together on the silverware.

When it was done, Caroline looked up at the door to the kitchen and found Pop smiling at her.

"How's that?" Caroline asked him, indicating the table.

Pop nodded, but he didn't look at the place settings. "Looks pretty good to me."

Caroline realized she had just passed her first test, and it was a wonderful feeling. "Now what?" she asked.

The back door slammed, and a strident voice interrupted. "Is it time to eat yet?"

"No, but it's time for you to wash up," Pop called back. "And stop slamming that door."

Sam came trudging into the dining room, covered in dirt from head to foot. "Oh. Hi, Doc," he said when he saw Caroline.

"Hello, Sam. I...uh...understand you won your first baseball game last week."

"Yep. We beat the Cougars twelve to zip. I pitched a two-hitter and racked up ten K's."

K's? Caroline wondered. Did she dare ask. "Kilometers?"

Sam rolled his eyes. "Strikeouts. You know, one, two, three strikes you're out?"

She shrugged. "I'm sorry, Sam. I guess you're going to have to teach me everything I need to know about baseball to keep me from looking like an idiot."

"Sure. Lesson number one." He flicked his wrist and a white sphere came whizzing across the table toward Caroline. Only quick reflexes kept it from hitting her in the chest.

"That's a baseball," Sam told her as she snagged it in midair.

Caroline looked at it. "Thanks for the tip."

"Lesson two." He held up his left hand and pointed to it with his right. "The glove. But maybe we should save that advanced stuff for after supper. You are staying for supper, right?"

Caroline couldn't help but laugh. Someday, Sam's humor would be every bit as engaging as his father's. "Yes. I'm staying."

"I figured as much. I was pretty sure my dad had the hots for you."

"Sam, go wash up!" Pop ordered.

"What's the hots?" Ruthann asked, but no one answered her.

Caroline tossed Sam the ball as he headed for the stairs.

"You'll have to forgive my brother," Janis said. "Daddy tried to teach him manners, but I think Sam has a learning disability."

"Really?" Caroline asked.

"No," Pop interjected. "He's just ten years old. That's a disability in itself, but we keep hoping he'll grow out of it."

Pop poured glasses of iced tea for everyone, and when Sam returned five minutes later, the group had drifted out to the back porch.

"Hey, Doc?"

Since everyone in the house seemed to have a nickname, Caroline didn't see any point in challenging the one Sam had chosen for her. "Yes?"

"Do you really want to learn about baseball?"

"I'd like to."

"Come on. I'll give you your first lesson while we're waiting for Dad. He could take a while." He grabbed his sister's glass of tea, finished it off in one massive gulp, then marched out.

Caroline looked at Pop, who just shrugged his shoulders as if to say, "It's up to you."

As soon as Caroline began to follow Sam, Ruthann naturally followed her, leaving only Janis and Pop.

"Don't you want to go, too?" Pop asked Janis.

"Is Daddy really dating Caroline?" she asked bluntly.

"That's what he tells me. Why aren't you jumping up and down? That *is* what you wanted, isn't it?"

"Yeah. Sure."

Pop frowned and went back into the kitchen.

IT WAS twenty minutes before Mitch arrived. He began humming happily when he spotted Caroline's car in the driveway, but there was no sign of her anywhere when he went into the house. The living room was empty. The table was set in the dining room. But no Caroline. And no kids, either. He finally found his father in the kitchen, muttering because his roast was drying out.

"Well, it's about time," Pop groused. "Normally I expect you to be late, but I figured you'd be home *close* to on-time since we have a guest."

"Sorry. I got away as quickly as I could. Where is she?" he asked.

"Sam's got her."

"Oh, Lord. Has he got her hog-tied, sticking bamboo shoots under her fingernails?"

Pop hitched his thumb in the direction of the hall. "See for yourself. They're in your office—all except for Janis, who hightailed it upstairs."

Mitch didn't understand that, but he didn't question Pop. Instead, he headed for his study, where one of their two home computers resided. When he reached the door, he found Caroline in his office chair with Ruthann in her lap and Sam sitting on the arm, patiently instructing her in the fine art of computerized baseball.

"Okay. What do I do now?" Caroline asked. "I've got runners on first and third with only one out. Should I have the batter bunt?"

"That's right. You're a quick learner," Sam complimented her.

"I don't have all those letters after my name for nothing," she replied as she made the appropriate play with the computer mouse, then passed the device to San..

"I guess Janis will have those after her name one day, too. She's an egghead like you."

"Is that bad?"

"Sure it's bad. Every teacher I've ever had expected me to be as smart as she is. It's a real pain."

"That gives you a lot to live up to, doesn't it?"

"Yeah." He shrugged. "But I guess Janis isn't so bad as a sister. She helps me with my homework sometimes, and she does like camping. She can bait her own hook when we go fishing and she really knows her way around the hiking trails near Grandpa Lew's cabin."

"Grandpa Lew?" Caroline asked.

"My mom's dad," Sam explained. "He and Grandma have a cabin up in Big Sur where we always go camping the last weekend in July."

"Oh, right." Caroline vaguely remembered that Sam had mentioned a family camping trip the last time she was here. It was a vacation tradition that Mitch and his late wife had started even before the children were born. "Well, Janis is certainly one up on me there," Caroline told him. "I've never been camping in my life."

Sam looked at her in disbelief. "You're kidding?"

"No, I'm not."

"Geez, and I thought Janis was a geek."

"Sam, don't call your sister a geek," Mitch instructed from the door.

Everyone whirled around in surprise and Ruthann scrambled off Caroline's lap to fling herself at her father. "Thank you, Daddy. Car'line came back."

"I noticed." He picked her up and accepted her hug.

"Now you'll make her stay and never go away, won't you?"

"That remains to be seen," Mitch said cautiously, but the look he gave Caroline indicated that he was in perfect agreement with his daughter. Caroline blushed, and he grinned.

"You won't believe this, Dad," Sam said, moving toward his father. "Caroline has never been to a baseball game and she's never been camping. Never."

"Oh, my. We'll have to rectify that, won't we?"

Sam turned to Caroline. "You wanna come to my game next Saturday? I'm pitching."

Caroline took Sam's invitation as a good sign, and wouldn't have dreamed of refusing. She didn't have time for baseball games, but if she wanted a relationship with Mitch, she knew she had to start making time for the things that mattered to him and to his kids. "Thank you, Sam. I'd love to come."

"Great."

"Car'line will come camping, too, won't she, Daddy?" Ruthann asked.

"I certainly hope so," Mitch replied, casting a speculative look at Caroline. "Four days at a rustic cabin in Big Sur. Fresh air, sunshine, hiking, fishing—"

"Cooking over an open camp fire," Sam added. "You'll love it. It's great."

Caroline had her doubts about that. "Uh, we'll see," she replied hesitantly. A baseball game was one thing, but a family vacation was something else entirely. Caroline wasn't sure she was ready to plunge in quite that far yet.

The look Mitch gave her seemed to suggest that he understood that she was suddenly feeling a bit overwhelmed, and he bailed her out by changing the subject. "Listen, Pop's throwing a fit because I'm late. If we want peace and harmony in the family, we'd better get to the dining room quick. He's been known to mutiny."

Sam was the first one to hit the door, and Mitch thrust Ruthann into his arms. "Here. Make sure your sister's hands are clean. I thought I detected a little Popsicle residue."

"Aw, Dad," he groused, but marched out with her, anyway.

Caroline went to the door more slowly and when she got there, Mitch was waiting to take her into his arms.

"You're wonderful," he said, giving her a kiss that had far less wattage than he would have liked.

It was still enough to take Caroline's breath away. "What did I do to deserve that?"

"You're learning how to play baseball. I am sure that's not a high priority in your life right now."

"It didn't cost me anything to listen, and I learned something."

"But you're not sure you want to learn about camping, are you?"

Caroline sighed. "I don't know, Mitch. It seems like a very big step to take this soon. And besides, it's a family thing...."

"You can be part of this family if you want to, Caro," he said tenderly.

The thought of being part of a family made Caroline feel very warm inside, but it also brought a surge of fear. Suddenly she realized that she was afraid of the thing she wanted most.

"I'll think about it," she promised. If the trip wasn't until the end of July, she had plenty of time to make up her mind. In the meantime, she wanted another change of subject. "Mitch, did you talk to Ed Newton today? He said he was going down to the station to file an official report."

Mitch nodded and dropped the topic of the camping trip. "Yeah. We started the background checks on Media-Tech's employees."

"So you're launching a department investigation?" she asked expectantly.

"No," he replied regretfully. "I can't involve the force officially until we have something more solid to go on. Department policy says it should be your in-house investigation at this point, but Ed and I are going to work together."

She would rather have heard that he was putting all the resources of the Hilliard PD on the case, but she understood he had rules to follow. "Thank you, Mitch. Have you come up with anything?"

"Not yet, but we will. I'm going to stop Richmond in his tracks for you."

"And I'm going to learn about baseball and fishing," she said wistfully. "Then we'll all live happily ever after. Is that how it's supposed to go?"

He nodded. "That's it."

"It doesn't always work that way, Mitch," she warned him softly. "In fact, the odds are against us."

"I'm not a gambler, Caroline. I don't believe in odds, but I do believe in love. I just have to make a believer out of you." He brought his lips to hers, and Caroline slid her arms around his shoulders, giving herself over totally to his kiss.

"Hey, you two! I got a dry pot roast and cold gravy!" Pop shouted from the dining room. "Get in here."

Mitch and Caroline separated like a couple of guilty teenagers, then laughed.

"Yes, sir!" Mitch shouted, then slid one arm around Caroline's waist again, keeping her close as they strolled in to join his family.

Despite Caroline's anxiety, dinner was very pleasant. Since Janis was so quiet, Sam had a chance to dominate the conversation. Caroline listened patiently to him, but she also tried to draw Janis out, asking her questions about how she had enjoyed her first week at MediaTech. All she got for her efforts were monosyllabic answers.

After dinner, they all pitched in to help with the dishes. Sam challenged Caroline to another game of baseball, and everyone except Janis and Pop ended up in the study playing video games for most of the evening. Ruthann kept herself plastered to Caroline's side until it was her bedtime. But the little girl refused to go unless "her Car'line" read her a story.

With Mitch sitting on one side of the bed, Caroline on the other and Ruthann sandwiched happily between them, Caroline read her the story of the "Princess and the Pea." She made it only partway through before half of her audience dozed off, but Caroline was reluctant to stop. Fairy tales, like television, had been disdained by her parents.

Mitch finally succeeded in getting the book away from her by reassuring her that Ruthann would demand she finish it next time.

"See, that wasn't so bad, was it?" Mitch asked as he walked her to her car about an hour later.

Caroline slid her arm around his waist. "No, it wasn't. It was fun. So much so that I feel guilty," she confessed.

"Why?"

"I should be working. Trying to solve the riddle of why Scarlett lost the astronomy data base."

"You'll figure it out, Caroline," he assured her. "But it doesn't have to consume your whole life."

She nodded. "I know you're right. But please bear in mind that I'm fighting habits that took a lifetime to build, Mitch."

"I know. I understand," he said, turning her in his arms. "It's hard for me to leave my work at the station sometimes, too."

"Particularly when you have to go on midnight stakeouts," she said wryly.

Mitch groaned. "I wish I could come home with you, instead," he said huskily. "You're much better company than cold coffee and the grumpy detective I'm sharing the watch with."

"There'll be other nights," she promised him.

"I'm counting on it." He gave her a long, slow, languid kiss that made them both ache for something that wasn't going to happen that night.

Mitch had his arms wrapped around her, and Caroline rested her head on his shoulder, unwilling to let go just yet. They stood there next to her car, soaking each other up like sponges, while they tried to decide when they would be seeing each other again. They settled on a date Friday evening.

"With or without the kids?" Caroline asked.

"Without," Mitch replied, grinning devilishly. "I don't plan on sharing you with them *all* the time."

"I think I can handle that," she said coquettishly, then sobered. "Mitch, is something wrong with Janis?"

"That's a good question," he replied, a puzzled frown coming over his face. "She's a hard kid to gauge."

"But she was so quiet tonight. It was almost as though she resented my presence in the house."

"No, you're wrong about that," he assured her. "She was furious with me last week when I told her you and I weren't going to be dating. What you have to realize about Janis is that the bubbliness you've seen in her up till now is very atypical. She's usually very quiet... off in her own world, like she was tonight," he told her.

"But maybe she's been the woman of the house for so long that it's natural she might be having second thoughts about the possibility of sharing you."

"Maybe," he conceded. "More likely she's got a new idea for improving IVAR and can't think of anything else."

"I hope you're right."

Mitch looked down at her. "I know I am. Janis thinks you're the most wonderful woman in the world. And so do I," he murmured, closing in for another kiss.

It was a long time before he finally let her go home, and they both knew that it was going to seem like an eternity to the weekend.

CHAPTER FOURTEEN

MITCH CALLED Caroline every day that week, and his calls provided the only light in a dismal tunnel. Despite the team's best efforts, no one could find any reason why Scarlett kept losing data. Nothing catastrophic happened, but Caroline's fear of a total breakdown increased every time she activated her computer.

Word of The Richmond Group's successful demonstration of Vic had spread through the industry like wildfire, and everyone at MediaTech was understandably upset. The board of directors was exerting pressure on Caroline to isolate Scarlett's problem and fix it so that they could launch before Richmond, but having eight men in suits calling her every day and issuing threats didn't solve any of her computer's problems.

Caroline, in turn, put pressure on Ed Newton to get results in his investigation, but she was no more successful than the board members were. Ed's consistent counsel for her to be patient didn't sit well with her. Nor did it help that Mitch was telling her the same thing. By the end of the week, Caroline had to do something herself. She had to find some solid proof—something more than her own conviction and Mitch's suspicions. Until she did, Mitch wouldn't be able to launch a full-fledged investigation.

When she called Ed on Friday morning and he politely told her for the umpteenth time she was expecting too much too soon, Caroline decided to take matters into her own hands. She knew Mitch wouldn't approve, but she was beyond caring. She called The Richmond Group and invited her ex-husband out to lunch.

"I HAVE A FEELING you're not interested in eating," Evan said almost the moment they sat down in the out-of-the-way sandwich shop Caroline had chosen.

"No. I'm not," she replied. "In fact, I haven't eaten much at all this week. It's hard to think about food at a time like this."

He looked very sympathetic. "Caroline, I know it's distressing to you that we succeeded in getting our computer ready before yours, but—"

"It's *how* you succeeded that concerns me, Evan," she said, cutting him off.

A frown rearranged his thin, hawkish features. "What do you mean by that?"

Caroline felt that three years of marriage to this man had earned her the right to be direct. "Tell me everything you know about Vic's information data base."

"Caroline, you know I can't divulge secrets—"

"I'm not talking about secrets. I want to know what happened last year after the data base crashed. How did Howard reconstruct it so quickly?"

He smiled and relaxed. "There's no great mystery there, Caroline. The data base didn't crash."

"But I heard that Dean Eddington—"

"What you heard were the rantings of an employee who was fired because of his incompetence. It happens all the time in this business. There *were* problems with Vic's data base, but it never crashed. Howard brought in a new programmer to go back and correct the errors Eddington had made, and he did an incredible job."

"Do you know that for a fact or is it just what Howard wants you and the rest of the staff to think?" she asked, unwilling to believe Evan could be correct. If Vic's data base had been sound, Richmond wouldn't have had a reason to pirate Scarlett.

"Why would he lie?" Evan asked.

"Because somehow Howard Richmond got his hands on the OHARA data base."

The accusation rocked Evan back in his chair. "Caroline—"

"Hear me out, Evan, please," she begged, leaning forward. "Vic answered every question on Monday in the exact way Scarlett would have—including the question about the nonterminating decimal, which could have sent Vic into an infinite loop and shut the system down completely. Yet Howard wasn't worried about that. But when I asked about friends, he wouldn't let the computer respond. Why? What harm would it have done to let Vic answer?"

Evan seemed genuinely puzzled. "I don't know. I figured he stopped you because we've tried not to introduce personalities into the VIC data base. What did you expect it to say, anyway?"

"I was hoping it would say my name," she replied. "I'm sure that after Howard got hold of Scarlett, he or that new programmer of his erased or replaced everything he could think of that pertains to MediaTech, me and all the other employees who worked on Scarlett, but he can't have gotten it all. There has to be something left inside Vic's memory banks that programmers at Richmond never would have taught it."

"That's insane."

"No, it's not. I'm telling you, Evan. Vic is Scarlett," she said forcefully. "And you have to help me prove that. I need a close-up look at your computer."

"What? I can't do that, Caroline," he protested. "I can't risk my job. I'm not the chief designer on this project. I don't have unlimited power the way you do at Media-Tech."

"But you do have access to Vic. You can get me into the lab."

"No, I can't," he argued.

"You mean you won't," she countered, then reached for his hand. "Evan, please. You know better than anyone how important this is to me. Scarlett is my life's work, and someone has stolen it from me."

For the first time, Evan's face turned cold, reminding Caroline of some of the more disturbing arguments they had engaged in during their brief marriage. "I don't believe that, Caroline. And for your information, Vic is no less important to me than Scarlett is to you. Frankly, I find your suggestion that we were only able to complete this computer by thievery insulting."

"I'm sorry," she said sincerely. "I'm not trying to take anything away from your work and I'm certainly not accusing you of being involved in the theft. But you just said yourself that you don't have control of this project. You can't know for sure what Howard did or didn't do to the VIC data base, now can you?"

She had him there. "No. But I still don't believe it."

"Then prove me wrong. Let me talk to Vic."

Caroline was certain he was going to refuse, but after a moment's careful meditation, he surprised her. "All right. If that's what it will take to convince you, I'll get you into the lab. I can't let you have direct access to a terminal, but you can talk to Vic."

Caroline smiled and covered his hand with hers again. "Thank you, Evan."

"But if Vic doesn't say anything that proves your ridiculous theory, I don't want to hear any more about it," he said sternly. "Do we have a deal?"

"Yes. When can I talk to Vic?"

He thought a moment. "It'll have to be tomorrow morning when the lab is deserted. I sure as hell can't go waltzing in there with you today. I'll meet you in the parking lot at ten.''

"I'll be there. Thank you, Evan." She gave him an impulsive hug and was surprised again when he held on to her for a long moment.

When he finally released her, his smile had all the boyish charm she remembered from their days in college. "If I get fired because of this, I expect you to give me a job," he told her

"You've got a deal," she replied.

THOUGH IT MADE her feel terribly guilty, Caroline said nothing to Mitch that night about her meeting with Evan or her plan for the next morning. He would only try to talk her out of it, or worse, forbid her to go, which would lead to an argument, because she wasn't going to back down. Silence seemed like the best course.

They had dinner at a small steak house and went back to her place to talk—and to make love. As before, it was an earth-shattering experience; and also, as before, Mitch left shortly after midnight to return home. Saturday mornings were a special time he usually devoted to the kids, and he didn't want to interrupt that routine.

He asked Caroline to come by early so they could all have breakfast and go to Sam's game together at noon, but she begged off. Mitch didn't seem at all suspicious when she told him she had to work and would meet him at the ballpark, instead.

Caroline slept very little after Mitch left. Instead, she sat at her home computer most of the night, making a list of questions to ask Vic and committing it to memory. She readied a microcassette tape recorder, which she would carry in the pocket of her casual blazer. She knew Evan would protest if he found out she was planning to tape the interview.

By nine the next morning, she was ready. By ten, she was sitting in The Richmond Group parking lot, waiting for her ex-husband.

"WHERE'S MY Car'line, Daddy?" Ruthann whined for the hundredth time. "I want my Car'line. Make her come."

"She'll be here, Short Stuff. Now just settle down and watch Sam, okay? See him? He's out there on the pitcher's mound," Mitch said, pointing.

"I don't wanna watch Sam. I want Car'line," the child said petulantly.

Mitch glanced at his watch, then at his father, who was sitting next to him. Caroline was thirty minutes late. Obviously she had gotten involved in something at Media-Tech and lost track of the time.

Though he knew he shouldn't be too upset with her, Mitch couldn't help being a little irritated. Ruthann was counting on seeing her, and Sam seemed very excited about showing off for his dad's new girlfriend. The boy had given Mitch endless instructions on the things he was supposed to explain to her during the game. Janis, who wasn't interested in baseball, had chosen to stay home, but Mitch planned to pick her up after the game for a family outing to a nearby amusement park.

Everyone, including Mitch, would be disappointed if Caroline didn't show up. If she was going to be this unreliable, he would have to be more careful about the plans he made and what he told the kids. He disappointed them often enough because of his own work. They didn't need it from the woman in his life, as well.

Sitting on the wooden bleachers with Ruthann wiggling impatiently on his lap, Mitch did his best to concentrate on the game. Sam was doing a fine job and he would expect his dad to be able to discuss his pitching performance in detail.

By the fourth inning, Ruthann was getting wilder by the minute. She couldn't seem to sit still, and Mitch refused to let her run up through the crowd.

"How would you like a snow cone, Short Stuff?" Pop asked.

"Yes, yes, yes! Grape, grape, grape."

Mitch grinned as he shot his father a grateful glance. "Is bribery good parenting?"

He shrugged. "It worked with you."

"Here. See what you can do with her," Mitch said as he handed her over.

Pop carried her out of the bleachers, then put her on the ground and let her dance beside him as they disappeared behind the stands where the concessions were located.

Mitch breathed a sigh of relief, but he also checked his watch again and wondered about Caroline. The small, scattered crowd set up a roar and Mitch jerked his gaze back to the playing field to see what he had missed. Sam was doing a little dance himself as he ran from the pitching mound to the dugout, and Mitch guessed that his son had been instrumental in making a double play that ended the inning.

Mitch was going to catch hell for missing it. He followed Sam's progress to the dugout, and when the boy disappeared, Mitch looked once again in the direction of the parking lot. He felt simultaneous surges of relief, pleasure and irritation when he saw Caroline in front of the bleachers, scanning the crowd.

Mitch stood and waved to her, capturing her attention, and a breathtaking smile lit her face as she hurried up the steps and across to him.

"I'm sorry I'm late, Mitch," she said, giving him a quick hug before they sat.

She looked so radiant that it was impossible for him to be upset with her. "You look like you have good news," he said happily. "Did you single-handedly solve the mystery of Scarlett's memory losses this morning?"

Her smile dimmed a bit. "No, but I've got something almost as good." She dug into her purse and handed Mitch a microcassette.

He turned it over, but didn't find a label. "What is it?"

"Proof that Howard Richmond constructed Vic from Scarlett's data base."

"What?"

"You heard me."

Mitch shook his head. "What kind of proof? How did you get it?"

Caroline was too excited to worry about how he was going to react. "Evan took me to the Richmond lab this morning so that I could talk to Vic. That's a recording of our conversation, and it contains something that Vic couldn't possibly have known."

Mitch didn't believe what he was hearing. "Caroline, that was stupid! What do you think you've accomplished?"

She bristled at his scolding tone. "A lot," she replied defiantly. "I have proof now."

"So what? A recording like that won't stand up in court."

"I know that, but now I have something more than suspicions to give to Bob and my board of directors. If you and Ed can't find any proof of criminal activities, at least I'll have a basis for convincing the board to initiate a civil suit. I'm going to stop Richmond one way or another."

"Caroline, don't you understand that you've just left yourself open to civil—maybe even criminal—prosecution?"

Caroline shook her head. "No one but Evan knows that I was at Richmond today."

"He got you past security?" Mitch asked skeptically.

"Not exactly. We had a stroke of luck. The guard was the same one who admitted me to the demonstration Monday. He remembered me as Dr. Leister and Evan just signed me in as his guest."

Mitch ran one hand through his hair. "Great. Now they can charge you *and* your ex-husband with fraud and industrial espionage."

Caroline gritted her teeth. "Mitch, all I did was talk to Vic. I didn't get close to a monitor and I had no contact with its base programming."

"Prove that in a court of law," he challenged.

"Why are you being so negative?" she asked irritably.

"Because this could land you in a heap of trouble," he snapped. "Don't you realize that?"

"I realize that you and Ed haven't accomplished a damned thing."

"What do you expect in a week?"

"Results! Something. Anything." She reached for the cassette, but Mitch held it out of her grasp.

"I'll listen to it, Caroline," he told her with a weary sigh.

"Gee, thanks," she said sarcastically.

"Car'line!"

At the foot of the bleachers, Ruthann was straining against Pop's hand to get to her, and Mitch shot Caroline an exasperated glance as he slid the tape into the pocket of his polo shirt. "We'll talk about this later."

"Don't do me any favors," she muttered.

Ruthann's snow cone was dripping like a faucet and tottering precariously as she came up the stairs. Pop snatched it out of her hand just in time to save Caroline from a messy disaster when Ruthann hugged her, but there were still purple handprints all over her shirt before the little girl was finished.

Ruthann ended up on her knees in Caroline's lap, and she brought her face close as she wagged a finger under Caroline's nose. "You're late."

"I'm sorry, Ruthann. What have I missed?"

"Sam striked out."

Caroline looked at Mitch. "Did he fail at bat or oust an opposing batter?"

Mitch sighed and tried to let go of his irritation. Somehow he was going to have to convince Caroline that playing Mata Hari wasn't in her best interests, but that would have to wait until later. "He struck out the batter," he replied.

When Mitch didn't elaborate, Pop caught her up on the score and Sam's performance so far. Ruthann settled onto Caroline's lap, chattering like a magpie, and Caroline tried to redirect her focus to Mitch's children. It wasn't easy. She felt as though she were living two lives; or three, actually, if she included her newest role as detective. She was a computer designer tottering on the brink of disaster who felt guilty for the time she was spending away from her work. She was also a woman falling in love and trying to carve out a place for herself in her lover's family. Both were new and equally frightening experiences.

As the game proceeded, Pop gave her a running commentary of what was happening. He kept casting curious glances at his quiet son until Mitch finally loosened up and took over the job of teaching Caroline the finer points of Little League baseball.

When it was over, Sam's team had won by only a tiny margin, but the victory was enough to keep him bragging and reliving the game all the way home. The triumphant baseball hero took a quick shower, then everyone but Pop piled into the car and headed for San Jose.

When Sam learned that Caroline had never been to an amusement park before, he rolled his eyes in disbelief, but he also took it upon himself to educate her. They all laughed at Caroline's reaction to her first dizzying roller-coaster ride. They ate junk food shamelessly, screamed their way through a house of horrors ride and laughed until they were giddy. Even Janis seemed to enjoy herself more than she usually did on her dad's frivolous family outings, and Sam paid Caroline the most extravagant compliment imaginable when he told her, "You know, Doc, for an egghead, you're a lot of fun."

Overall, it was an amazing—and quite successful—experience. But Caroline knew better than to place too much store in it as a gauge of how successful her relationship with Mitch was going to be. As she had told him, life wasn't an amusement park. Children and relationships took a lot of work and a special kind of understanding that Caroline still wasn't sure she possessed.

Ruthann fell asleep in the car on the way back to Hilliard. She was exhausted from too much excitement, and the fit she had thrown because Mitch insisted she ride in a seat belt instead of on Caroline's lap had worn her out totally. It was late when they arrived at Mitch's, and the little girl barely stirred as her father carried her upstairs, peeled off her outer clothes and covered her up.

Sam went to bed without a fuss, either, and Janis disappeared into her room, as usual. Pop took a subtle hint from his son and went off to his room, leaving Mitch and Caroline alone.

They collapsed onto the sofa together, and Caroline let her head fall on Mitch's shoulder. "I'm beat," she told him. "You forgot to warn me that having fun was so exhausting."

Mitch rested his cheek on her forehead. "Did you really have a good time?"

"Of course. Couldn't you tell?"

He was silent for a moment. "Which did you enjoy more? The amusement park, the ball game or breaking into The Richmond Group?"

Caroline sat up and looked at him, ruffled by his cool tone. "Actually, I enjoyed them equally but for different reasons. I love being with you, and for some reason I haven't defined yet, the kids make me feel good about myself. On the other hand, talking to Vic made me feel that I had accomplished something that will enable me to prove that Howard Richmond stole my work. Is that a satisfactory answer?" she asked archly.

"No, it's not," he replied. "Talking to Vic didn't accomplish anything."

"How do you know that? You haven't even listened to the tape yet."

"It doesn't matter what's on it, because it won't be admissible in court."

"But it might be enough to allow you to open this case officially," she argued. "I want more than just a piddling in-house investigation and your help on the side. I want the Hilliard Police Department doing everything it possibly can to prove that Scarlett's data base was stolen."

Mitch sighed. "Caroline, department policy—"

"I don't give a damn about department policy," she said, twisting around so that she was on her knees facing him. "I've made a legitimate accusation against The Richmond Group, and I want it investigated. If a private citizen came to you and said she'd seen Howard murder someone, you'd check it out, wouldn't you?"

"Yes," he conceded. "But if there was no body and no physical evidence, it would be a very short investigation."

"That tape is physical evidence, Mitch!"

He sighed again. At the moment, the tape was in a drawer in Mitch's study where he'd put it for safekeeping earlier that afternoon. He was too tired to listen to it tonight, though. "Tell me what's on it and I'll decide that for myself," he said after a moment.

"Let me start at the beginning," she said, smiling with relief as she told him about her conversation with Evan yesterday and the line of questioning she had taken with the computer this morning. "In areas of general information, Vic answered everything almost precisely as Scarlett would have, but when I got into personal information, he started drawing a blank. He doesn't remember me or any of my staff—" she grinned "—but he does know about a certain police lieutenant named Mitch Grogan."

Mitch sat up a little straighter. "You're kidding?"

"No, I'm not," she said with mounting excitement. "And what's more, the computer also remembers that you have a daughter named Janis. When I asked how he knew about the two of you, he said he had met you and even gave the exact date. But Howard has substituted all of Scarlett's factual information about where she was created and by whom, because Vic claimed to have met you at The Richmond Group, not at MediaTech."

She looked at him triumphantly. "*Now* tell me you don't have enough to launch a full-scale investigation."

Unfortunately, he couldn't give her what she wanted just yet. "What did your ex-husband have to say about all this, Caroline?"

"Evan was floored when I explained the significance of Vic's answer. I know I could have found more anomalies if I'd had the chance, but he was afraid to risk having us discovered."

"He claims to have no knowledge of the theft?"

"Evan was genuinely shocked, Mitch," she assured him.

"Is there any chance that he would be willing to work with us? Having an informer on the inside looking for solid evidence would—"

"He offered to try, but I told him not to do anything until he heard from me. I'm not sure that Evan is cut out to be a spy, and I wasn't too clear on the legalities of that. If something went wrong, Howard could have him brought up on industrial espionage charges and he'd be able to make them stick. I don't want to get Evan into trouble."

She was right. "Okay. Have him sit tight and pray that no one questions him about the guest he brought in today. For the time being, he's just a potential source of information. Nothing more."

"Does this mean you're opening the investigation officially?" she asked, holding her breath.

"Maybe," Mitch said cautiously. "I want you to ask Scarlett all the same questions and give me a printout of her answers. Have the tape transcribed, too, and if they match in significant detail, I'll open the case."

A surge of victory coursed through her. "Thank you, Mitch!" she said, throwing her arms around him. "I knew you wouldn't fail me."

Mitch chuckled. "You're not just dating me because I'm the greatest detective the world has seen since Sherlock Holmes, are you?"

Caroline pulled back and looked at him. He seemed to be joking, but she thought she detected a slight undercurrent of doubt. "Mitch, if you have to ask that, I should walk out of here and not come back."

He ran the back of his hand lovingly against her cheek. "Don't do that. I don't think I could handle it."

His eyes were filled with emotions that were almost too powerful for Caroline to cope with. "You're a good cop, Mitch. I don't think it would be necessary to seduce you in order to get you to do your job."

He grinned wickedly. "If I recall, I'm the one who did the seducing," he reminded her.

"I'll return the favor one of these days," she said huskily, then blushed at her boldness.

"Now, *that* I'm looking forward to. Would you care to give me a preview?"

The color on her cheeks intensified, but Caroline couldn't refuse him. She wrapped her arms around his neck and delivered a slow, languid kiss. When she finally pulled away, Mitch had to take a deep breath.

"If that's the preview, I can't wait for the feature to begin. Why don't you stay over tonight, Caro?"

"Oh, Mitch, I couldn't. The kids..."

He shook his head. "I wasn't suggesting that. I'd just like to know that you're close. I can bunk in Pop's room or on the sofa."

For some reason, the offer wasn't even tempting. "I still don't think it's a good idea, Mitch," she said gently. "It would send a signal to the kids that I'm not ready to transmit."

"I guess you're right. Will you come for Sunday brunch, at least?" he asked hopefully, but she shook her head.

"I need to work tomorrow morning—for real, this time, I promise. I've got to question Scarlett and transcribe the tape. Maybe another Sunday."

Mitch tried not to be too disappointed. "When will I see you again?"

She thought it over. "I could fix you dinner one night this week. Thursday?"

He grinned. "Tuesday would be better."

"Why?"

"Because I don't think I can wait until Thursday," he said, gathering her close for another stirring kiss. By the time it ended, they were both gasping for breath, and Mitch stood up, offering Caroline his hand. "Come on. I'd better walk you out to the car before we start something we can't finish with a houseful of kids."

Mitch retrieved the tape from his study, then walked hand in hand with Caroline to the door. Just as they reached the foyer, Janis appeared at the top of the stairs, still dressed, and wearing a scowl that made her seem a dozen years older. "Daddy?"

Mitch looked up to the second floor landing. "Are you still up, Angelface?"

"It looks that way, doesn't it? Are you going to Caroline's?"

Mitch felt Caroline's hand tighten on his. "No. I'm just walking her to her car."

The scowl softened. "Oh. Okay. Good night, Caroline."

"Good night, Janis," she replied.

The teenager disappeared into her room and Mitch opened the front door. "I gotta tell you, there's something spooky about getting old. It used to be my mom who stood at the top of those stairs looking stern when I came in late. Now my daughter is policing my romantic activities. I've come full circle, I guess."

Caroline didn't smile at his comment. "Mitch, something is wrong with Janis. I think she really resents the presence of another woman in her domain."

This time Mitch didn't argue. His daughter was behaving strangely. "I'll have a talk with her, Caroline."

"And if she doesn't come around?"

"She will, Caroline. It may take some adjustment, but she'll learn to be as crazy about you as Ruthann and Sam are."

Caroline hoped so, because Janis's standoffishness was becoming increasingly disturbing. Every time she thought that it might be eroding, like today at the amusement park, something always happened to turn Janis to ice again. "Do you think I should say anything to her?" she asked Mitch.

"No, let me try," he replied.

"Do you think it's possible that I said something that hurt her feelings?"

"I don't know. It's hard to tell what's going on in that brilliant head of hers," Mitch said, slipping his arm around Caroline's waist. "But don't you worry about it."

"I'll try not to," she said, leaning her head against his shoulder. "Thank you for another wonderful day."

"It was my pleasure," he murmured. "Just promise me that you won't play Mata Hari again, okay?"

"Yes, sir." She lifted her face to his and received a lingering good-night kiss. When she looked into his eyes after it ended, she found that same wealth of emotion that had been there before.

"I love you, Caroline."

For just a second, she couldn't breathe and the world tilted a little. She parted her lips, but words wouldn't come, so she pressed a kiss to his mouth, instead. "See you Tuesday, Mitch," she said, then quickly slipped into her car.

CHAPTER FIFTEEN

CAROLINE'S TRANSCRIPTS of the tape were convincing enough to justify launching an official investigation, but as the next month crept by, Mitch and his detectives turned up very little in the way of hard evidence. He personally conducted most of the interrogations of Caroline's employees, beginning with her programming staff and working out in a spiral that included everyone who had had any contact with the computer.

He also tried to contact Dean Eddington, the Richmond programmer who had made the claim that the VIC data base had crashed last year. Unfortunately, Eddington was in Tokyo programming a computer system for a new theme park. Since he was expected to return in mid-July, Mitch decided to wait to interview him; it was too hard to gauge whether or not someone was telling the truth over the phone.

Though Mitch did conduct one amicable interview with Evan Converse, he didn't make any attempt to interrogate Howard Richmond or anyone else at The Richmond Group. Richmond wasn't going to confess, and a direct confrontation would only lead to threats of slander and harassment suits. He knew it was frustrating for Caroline, but Mitch wasn't too disappointed because he knew from experience how difficult cases like this were to build.

Mitch's life away from the police station was no less complicated, but it was far more enjoyable. Except for the continued reserve Janis exhibited toward her, Caroline was fitting into his family seamlessly. It was clear to Mitch that she was trying very hard. It became something of a ritual for her to bring Janis home from MediaTech on Friday afternoons and have dinner with them, and she even threw a small surprise party at her own home to celebrate after Janis won the State Science Award of Merit for IVAR.

That night, Mitch had taken his unsuspecting daughter to Caroline's and watched her face when she saw the congratulatory banners, cake and the girlfriends Caroline had thoughtfully invited. Janis had been so touched and so excited that Mitch was certain her reserve toward Caroline had finally thawed, but instead, she became even more guarded, almost suspicious, after that night. Yet whenever Mitch asked her if anything was wrong, she insisted she was fine.

It was beginning to worry Mitch because he knew that Caroline was taking it as a personal failure. She was taking an interest in baseball to please Sam, showing up at all of his games even though it cost her time she felt she should be spending with Scarlett. She was patient and loving with Ruthann, who gave so much love back to Caroline that sometimes it seemed to frighten her a bit. Yet she didn't back away from them. Instead, she reserved that for Mitch. She was loving, passionate and considerate, but every time Mitch tried to tell her he loved her, she found a way to redirect the conversation. It was almost as though she had a sixth sense about it. She seemed to know when he was becoming too serious and she always managed to deflect his declaration of love.

It was frustrating, because Mitch wanted to hear Caroline say the words, too. In fact, he *needed* to hear them more with every passing day. He tried not to press her, though. He wanted to give her all the time she needed to be certain of her feelings, but hearing her say that she loved him would have made waiting for a more formal commitment a lot easier.

Until she was ready for that, he had to be content with Saturday ball games, private once-a-week dinners at her place and their Friday nights with the family at his.

"WILLIE MCCOVEY."

Caroline picked up a pot holder and opened the oven door to check on her cherry cobbler. "Lifetime batting average of .270. Five hundred and twenty-one home runs."

"Pretty good," Sam said appreciatively from his perch on the stool across the Grogan kitchen. "What year did he enter the Hall of Fame?"

"Nineteen eighty-six."

"Okay. Ted Williams."

The cobbler looked fine to Caroline and she closed the door. "Batting average of .344, the sixth highest of all time, right?" she asked as she turned to her inquisitor.

"Right. Babe Ruth?"

Caroline quoted the stats on the Babe, then turned the tables on him. "Edgar Smith," she said with a smug glint in her eyes.

Sam sighed and stuck his tongue in his cheek. "You mean Ozzie Smith, don't you?"

"No, Edgar Smith. Come on," she prompted. "Lifetime batting average. What is it?"

Sam frowned. "I don't know."

Caroline grinned triumphantly. "Gotcha. Edgar Smith. Boston. National League... 1883...he played thirty games and averaged .217."

"Oh, come on, Doc! 1883? That's no fair," Sam protested, but he was grinning.

"Where I come from, a statistic is a statistic," she informed him, crossing the kitchen. When she reached him, she eyed the dirty palm prints he had left on the counter of the bar. "You know, Sam, it amazes me that you can hold all these baseball stats in your head but you can never remember to wash up for dinner."

"A man's got to have his priorities straight."

He sounded so much like his father that Caroline almost reached out and ruffled his blond hair. But despite the apparent bond that had formed between them over this past month, Caroline still wasn't quite comfortable enough to take a liberty like that.

Sam looked down at his hands. "I guess that was a hint, huh?"

Caroline nodded. "Unless Mitch is late, we'll be eating in about fifteen minutes."

"Great. I'm starved." Sam jumped off the stool to head for the bathroom. When Caroline turned, she found Pop standing in the kitchen door, smiling at her.

He did that a lot—observing her when she wasn't looking. At first, it had bothered her somewhat, but now she didn't mind because there was nothing but benevolence in the contemplative looks he gave her. "How am I doing, Pop?" she asked him.

He crossed to the stove and sampled the spaghetti sauce she had started making the minute she'd walked in the door with Janis. "Tastes good to me."

"No," she corrected him, her voice soft. "I meant how am I doing with the kids?"

They looked at each other, and Caroline got the feeling he had just been waiting for her to ask that question. "Pretty good for someone with no experience," he replied honestly. "How do you think you're doing? That's what counts."

Caroline started placing dinner rolls on a cookie sheet. "I don't know exactly," she said, searching her own feelings, which were often jumbled these days. "Ruthann is easy. All you have to do is give her lots of hugs, attention, and learn to say no once in a while. Sam is . . . I don't know what Sam is," she said with a chuckle. "Sometimes I think he's convinced I'm the stupidest person on the planet, and other times I think he really likes me."

"He does," Pop assured her. "He's a smart kid and he knows how hard you're trying. I think he likes you a lot."

Caroline gave him a grateful smile. "I'm glad you think so."

"And that leaves Janis."

The smile faded. "She's the big surprise. She seems fine at work, but I don't have a lot of contact with her there, of course. Mitch keeps asking her what's wrong and she keeps swearing she's fine. How do you fight that kind of silent treatment?"

"With Janis, you don't. She's never been one to talk about her feelings. Not since her mother died, at least."

"Maybe that's the problem," Caroline said thoughtfully. "She has more memories of Becky than Sam does. I tried to tell her once that I just wanted to be her friend and that I had no intention of trying to replace her mother, but it was the wrong thing to say. That look came over her face again, she muttered something about not being surprised and dashed off to her room."

"Beats me," Pop said with a shrug, then he grinned. "What about Mitch?"

A blush and a smile crept across Caroline's face. "What about him?"

"Do you love him?"

Caroline turned to the stove to stir her sauce. "I don't know," she said after a moment.

"I'm sorry, Caroline. I shouldn't have asked that. I thought I knew the answer, but I guess I was wrong."

"I've still got doubts and I'm still scared, Pop," she admitted softly without looking at him.

He placed a fatherly arm around her shoulder. "Then the best advice I could give you is not to commit to anything until the doubts are gone," he told her. "There are a lot of people around here who stand to get hurt if you make the wrong decision—including you."

"Hey! What is this?" Mitch demanded from the kitchen door. "Are you trying to steal my girl, Pop?"

The couple at the stove turned, and Caroline stepped away from the father to give the son a welcome-home kiss. "Hi, there, sailor."

"Hi, yourself. What smells so good?"

"Spaghetti, Italian rolls and cherry cobbler."

"And she wouldn't let me lift a finger," Pop interjected. "She gets all the blame tonight."

Mitch sampled the sauce and Caroline popped the rolls into the oven while the rest of the family trooped in to see Mitch. The kitchen and dining room turned into the kind of free-for-all chaos that Caroline had finally grown accustomed to. She managed to get supper on the table with Janis's silent assistance, and sat back to let the warmth in the room flow around her.

To anyone else, it might have seemed like an ordinary meal on an ordinary day, but to Caroline it was special. She had spent most of her life feeling like an outsider peeking in through a window, but never belonging anywhere that didn't have antiseptic corridors and electronic circuits. Now she was starting to belong someplace warm and comforting. It was a wonderful feeling.

When she glanced around the table and discovered that Mitch was looking at her, she had the feeling that he was reading her mind. His blue eyes caressed her, and a sensation of perfect contentment washed through her. At that moment, she wouldn't have wanted to be anywhere else on earth.

"...but it's got a real stinky smell. Dad? Yo, Dad? Are you in there?"

This time, it was Mitch whose face got a little red as he turned to his son. "Sorry. What did you say, Sam?"

"I said I gotta have a new sleeping bag for the camping trip. You do remember the camping trip, don't you?" the boy asked with a touch of sarcasm. "Big Sur, fresh air, fishing..."

"Yes, I remember that we're going up to the cabin next week, Sam. I'm not senile yet. What's wrong with your sleeping bag?"

"It's smelly. Truly gross-out time."

"Did you remember to let it dry out after your trip with Todd and his family?"

Sam pursed his lips. "Uh, sure I did," he said somewhat belatedly.

Mitch shook his head. "Give the bag to Pop tomorrow and let him see what he can do with it. I'm not buying you a new sleeping bag."

Sam turned a smile that passed for charming on Caroline. "You work on him, will you, Doc? Get him to change his mind. You don't want to spend a l-o-o-o-ng four days in the mountains smelling my yucky sleeping bag, do you?"

Actually, Caroline didn't want to spend four days in the mountains, l-o-o-o-ng or otherwise. When the invitation had been issued to her over a month ago, she had promised to think it over and she had done that—at great length, in fact. She had decided that she didn't belong at a cabin owned by Mitch's in-laws, a place that had been very special to his late wife and her two oldest children.

Yet somehow, all the Grogans had come to the conclusion that Caroline was accompanying the family to Big Sur. She had been trying to tell Mitch for weeks that she didn't want to go along, but either she had been too subtle in expressing her reservations or he just hadn't been listening.

Either way, Caroline knew that she was going to have to make her feelings clear as soon as she had a moment alone with him.

"I think you should leave me out of the sleeping bag debate, Sam," she said mildly. This wasn't the first time he had tried to play her against Mitch, and she hadn't fallen into that trap yet. "Since your father would be paying for the bag, he has to decide whether it's a worthwhile expense."

That wasn't what he wanted to hear, and he made Caroline pay for it. "Don't you ever talk like normal people, Doc?" he asked irritably. "Couldn't you just say, 'No, it costs too much'?"

"Sam! Apologize," Mitch ordered.

"Yeah, Sam," Ruthann piped up. "Don't be mean to Car'line," she said, wagging a finger at him.

"Who was being mean?" he said defensively. "I just said she talks funny. And she does. Geez, when did telling the truth get to be a big crime around here?"

Mitch glared at him. "Sam, do you want to go to your room?"

"No."

"Then apologize."

"Sorry, Caroline," he said grudgingly.

The cocoon of warmth that had enveloped Caroline slipped away. She hated being at the center of these occasional family squabbles. "It's all right, Sam. I suppose my speech must sound very formal to you. Maybe you could teach me some slang to loosen it up a bit."

"Sure," he said, brightening a little. "We'll work on *hasta la vista, baby* after supper."

He spoke the Spanish phrase in an accent that would have gone completely over Caroline's head two months ago. Mitch and the family had been introducing her to movies, though, and now she recognized the line Arnold Schwarzenegger had popularized in one of Sam's favorite sci-fi films. "No *problemo,*" she said, calling on another of the movie's catchphrases, and earning an approving smile for her efforts.

Mitch was smiling at her, too, but not because she had a good memory. Apparently, she had handled the situation correctly, and he was proud of her. For some strange reason, that notion irritated Caroline, but she said nothing.

Dinner proceeded without further mishaps, and Sam was especially complimentary about her cooking to make up for having insulted her. Pop volunteered to do the dishes, but Caroline and Mitch vetoed him. Sam ran off to a neighbor's to play, Janis went into her room, and Pop enticed Ruthann to come into the living room with him to reduce the risk of damage to the good china Caroline had set the table with.

"You really impressed Sam when you threw that line from *Terminator 2* back at him," Mitch told her once the table had been cleared and they were alone in the kitchen.

"I've found that having a good memory has helped me where Sam is concerned," she replied.

"Yeah, for some reason, he really likes teaching you things," Mitch said.

"I know. I think it's because of Janis."

Mitch frowned. "Janis?"

Caroline nodded. "She's the smart one, and he's never been able to compete until now. My ignorance about the things that are important to Sam has allowed him to be intellectually superior to someone around here for the first time in his life."

Mitch was impressed with her reasoning. "Do you realize what incredible instincts you have, Caroline?" he said warmly. "You're great with those kids."

"I'm learning, I guess," she admitted, but she wasn't entirely comfortable with the concession. That realization brought her around to something else she wasn't comfortable with. "Mitch, about this camping trip..."

"Oh, we're going to have a great time," he said, his face lighting up with excitement. "Even Janis loves camping up at the cabin."

"I'm glad, Mitch, but—"

"Did you get those hiking boots I recommended?"

"Not yet."

Mitch shook his head. "You really ought to do that and start breaking them in. It's only a week until we leave, and one good blister can spoil the whole trip for you."

Caroline stopped what she was doing and faced him. "Mitch, I'm not certain this camping trip is a good idea. For me, I mean. The amusement park was fun and I've enjoyed an introduction to movies, picnics and baseball. But camping—"

Mitch took her into his arms. "You'll love it, too," he assured her. "The mountains are beautiful at this time of year, the fishing is great and it's the most relaxing environment you can possibly imagine." When she opened her mouth to protest, he cut her off. "Caroline, trust me. You'll have the time of your life."

He gave her a quick kiss, then went back to the sink.

Caroline didn't know what to do. She had tried to be a good sport about so many things, but she just couldn't visualize herself as the outdoorsy type. But this seemed so important to him, and to his children, as well. Even Janis was looking forward to the trip. Caroline suspected it was because the girl had a lot of memories of times up there with her mother. Becky, apparently, had been a skilled outdoorswoman, but Caroline wasn't. Where Janis and Sam were concerned—and possibly Mitch, too—Caroline wasn't going to measure up.

She smelled a disaster in the making and she wanted to avoid it. "Mitch, you're not listening to me," she said more forcefully.

He grinned at her. "That's because you're not saying anything I want to hear." When she didn't seem to find that amusing, he turned and took her into his arms again. "I'm sorry. I didn't mean to be flippant."

It was always hard to think when he was holding her, and even harder to argue, but she did her best. "I don't want to go, Mitch. I'm not..."

"Not what?" he asked when she hesitated.

"I'm not Becky," she said quietly.

He frowned. "Caroline, no one expects you to be."

"Sometimes I think you do, Mitch," she argued gently.

"Because I want you to go camping with us? Caroline, this is just a family tradition that I want you to be part of."

"A tradition that was started by you and Becky—together."

"And now she's gone."

"But you've carried on the tradition. When I hear you and the kids talk about that cabin, it's almost as though you cherish it as a shrine to your late wife. And there's nothing wrong with that," she hastened to assure him when it seemed that he was going to protest. "All your children should have something that is uniquely and totally their mother's... and I shouldn't have to try to measure up to their memories of her."

"Caroline, you're making way too much out of this," he cautioned her. "It's just a little hiking, some fishing, songs around the camp fire... That's all."

"Then why doesn't Pop ever go with you and the kids?" she asked shrewdly.

"Because he's not that wild about camping," he countered.

"You told me once that he used to take you and your brother when you were kids," she reminded him.

"Only under duress. Most of the time, Tom and I went camping with friends."

Caroline suspected there was more to it than that, but she didn't challenge him. No matter what she said, he was going to have an answer for it. "Mitch, if you can understand and accept the fact that your father doesn't like camping, why can't you show me the same courtesy and let me off the hook?"

"Because it's something you've never tried. Please give it a chance," he implored her. "If you absolutely hate it, I'll never ask you to go back."

It was hard to argue with that logic. And he had been right about the other things he had introduced her to—roller coasters, movies, passion...even his children. Maybe he was right this time, too. "All right," she said finally. "I'll buy the hiking boots tomorrow."

The way his blue eyes started sparkling was almost enough to make her glad she had acquiesced. "Thank you," he said, kissing her soundly.

Caroline sighed and threw herself vigorously into the kiss. She cherished the security and comfort she felt at times like this almost as much as she relished the passion he evoked in her.

The kiss ended abruptly, though, as they both realized where they were and who might walk in on them. Mitch's eyes were dark with longing as he looked at her, and she realized that he was about to say he loved her again.

"Correct me if I'm wrong, sailor, but aren't we supposed to be doing dishes?" she asked brightly as she slipped away from him.

Caroline heard the weary sigh Mitch heaved. He'd been very sensitive this past month about not pressing her, but she was afraid it wasn't going to last much longer. Sooner or later, she was going to have to explain why his expressions of love made her so uncomfortable, and that was going to be very difficult to do because Caroline didn't understand it herself.

But this wasn't her day of reckoning. "Am I washing or drying?" he asked, joining her at the sink.

"Drying," she announced, casting a quick glance at him. Whatever disappointment he felt was completely hidden from her now. In fact, she found a hint of a mischievous twinkle in his eyes that made her very suspicious.

"Why are you looking at me that way?"

"What way?" he asked innocently.

"Like a cat that just heard the dinner bell at the aviary."

"Don't be ridiculous. I was just thinking that since you're being such a good sport about the camping trip, you deserve a reward."

"Such as?" she asked skeptically.

"I'm taking you to San Francisco with me next Monday."

Caroline frowned and forgot all about being playful. "Mitch, I can't afford another day off from work, especially if I'm going to take next Friday and the following Monday off for the camping trip."

"Well, okay," he said nonchalantly as he began searching for a dish towel. "If you don't want to talk to Dean Eddington, so be it."

Caroline's heart leaped into her throat. "Eddington is back from Tokyo?" she asked with a rising sense of excitement.

"That's right. I've made an appointment to see him next Monday afternoon, but if you don't want to talk to him—"

"Of course I want to talk to him! You know I do! Right now, he's the only person we know who might be willing to confirm our contention that Vic crashed last year. He may even have proof of it."

Mitch decided it was time to stop teasing her. "I know. That's why I want you there. If he spews a lot of technical jargon about optical interface computers at me, I want someone along who can translate."

"Thank you, Mitch." Caroline gave him a big hug, and Mitch held on to her.

"You're welcome," he said, his eyes twinkling again. "And I confess, I do have an ulterior motive. There's something very appealing about getting you alone in San Francisco. I have this nifty little fantasy about taking you out to dinner at a fine restaurant, then, maybe, back to a nice hotel for a night of uncontrollable lovemaking." He wiggled his eyebrows suggestively. "How does that sound to you?"

"A lot better than a rustic cabin in the woods," she replied as she pressed her lips to his.

CHAPTER SIXTEEN

"I'M SORRY, Lieutenant Grogan, but there's nothing I can tell you about The Richmond Group," Dean Eddington said three days later when they met him in his office at a San Francisco computer systems firm. He was in his mid-thirties with dark hair, a ruddy complexion and a manner that suggested he was extremely edgy about discussing his former employer with the police—or anyone else.

He had looked nervously over his shoulder and closed the door behind them when they arrived, and so far, he had given noncommittal answers to every one of the questions he had been asked.

Caroline sensed his reluctance. "But you were willing to talk to the press after Howard Richmond fired you," she reminded him.

"And because of it, Richmond slapped a lawsuit on me, charging me with violating my nondisclosure agreement," he said testily. "The suit was dropped on the condition that I keep my mouth closed, but if I talk to you and he gets wind of it, I'll be in hot water all over again."

"I could subpoena you to give a deposition," Mitch said casually.

"Only if you've got a good case against Richmond," the programmer countered.

He was right about that. Mitch tried another tactic. "So you won't confirm or deny the allegations you made that the VIC data base suffered a complete collapse?"

"That's right. I won't."

"Are you aware that Howard Richmond denies the collapse and has told the rest of the staff he fired you for incompetence?" Caroline asked.

Eddington stiffened in anger but he brought his temper under control quickly. "I was not incompetent," he said tightly. "Howard tried to go too fast because—" He clammed up.

"Because of what?" Mitch asked, sensing that Eddington was close to telling them something that could help the case.

But the programmer shook his head. "Sorry. I can't say any more."

"Then answer this," Mitch said. "If we succeed in bringing Richmond into court for criminal prosecution, would you be willing to testify—assuming you have any information that would be pertinent to the case, of course. He wouldn't be able to sue you for telling the truth in a court of law."

Eddington leaned back in his chair and thought it over. "Yes. If you can get the case to trial, I'll testify."

"All right. Good," Mitch said, rising. Caroline followed suit. "Thank you for your time, Mr. Eddington."

The programmer stood up and accompanied them to the door. "Exactly what are you trying to charge Howard with, anyway?" he asked cautiously.

Mitch shot a quick glance at Caroline and decided to tell Eddington the truth. "We're trying to prove that he created the VIC computer with stolen technology."

Caroline seized the opportunity to ask, "Do you think you could give us any help along those lines?"

Eddington met her gaze steadily as he wrestled with a decision, then a big grin split his face. "Let me put it to you this way, Dr. Hunter. I'll make a very good witness for the prosecution."

"RICHMOND'S GOT a tight gag on him," Caroline said vehemently as soon as they reached the privacy of Mitch's car.

"Actually, there may be even more to it than that," he replied with the mounting excitement he always felt whenever a case started heating up. "Eddington is afraid, but not just of a lawsuit."

Mitch started the car to cool the interior but made no effort to drive away and Caroline turned in her seat to face him. "What do you mean?"

"I've been doing some checking into Howard Richmond's background, and he's got an investor who might be considered shady, at best. Seems Richmond got into some financial trouble a few years back and had to take on a silent partner."

"Who?"

"Syndey Grisham. He's been brought up on racketeering charges three times and has managed to wiggle free, I might add, because no one is willing to risk testifying against him."

Caroline was astounded. "You think Richmond or Grisham threatened to harm Eddington?" she asked incredulously.

"That's a possibility," Mitch answered. "In fact, it might be worthwhile to find out if our reluctant informant has spent any time in the hospital in the last year."

"This is scary, Mitch. You haven't talked to Howard directly, but he has to know we're investigating him. And he has to know *I've* been making accusations."

Mitch reached for her hand and squeezed it reassuringly. "Don't worry, Caroline. Richmond isn't going to make a move against you. What would be the point? He has to know he couldn't threaten you into withdrawing your claims because he'd also have to threaten Bob Stafford and every member of the MediaTech board of directors—not to mention me—to stop this investigation."

She relaxed. "You're right, of course."

"I know I am. Richmond's only course of action right now is *inaction*. He has to stay put, keep his mouth shut and pray that we can't come up with enough information to get a judge to order him to open Vic's data base files to us."

"Are we going to be able to do that? We haven't got much right now."

"It might be easier if I could prove that threats were made against Dean Eddington, but at least we've got a lead to follow, for a change. Don't worry. It'll take us somewhere eventually. Now—" he grinned and put business behind them temporarily "—how do you want to kill the rest of the afternoon? Our dinner reservation isn't for another three hours."

"Didn't you mention something about a hotel?" she asked with a coquettish smile.

"Your wish is my command, my love. One romantic retreat, coming right up."

AUNT LIDDY would have been proud of the way Caroline had spruced up her wardrobe in recent weeks—particularly as it pertained to what she wore *under* her clothes. Weeks ago, she had bought a daringly lacy teddy and Mitch had been so appreciative of it that she had splurged on an outrageously sexy strapless corset complete with garters and matching bikini briefs.

When they got back to the hotel that afternoon, Mitch got the shock of his life when he helped her out of her prim blue suit and discovered the provocative scraps of lace underneath. His commentary—verbal and otherwise—made her turn almost as red as the lingerie.

They teased each other mercilessly, sending their fore-play to new heights and their lovemaking to a joyous new depth. They were both almost too exhausted to move later when it was time to prepare for dinner. Caroline was the first to succumb to practicality. She slipped out of bed and began donning her lacy underthings.

Mitch lay back, obviously enjoying the show. "Are you sure you wouldn't rather order room service, Caroline? I don't want you to put on any more clothes than that, and I'm sure the management of the restaurant wouldn't ap-prove."

"Control yourself, handsome," she said, wrinkling her nose at him. "The night is still young." She sat on the bed and raised one leg so that she could slide it into a sheer stocking.

Mitch sighed happily. "Do you know that when we met, I nearly went crazy wondering if your legs were as gor-geous as I imagined they were?"

"Really?" she asked, amazed that anyone would have such lustful thoughts about her. It made her feel empow-ered, somehow.

"Absolutely. It was all I could think about for days."

Caroline fastened the stocking to the garters and lifted the other leg, stretching it out and turning her ankle to study it—and letting Mitch study it, too. "Were you dis-appointed?"

Mitch shifted his position on the bed until he was close enough to run his hand up one shapely calf and onto her thigh. "Not a bit," he said huskily. "It's a beautiful leg. It belongs to a beautiful woman." He sat up and pulled her closer, running his hand through her silky hair. "I love you, Caroline," he murmured, then kissed her before that hesi-tant look he hated so much could spoil the moment. By the time he finished stealing her senses, there wasn't a hint of uncertainty in her eyes.

"Marry me, Caro."

Caroline's breath caught in her throat. "Mitch . . ."

The look was back, and Mitch almost cursed aloud. "Not right this minute," he said lightly, trying to disarm the heaviness in the atmosphere before she could muster her senses and mount an argument. "And not tomorrow, either. I just want you to know that *someday* I want to marry you."

She didn't relax. "Mitch, it's too soon for us to even *think* about marriage," she said, slipping out of his embrace.

Her retreat made his frustration level shoot off the scale. "I suppose you're right. But it's not too soon to know if we're in love," he said tightly. "I am. How about you?"

"Mitch, please," she said, snatching up her other stocking.

"Please what?"

"Don't ask me for something I'm not ready to give."

"Caroline, what's so hard about saying that you love me?" he demanded. "And why does it make you so nervous when I tell you I love you?"

"Because this is too new. It's unfamiliar territory that is riddled with buried land mines, booby traps and God knows what else."

"Gee, thanks," he said as he rose and began reaching for his clothes. "It's good to know that you view the time you've spent with me and the kids as a war zone. And here I thought you were enjoying yourself for the first time in your life. Silly me."

"Mitch, please don't be angry with me," she begged.

"I'm not angry!" he snapped. "I'm frustrated because I don't understand what the problem is. You've worked so hard to get close to my kids. You give of yourself so freely, even joyously sometimes, yet you can't admit that you love me. What is it, Caroline? Is my family just a scientific experiment to you? Are we a new theory that has to be tested and examined under a microscope?''

"That's unfair, Mitch." She shrugged into her blouse and began buttoning it. "This situation is very complex. If it were just you and me, it might be different, but it's not. There are also three children involved who represent an enormous responsibility."

"Which you knew you were taking on when you agreed to date me," he reminded her hotly.

"I said I would try, and I have!" she retorted. "I've sacrificed untold hours of my work, made concessions, adjusted my schedule to accommodate you and your children... I've given all I can give, Mitch! Don't ask for more yet. I'm not ready!"

He knew she was right. He had to stop pushing. "I'm sorry," he said, taking a deep breath to calm himself. "I just need to hear you say that you love me. And I need to be able to tell you how much *I love you* without having you pull away from me."

"Then stop testing me," Caroline urged hotly.

Mitch frowned. "What do you mean?"

"Exactly what I said. Stop making everything that we do a proving ground for Caroline's suitability as a wife and mother."

Mitch was floored. "I'm not doing that."

"Yes, you are," she argued. "You sit back and watch me with the kids, passing judgment on how well I handle every situation. Can she read bedtime stories to Ruthann? Can she placate the child when she's fussy? Can she handle Sam's rudeness without alienating him? Can she cook supper for the family? Is she understanding about being stood up when you have to work late? *Everything* is a test!"

"That's not true, Caroline."

"Really?" She grabbed her skirt and slipped into it with hurried, graceless motions. "What about this camping trip? If that's not a test, I don't know what it is."

"It's a family ritual, for crying out loud! It's not a pop quiz to see if you've been doing your homework. Caroline, if you feel the pressure of being tested, it's something you're applying to yourself."

She wasn't listening to him. "You know what really amazes me, Mitch? I am frankly amazed that you mentioned marriage since I've failed so dreadfully with Janis!"

He frowned. "Is that what this is all about?" He moved around the bed, and when Caroline tried to skirt around him, he took hold of her arms. "Answer me, damn it. Have you been holding back because Janis is so cool toward you?"

She lifted her head defiantly. "I'm holding back because loving you isn't simple. It's loving Ruthann, Sam, Janis and Pop, as well. It's committing myself to being a parent to another woman's children. It's all well and good for you to say you love *me* because I'm just one person, but if I say it back, you're going to start expecting more from me than I'm ready to give."

"You're right." He let go of her and sat on the edge of the bed. "I've been expecting too much. You handle everything so well. You seem so happy. I didn't realize that to you it's all been research for a dissertation on parenthood," he said without rancor. "You're not going to add M.O.M. to the string of letters after your name until you've passed the final exam to your own satisfaction."

Caroline sat on the bed next to him. "Is that so bad?"

He nodded as he tilted his head toward her. "Yeah, I'm afraid it is, because you're a perfectionist. If you've been taking a test, you're grading yourself a lot lower than I have. As Sam could tell you, you don't have to bat a thousand to be a good ball player. You don't have to be perfect to be a good parent.''

She placed a hand on his arm. "I just need more time, Mitch. I have to be sure of what I feel.''

"What do you feel?" he asked. "Can you tell me that, at least?''

Caroline sighed. "I like your kids, Mitch. They scare me, but they also make me feel warm inside. When Ruthann snuggles up to me or Sam tells me I'm a lot of fun despite being an egghead, I feel a sense of accomplishment, and I wonder why my own parents never wanted or needed that kind of approval from me. It makes me want to give them what they need, but it also makes me afraid I don't have enough.''

"You do," he said. "The beauty of love is that the more you give, the more you get back. And the more you get back, the more you have to give in return. It's an infinite loop.''

"But a loop doesn't have a beginning or an end, Mitch. It's a continuous circle, and I haven't connected it yet. You're at one end, the kids are at the other, and I'm in the middle. If I can't put those ends together and bind the seam tightly, the loop will eventually break.''

She was right. Mitch had already connected the ends of the loop in his own mind and heart, but he had to give Caroline time to do the same. "All right, Caro. I'll stop pushing. If you want me to, I'll even stop telling you that I love you.''

She shook her head. "Don't do that, Mitch.''

"Will you stop retreating every time I say it?''

"Yes," she promised. "Just don't expect me to say it back until I'm sure.''

"All right," he said, unable to deny that he was disappointed. And he also felt a terrible fear that hadn't been there before. The connection Caroline wanted to make might never be strong enough to satisfy her. She didn't understand that failure was part of life; that perfection was impossible to achieve. Her standards were so high that no one could ever live up to them—not even Caroline herself.

But he didn't give voice to that fear because he knew that if he did, he'd have to face the fact that their relationship was doomed.

Then they continued dressing and went out for dinner.

THURSDAY AFTERNOON, Caroline left work early and went to do a few last-minute errands before going home to pack for the camping trip. For once, she didn't regret the time away from her lab because working with Scarlett had become so frustrating that she was relieved to escape the pressure. Her staff had finally completed the line-by-line analysis of all the computer's programming, but not a single error had been found. In theory, the OHARA computer was flawless. In fact, it was now losing pieces of information nearly every time Caroline brought it on-line.

Her personal life didn't seem to be functioning any more smoothly, either. After her fight with Mitch, they had kissed and made up, but she sensed a reserve in him now that hadn't been there before. She couldn't blame him for it since she was holding back far more than he ever had, but it created a tension that was difficult to cope with.

She was looking forward to the camping trip tomorrow with all the enthusiasm she had felt the last time she'd had a wisdom tooth pulled, but she couldn't back out of it. Mitch was counting on her, and so were the kids. She would have gladly traded places with Pop and stayed home, though.

Exhausted, Caroline kicked her shoes off the moment she came through the door, and dumped her armload of packages on the nearest chair. The hiking boots she should have purchased over the weekend spilled out of their box onto the floor, but she was too tired to care. She left them there and collapsed on the sofa to sort through her mail. The phone rang before she managed to slit open the envelope of the first bill. She considered letting her answering machine pick it up, then changed her mind because she couldn't eliminate the possibility that it was Mitch calling to give her the good news that the camping trip had been canceled.

"Hello?"

"Hi, Caroline. It's Mitch."

She didn't need the identification. She'd have recognized that sexy, gravelly voice even if they'd been conversing over two tin cans. "Hello, Mitch. What's up?"

"I tried to catch you at the lab, but you'd already left," he said. "Are you getting packed?"

Oh, joy. The trip was still on. "Not yet. I just walked through the door and collapsed."

"Hard day?"

"About the same as always."

"Sorry. I have some news on the case that might cheer you up, though."

Caroline sat up and dropped her feet to the floor. "What's that?"

"Just a few days after Dean Eddington was quoted in *PC Imaging* as having stated that Vic collapsed, he was treated at Mercy Hospital here in Hilliard for a broken rib, cuts and contusions. The doctor on duty in ER that night doesn't remember Eddington specifically, but he looked at Eddington's medical chart and said that the damage was consistent with a severe beating."

"Eddington didn't report it?"

"No. Evidently, Howard's henchmen put the fear of God in him. That's why he's clammed up."

"Are you going to ask Eddington about it?"

"Not just yet. I've got my men digging a little deeper into Richmond's association with Sydney Grisham."

"The racketeer you mentioned?"

"Yes," Mitch replied. "I suspect that Eddington knows about him. I just have to figure out a way to get him to open up."

Caroline asked him how he planned to do that, and Mitch replied, "I have to give him more confidence in us. Monday we were just taking shots in the dark and he knew it. If I can go back to San Francisco and tell *him* who beat him up and why, he might admit that it happened."

Caroline sat back again. "Keep a low profile, Mitch, please," she begged him. "This is starting to scare me. Before, I was just angry because Richmond was passing my work off as his own, but things have changed. We could be walking in very dangerous territory."

She heard a smile in his voice when he responded, "Caroline, don't worry. This is what I do for a living."

"I know. Just be careful."

"I will." There was a short pause. "How long will it take you to pack?" he asked.

Caroline glanced at the packages on the chair. "I haven't even started."

There was another pause. "Caroline, if you really don't want to go—"

"Thanks, Mitch, but I think it's a little late to back out now, don't you?"

He sounded relieved when he said, "Just remember that it's not a test. It's just a camping trip."

She chuckled. "That's like saying Tyrannosaurus rex is just a big lizard."

"Haven't you heard? The latest theory is that dinosaurs were birds, not lizards. Keep up or drop out, kid," he said jokingly.

"Thanks for the advice. What time are you picking me up in the morning?"

They completed the call by finalizing their plans for the next day, then hung up. Caroline went back to sorting her mail because it was the only way she could think of to avoid packing. She put the bills in one pile, catalogs in another and tossed the junk mail onto her coffee table to be disposed of later.

She stopped sorting when she came to a plain white envelope with her name and address in bold type, but with no return address. Curious, she split it open and pulled out a single sheet of paper that read in the same typeface:

This is Vic's trapdoor. Use it and you'll find everything you need to know.

A series of numbers and symbols followed the terse message.

Caroline sat upright and checked the envelope. No return address, but it was postmarked Menlo Park, just south of San Francisco. She looked at the message again.

Vic had a trapdoor.

A stab of excitement coursed through her, because if what the anonymous note said was true, she was holding the means of accessing Vic's memory core in her hands. Trapdoors were unique codes that most designers built into their computers as a way of reaching the core programming in the event of a massive systems shutdown. They could be designed to bypass security systems, and a truly clever designer could make the code completely undetectable.

If Vic did, indeed, have a trapdoor, Caroline could access Howard Richmond's computer from the comfort of her very own home, compare its programming line by line with Scarlett's and have all the proof she needed that the data base had been stolen.

Unfortunately, she would also be breaking the law and leaving herself open to criminal prosecution in order to obtain information that would never hold up in a court of law. She had a gold mine, but she couldn't use it.

Caroline looked at the envelope again. It was no wonder that her mysterious benefactor had omitted his return address. Anyone who had this level of high-security information about Vic had also signed an agreement that made divulging such information illegal. Caroline could think of only two people who might have been willing to take that risk: Dean Eddington and Evan Converse.

Considering the threats that had been made against Eddington, he couldn't afford to help her outright, but he was so bitter he might have been willing to do it covertly. Evan, on the other hand, wasn't bitter, but he was afraid to put his job in jeopardy. This was just the sort of anonymous risk he might be willing to take.

For an instant, Caroline was tempted to call and ask him, but she decided against it. If he *had* sent it, he would only deny it. If he hadn't sent it, it was probably best that he not know that Caroline now possessed the trapdoor code. Since Evan wasn't the chief designer of the VIC, there was a good chance he didn't even know about the trapdoor. She trusted Evan, but now that she knew Richmond had ties with dangerous criminals, she didn't want to risk putting anyone at peril.

The temptation to use the code was overwhelming, but Caroline resisted. She couldn't resort to an illegal, unauthorized entry, but the codes were so appealing...

And they were also familiar.

That conviction jolted Caroline and it took her a moment to figure out why she had the feeling she had seen this code before. The format was almost identical to the one someone had used in the attempted break-in nearly three months ago. Had someone been trying to use Vic's trapdoor on Scarlett?

Or did Scarlett have a trapdoor that Caroline didn't know about?

Caroline was on her feet in an instant and within a few seconds she had linked her home computer with Scarlett at MediaTech. She bypassed all of her computer's usual friendly greetings and called up the break-in code, which had been stored in a file for future reference.

She looked back and forth from the code on the screen to the one on the piece of paper.

The screen read: > >68092.if? > >yimrestp.894 > >interface
The paper read: > >90783.if? > >ssntrprs.701 > >interface

The same format with different letters and numbers. Three months ago, someone had been attempting to access Scarlett with a code that was remarkably similar to Vic's, but the code hadn't worked. Why? Had the user typed an incorrect symbol? Transposed two of the letters or numbers? Why had Scarlett rejected the code?

Caroline didn't even entertain the notion that she could be wrong in the supposition she was making. She *knew* beyond any doubt that Scarlett did have a trapdoor. It explained so many things. Not just how Richmond had gotten access to the data base, but the problems Scarlett was having, as well. What better way could there be to slow down Caroline's work than to create a mysterious recurring memory loss that couldn't be traced or detected? With a trapdoor, someone could access Scarlett a dozen times a day and Caroline would never know about it. One well-placed delete command, and *poof!*—the whole system was assumed to have a major flaw.

She had been running in circles like a hamster in a cage, trying to solve a nonexistent problem and accusing herself of incompetence.

Caroline was incensed, but at least she knew the source of the problem now, and she could correct it. All she had to do was figure out what mistake the unknown thief had made in the trapdoor code when he'd tried to access Scarlett. Once she had the code, she could use it herself to get inside and erase it. That was going to take a lot of time, because there were literally trillions of letter and number combinations that would have to be tried, but she could do it. Eventually.

First, though, there was one very important step she had to take. She had to create an unbreakable, protective code that would prohibit the thief from accessing his trapdoor. It was difficult since she didn't know exactly where the existing trapdoor was located, but an hour later, she had built so many layers of protective security into Scarlett's core that she was confident no one could get through it but her. She placed a quick phone call to Henry Bergman at his home, and informed him that until further notice, no one would be able to access any of the computer's systems but her.

She explained her reasons, what she had discovered and what she had done to protect the computer, and Henry was delighted that they were finally on the verge of solving the problem. He encouraged her to give him the new security codes so that she wouldn't be the only one with that critical information, but she refused. She wasn't taking any chances this time. She made a similar phone call to Ed Newton and told him she wanted someone stationed in the lab at all times to make certain no one could have any access whatsoever to Scarlett.

After she finished with the calls, Caroline asked Scarlett to run all possible number sequences associated with the first five digits of the inaccurate trapdoor code. If Scarlett hit the correct number, Caroline would automatically be admitted into the netherworld where the trapdoor resided. If the right number didn't come up, she would try the letters in the second part of the command, and if that still didn't work, she'd have Scarlett do both simultaneously. The search could take weeks, but eventually she would succeed.

Once the numbers were running, silently flashing with blinding speed, Caroline sat back. There was nothing for her to do now but wait.

And pack.

Mitch! The camping trip. The kids who would be disappointed if she canceled. A lover who would undoubtedly view it as a major failure on her part if she put her work above his children just this once. This stupid camping trip was important to him; so much so, that Caroline almost felt that their whole relationship depended on its success. Perhaps that was why she had resisted it so hard and why she dreaded it so much.

Now, she had an excuse to back out. Or did she? She couldn't leave her home computer linked with Scarlett for the whole weekend, but if she went to MediaTech, she could access Scarlett directly and let the computer chew on the problem while she was gone. Since it might take weeks to crack the code, there was no reason for her to sit and stare at the screen.

No, she didn't have an excuse. She had to go camping and that meant she had to pack. And she should probably call Mitch, too. He certainly needed to know what she had learned.

Before she could match thought to action, though, her doorbell rang. Hoping it was Mitch, she hurried across the room, threw the door open...

And discovered Evan Converse.

CHAPTER SEVENTEEN

"EVAN! What are you doing here?"

"Am I catching you at a bad time?"

"Actually, I am a little busy," she said, wondering how she should handle this ticklish situation. Vic's trapdoor was no longer of any concern to her now that she knew Scarlett had one, as well. She didn't want anyone at The Richmond Group, not even Evan, to know that she knew about it, though. Unfortunately, just across the room her computer monitor was flashing permutations of the code. If Evan didn't know about Vic's trapdoor he wouldn't recognize what her computer was running, but she hated to take the chance.

"I won't take up much of your time," Evan promised.

"All right." She stepped back to admit him.

Evan came into the room and almost tripped over the packages she had dropped earlier. He eyed the shoes, then Caroline. "Hiking boots?" he said skeptically.

"I'm going on a camping trip tomorrow," she told him. "That's why this isn't really a good time, Evan. I've got to pack."

"*You're* going camping? When did you become interested in the great outdoors?"

"Since I met a man who loves camping," she replied.

"Grogan? The cop?" he asked.

She had never accused Evan of not being perceptive. "That's right."

He just nodded. "I thought maybe you two were involved. When he talked to me the week after the demonstration, I detected a bit of hostility that seemed uncalled for."

Caroline didn't dispute that. Mitch no longer seemed to think that Evan was a viable suspect in the case, but he had other reasons to dislike her ex-husband. "I'd rather not discuss Mitch with you," she told him, moving across the room toward the computer. Evan drifted in that direction right along with her, and Caroline tensed. "Why don't you have a seat," she offered, indicating the sofa, but he ignored the invitation and looked at the monitor.

"What are you working on?" he asked.

Caroline punched a button and the monitor went black. Scarlett was still spewing out numbers, but at least Evan couldn't see them now.

She turned to him and managed a smile. "A new program that I'd rather my competition didn't know about."

"Oh." He turned away from the computer and sat.

"Sorry. Now what did you want, Evan?" she asked, dropping into the chair opposite him.

"I want to know how the case against Howard is going," he replied. "You and your new boyfriend made all these wild accusations that—"

"Accusations that I proved are true," she reminded him. "You heard Vic tell me that he had met Mitch Grogan and his daughter."

Evan sighed. "I know. And there is no other explanation for it, but I still find it hard to believe, Caroline. I suddenly find myself in a state of suspended animation, and I want to know what you're doing. Should I start looking for another job? Are you going to ask me to work on getting proof from the inside? What?"

Caroline was pretty sure Mitch wouldn't approve of her giving Evan any information. "I'm sorry, but I really can't tell you anything about the case."

"Why not, for heaven's sake? You were only too willing to drag me into the middle of it."

"I know. And if I had answers, I'd give them to you, but Mitch and Ed Newton, our security chief, are handling the investigation and they haven't found much. Frankly, I've had other worries on my mind."

"Like Scarlett's memory losses?"

Caroline stiffened. "How do you know about that?"

"It's all over the industry, Caroline," he said gently. "The rumor has been going around since long before the VIC launch."

"Oh, really?" she said tersely.

"Is it true? Is there a flaw in the system that causes it to lose data?"

It seemed wise to let him think that she considered the problem to be a flaw in the programming. "Yes. The rumors are true."

"I thought so. I'm sorry, Caroline," he said sincerely.

"Don't worry about it, Evan, I think I'm on the verge of a breakthrough," she said, then stood up. "Look, I really hate to rush you, but there's nothing I can tell you about the investigation. Mitch and the kids are picking me up at six tomorrow morning. I've got to finish packing and get some sleep."

"Okay. Hint taken," he said with a grin as he moved toward the door. Caroline walked along with him. "Tell me, is that 'kids,' plural? Grogan has more than one?"

"Three," she replied. "Ages four, ten and fifteen."

Evan winced. "You and Grogan are serious, then?"

"Do you think I'd be going to the mountains with him if it wasn't?"

"Good point. I've got to admit, I'm surprised," he told her. "Despite all the fuss you made about the baby before our divorce, I never really believed you wanted kids."

"I know. That's why we're divorced."

He stopped at the door and looked at her wistfully. "Isn't it amazing that you can think you know someone so well and not know them at all?"

She saw a certain sadness in his eyes that touched her. "Yes, it is amazing, Evan."

"Well, good night, Caroline."

"I'll be in touch as soon as I have any information that would affect you," she promised. He nodded and disappeared down the hall.

Caroline closed the door and tried to remember what she had been about to do before the interruption.

Mitch. She was supposed to call him and tell him what she had learned.

She went to the phone and promptly put her ex-husband's visit out of her head.

HOWARD RICHMOND slammed the door of his custom-built Rolls Royce and stalked across the parking lot to the building that bore his name. This had better be good. He'd received a frantic phone call from Evan Converse half an hour ago ordering him to get down to the lab immediately.

Imagine! That pip-squeak Converse ordering his boss around! Howard was going to have to get a few things straight with this pain-in-the-ass computer technician. Granted, Howard did owe Evan a debt—a big one—but that didn't give him the right to issue orders.

Richmond ignored the guard at the security desk and went up to the lab. He found Converse at Vic's primary interface console, his face ashen and his eyes practically bulging with panic as he pounded on the keyboard in front of him.

"What the hell is going on, Evan?" Howard demanded.

"Caroline knows about Scarlett's trapdoor," he snapped, not bothering to look up.

"What?" Howard gasped.

"You heard me." Evan looked at him. "I went over there tonight to see if I could get her to tell me anything about the investigation—"

"You idiot!" Howard roared. "That was stupid. Almost as stupid as giving her access to Vic after the demonstration!"

"I thought I had wiped everything out!" Evan yelled back. "How the hell was I supposed to know she told her damned computer about her boyfriend? If you hadn't panicked when she asked the question about friends—"

"All right! Enough," Howard said. "We've both made mistakes," he admitted. "I was afraid you'd missed something in the information replacement and you wanted the satisfaction of knowing you were putting a big one over on your snooty ex-wife."

Evan's face hardened. "I was afraid she'd get suspicious if I didn't agree to help her," he said tersely, though Richmond was right. He had wanted to gloat about his victory, and Caroline's absolute trust of him had made it all the sweeter. Imagine asking the man who was responsible for stealing your life's work to help you *find* the man responsible. It had been an opportunity too rich to pass up.

"It doesn't matter now," Richmond replied. "Just tell me why you think she knows about the trapdoor."

"Because I saw it on her computer when I got there. I only saw a flash of it, but I'd recognize that code pattern a mile away. Somehow she's figured out that the access code I botched last May is a trapdoor."

Richmond glared at him. "Wait a minute. You botched a routine access? You never told me that."

"Because it didn't seem important," he said defensively. "I made a simple typographical error. Scarlett rejected the code and automatically notified security. But I covered it. I typed in a few random letters and made it look like some hacker had been on a fishing expedition."

Richmond stiffened his jaw against the rage he felt. "If you covered it so well, why has she made the connection to your trapdoor after all this time?"

"I don't know. With Caroline, you can never tell. She's a fruitcake."

"That fruitcake built the world's first artificially intelligent computer," Howard reminded him with considerable glee.

"Yeah. Something you weren't able to do until I told you about the trapdoor I hid in her data base codes before I let her divorce me. It was an insurance policy that is going to pay off very handsomely for both of us," Evan retorted.

"Not if she accesses that trapdoor. It'll be proof that someone has been tampering with her computer, and knowing your ego as I do, I'll just bet you couldn't resist putting some little 'Kilroy was here' clue in there, could you?"

Evan couldn't deny it. "If she cracks the code, she'll know it's me," he admitted.

"God deliver me from idiots," Howard muttered, then slammed his hand on the desk. "Get that damned code out of there! Now! Erase every sign of it, because if you don't, we're both going to jail, sonny!"

"I can't erase it!" Evan shouted. "What do you think I've been trying to do for the last half hour? Caroline has put some new security code into place and I can't get near Scarlett!"

"I thought the trapdoor was designed to circumvent security."

"It is, as long as no one knows it's there. Now she knows, and there's nothing I can do to break through. Scarlett is running a sequence search. Eventually, she'll hit the right combination of letters and numbers, and it will be all over."

"Unless we get the new security code from her first," Howard said. Wheels were turning in his brain, but they were having to grind against his mounting fear. He was not going to go to jail.

"And how do you plan to get them without her knowledge? I can't imagine that she was stupid enough to write them down. They're engraved in that steel-trap mind of hers."

"Then we'll just have to get her to tell us."

Evan laughed shortly. "What good will that do? Then she'll know for sure that—" He stopped abruptly when he realized what Howard was suggesting. "No," he said, shaking his head. "I will not be a party to murder."

Richmond eyed him coldly. "Then you'll spend the next twenty years in prison. I hear they have great opportunities for career advancement in license-plate manufacture. And it will do wonders for your social life, I'm sure."

Evan shuddered. He didn't want to go to prison, but he didn't want the electric chair, either. "Howard, you can't."

"Oh, yeah? Watch me." Richmond headed out of the lab toward his office with Evan on his heels.

"What are you going to do?" he asked desperately.

"Place a call to a friend who has almost as much riding on Vic as we do. He'll have her taken care of tomorrow."

"You can't do that! You can't just have her murdered!" Evan protested, trying desperately to think of something that would stop Howard. "She's not even going to be in town tomorrow! She's going to the mountains with her cop boyfriend and his kids!"

Howard stopped and looked at him. "Big Sur?"

"I don't know. And if I did, I probably wouldn't tell you."

"No matter. Sydney Grisham has sources in police departments all over the state. If Grogan has put in for a vacation, Sydney will be able to find out where." Richmond turned on his heel and disappeared into his office, leaving Evan standing in the hall.

It was going to happen. Evan finally saw clearly that there was nothing he could do to stop it. The less he knew about it, the better, but he didn't want to see Caroline killed. He had just wanted to cut her down to size professionally. She had made him feel small and incompetent for all of the three years that they were married, and after the divorce, she'd landed on her feet so nimbly that it had made him hate her more than he had imagined possible. He still hated her, still resented her success. But he couldn't be a party to her death.

But he couldn't warn her, either. Thanks to his gangster friend Sydney Grisham, Howard Richmond had a very long and vengeful arm.

When it came down to the bottom line, Evan had to choose between saving his own skin and saving Caroline's.

It didn't take long for him to decide.

CHAPTER EIGHTEEN

"SYDNEY?"

A deep, sonorous voice came back to Howard Richmond over the telephone line. "Yes, Howard. What is it now?"

Richmond hesitated. Considering Sydney Grisham's long history with the authorities, it wasn't wise to be too specific about things like this on the telephone. "I just wanted to know if everything is in place regarding the problem we discussed last night. Did your man find what we were looking for?" he asked cautiously.

"We know where the item is, and my subordinate is on his way to pick it up now."

"Do you expect any problems?"

A weary sigh filled an otherwise silent moment. "No, Howard, I don't. Unlike you and other clumsy members of your staff, my people don't make mistakes. I'll let you know when I have the information you need."

The line went dead and Howard Richmond hung up the phone. He leaned back in his chair heavily and discovered that his heart was racing. But then, was that any wonder? He'd done a lot of unscrupulous and illegal things in his life, but this was the first time he'd ever been a party to murder.

"SAM! Janis! Come back here!" Caroline shouted in alarm as she came out of the cabin and spotted the older kids on a path that disappeared into the woods and led God knew

where. Ruthann was playing happily in the dirt in front of
the porch.

They had been in the mountains less than four hours and
already the trip was a nightmare of disastrous proportions. To Caroline, a "rustic cabin" was one that had a
quaint, old-fashioned charm. To Mitch, a "rustic cabin"
was one that might survive the next stiff breeze if no one
breathed too hard.

Their "home" for the next four days did have electricity
in all four of the small rooms, thanks to a functioning gen-
erator, but that was about all Caroline could credit it with.
The ramshackle cots in the side rooms and the homemade
furniture in the main living area were all liberally decorated with thick spider webs—many of which were still inhabited by their creators.

There was no running water because the pump that ser-
viced the well had stopped functioning and it had stub-
bornly resisted Mitch's best efforts to fix it. Bathroom
facilities for the weekend consisted of an ancient outhouse
twenty yards behind the cabin.

Caroline was horrified by the prospect of being trapped
here for four days. She *wanted* to be a good sport, but the
cabin was more than primitive—it was unsanitary and
downright creepy.

And worst of all, she was temporarily stuck there alone
with the kids because the breakdown of the pump had
forced Mitch to make a trip down the mountain to the
nearest store to buy drinking water. Sam and Janis hadn't
wanted to go with him, so instead of playing the bad guy,
Caroline had agreed to stay. She had quickly realized her
mistake when she tried to put them to work cleaning out the
cabin, though. They had protested endlessly, and between
their disapproval and a running battle with the mice and
spiders, Caroline was close to tears. Unable to bear their

constant complaining, she released them from the work detail but had insisted they remain close to the cabin.

So far, though, Ruthann was the only one complying with Caroline's edict. Sam and Janis seemed determined to go exploring no matter what Caroline said to the contrary. As they jogged down the trail, she had to shout at them a second time, though she was certain they had heard her the first time.

"Kids, I said come back here!"

They finally stopped and turned reluctantly toward the cabin. "We're just going up to Pigeon Bluff, Doc," Sam called back to her.

"No, you're not!"

"It's okay, Caroline," Janis said testily. "It's not far. We go there all the time."

"Not while your father is gone," Caroline replied.

"Come with us," Sam urged, but she refused.

"We're all staying here and that's final!"

"Oh, man," Sam muttered as he came back down the path. Janis trailed after him, kicking her feet at the rocks and dirt. The girl's behavior was worthy of Ruthann, but not a fifteen-year-old, and it made Caroline furious. Somehow, though, she managed to control her temper.

She tried to reason with them. She tried to distract them. She fed them snacks from the cooler and enlisted their aid in collecting firewood, but the tension kept mounting as long shadows began stretching eerily through the tall stands of oak and fir trees.

To a city dweller like Caroline, the setting was so alien that every rustle of the bushes brought frightening images to mind of the bears and mountain lions that were said to still inhabit these mountains. By they time they heard a car coming down the dirt road, she was a nervous wreck. The kids ran down the rutted lane to greet their father, and when

Mitch's car came lumbering through the trees, Caroline nearly cried with relief.

"Hail, the conquering hero! I bring water to refresh the palate and restore the soul!" Mitch said jubilantly as he climbed out of the car. He flashed his famous grin at Caroline and tossed her the large can of pesticide she had demanded he bring back with him. "Well, how do you like the mountains so far?" he asked. "Isn't it wonderful?"

Caroline glared at him, turned and stalked into the cabin with the bug spray.

WHEN CAROLINE finally went to bed that night wrapped in a lumpy sleeping blanket on the rickety cot with the creepy sensation of spiders crawling all over her, she knew that Saturday would have to be an improvement over Friday. She was wrong. Things just kept getting worse.

Mitch kept telling her that one day she would look back on this and laugh, but she knew better. She was failing every test, and for some reason, the kids seemed to take great delight in pointing out every mistake, gaffe and blunder she committed.

They made it through breakfast because Mitch didn't expect her to cook over an open camp fire. He cooked, instead, and then they took off for a long hike through the mountains. Though Caroline was in excellent physical condition, she had trouble keeping up with the others because after the first hour, her new hiking boots had rubbed enormous blisters on her heels.

Mitch politely refrained from saying "I told you so," but Sam wasn't as tactful. Every time they had to stop and wait for her, he complained endlessly because she was slowing them down.

Janis contributed to the festive atmosphere by reminiscing about her mother at every opportunity, and eventually, the fond memories deteriorated into blatant comparisons between Becky and Caroline. Needless to say, Caroline fell considerably short of the stature of Janis's mother, who had apparently been a cross between Davy Crockett, Smokey the Bear and the great frontier explorer John Freemont.

By the end of the day, Caroline had grown to hate Becky; not the woman who loved her children and had even given her own life to bring one of them into the world, but the woman who had achieved mythological proportions in the memories of those children.

By nightfall, Caroline's nerves were frayed to the breaking point. She desperately needed some time alone; there hadn't been a single minute all day that she had been out of sight of Mitch and the kids, but she couldn't go traipsing off into the woods by herself. Instead, she tried hard to keep her mouth shut and not comment on anything, because when she did, her voice was sharp. The kids responded predictably by snapping back at her, and the cabin turned into an armed camp with Caroline on one side, the kids on the other, and Mitch in the middle trying to play peacemaker.

Armed warfare broke out right after supper.

"Not like that! You're wasting water," Janis told Caroline with disgust. They were trying to do the dishes, but Caroline couldn't even do that to anyone's satisfaction.

"Don't yell at me, Janis," she snapped back. "If you can't keep a civil tongue in your head, you can do the dishes alone."

"That's fine with me."

"Whoa!" Mitch said. "That's enough from both of you. Janis, apologize to Caroline."

"Why should I apologize? She's the one who can't do anything right."

"I said that's enough!" Mitch sighed wearily. "All right. Leave the dishes. Everybody sit down. We're going to have a family powwow."

"Oh, goodie!" Ruthann exclaimed. She had napped through most of the fishing expedition and was ready to play again.

Mitch ignored the little one and explained to Caroline, "A powwow is—"

"I know what it is, Mitch. I haven't been living under a rock for the past thirty years."

"You couldn't prove it by me," Sam grumbled.

Mitch glared at his son. "That's enough out of you, too. Now sit. All of you. We're going to talk through the problems we've been having today."

Caroline's stomach knotted. "I don't think that's a good idea, Mitch," she said tightly.

"Yes, it is," he said gently. "We need to clear the air."

He moved to the camp fire and Ruthann took hold of Caroline's hand to draw her over, too. "Come on, Car'line. Powwow is fun 'cause Daddy always tells us stories."

If there had been anyplace to escape to, Caroline would have refused to go with the little girl. Instead, she let herself be dragged to the fire and sat on a split-rail log beside Mitch. Ruthann nestled between them and the other two kids sat on the ground opposite.

"All right," Mitch began. "Here's how it goes. Since everyone is unhappy, everyone gets a chance to tell why. We'll discuss it, find a solution and then everyone will be happy again."

"I'm happy now, Daddy," Ruthann said, leaning against Caroline.

"Then you don't have to take a turn," he said. "Just listen, okay? Sam, you go first."

The boy shrugged. "Well, she slowed us down on the hike because of her blisters and we didn't get to explore any of the caves because she was afraid there'd be snakes or bears in them."

Caroline noticed that he didn't have to preface his criticism or even identify who "she" was because it was a given that "she" was the source of all their problems.

Sam listed a couple of other complaints that had to do with the restrictions Caroline had placed on them yesterday, then he shrugged again. "I guess she is trying, though. She did okay with the minnows."

"All right." Mitch looked at his older daughter. "Janis?"

"I don't have anything to say," the girl replied.

"Oh, I think you have more to say than any of us," he answered.

Janis got up. "I'm going to bed."

"No, you're not. Sit down, young lady," he ordered.

"Mitch, let her go," Caroline said, her voice tight. "Frankly, I'm not in the mood to sit here while you all play 'Vilify Caroline.'"

"That's not what we're doing," he told her. "I just want to know what's going on."

"That's easy. We're having a terrible time and it's my fault," she replied testily. "I told you this would happen. I was not cut out for the great outdoors. I am not Becky. And I am not, as the saying goes, a happy camper! I don't want to be here."

"Why not, Car'line?" Ruthann asked, looking up at her adoringly. "We love you."

She looked down into the little girl's face and felt tears come to her eyes. She brushed a damp blond curl off Ruthann's forehead. "I love you, too, Short Stuff."

"Oh, bull," Janis snapped. "Give it a rest, why don't you? You don't even like any of us, except for Daddy."

The uncontrolled venom in her voice rocked Caroline. "Janis, that's not true."

"Yes, it is. If we weren't around, you'd be having the time of your life!"

"You know, you're right," Caroline replied. She was so exhausted and frustrated that her patience with the brilliant but difficult girl had completely dried up. "I would be happier if you weren't around because you haven't given me an inch since the day I started dating your father. I have put up with your silences, sullen looks and snide comments hoping that you would learn to accept me, and instead it just gets worse. Why do you dislike me so much?"

Janis fixed her jaw mulishly and glared at Caroline.

"Answer her, Janis," Mitch said firmly. "I think we'd all like to know what's been bugging you."

"Yeah, Janis," Sam added. "Why don't you ever cut Caroline any slack?"

"Yeah!" Ruthann said, just to be part of the conversation.

Having everyone gang up on her was too much for the girl. "You don't want to know," she told her siblings.

"Sure we do," Sam replied.

"She doesn't like you, all right! Not any of you!" Janis shouted. "She's just been pretending all this time. I heard Daddy tell Pop that she didn't want anything to do with him because of us!"

Mitch frowned. "When did I—"

"After my first day at the lab," she snapped.

It took Mitch a moment to remember that conversation with his father because it was something that had happened in another lifetime. "You were eavesdropping on me and your grandfather?" he asked sharply.

"I came down to apologize for yelling at you, and heard the whole thing."

"Why didn't you say something?" he asked.

"What was there to say? Caroline liked you but she didn't like us."

A few things were clear to Caroline now, but she wasn't sure how to undo the damage that had been done so long ago. "Janis, my first decision not to date your father had nothing to do with whether I *liked* you children or not. I've never had kids. I've never even been around them, and you know that. I was just afraid."

"Are you still afraid?" the girl asked shrewdly.

"Yes."

"Are you going to marry Daddy?"

Caroline shot a confused glance at Mitch and he said, "We're not ready to consider marriage, yet, Janis."

"I'd rather hear what Caroline has to say," she said shortly. "Are you going to marry Daddy and be our mother?"

Caroline couldn't lie to her. "I don't know."

"Because you don't love him? Or because of us kids?"

She didn't flinch. "Because I don't know if I can give you and Sam and Ruthann what you need."

"You mean if we weren't around, you'd marry Daddy in a minute, right?"

Caroline shook her head. "That's a moot point, Janis. You *are* here. That's the reality I have to deal with."

Janis looked triumphantly at her brother. "See. I told you she didn't like us."

Caroline came to her feet. "For heaven's sake, Janis, you're old enough to know that liking you—or *loving* you, for that matter—isn't the point. I have to decide if I can assume the responsibility of being your mother."

"And if you can't, you'll go away just as she did!" Janis shouted. "I wish you'd go away now and get it over with, because I don't want to lose two mothers!"

A choked sob escaped the girl's throat and tears suddenly flooded her cheeks. She turned and ran to the cabin.

Mitch was on his feet in an instant. He touched Caroline's arm as a gesture of reassurance before hurrying in to his daughter.

Caroline sat down heavily, trying to absorb the implications of what Janis had said.

"Why is Jannie crying?" Ruthann asked, crawling into Caroline's lap. "Doesn't she want you to be our mommy?"

Caroline wrapped her arms around the child and snuggled her close. "She's just afraid, honey."

"Of what?"

"That's hard to explain."

Ruthann looked up at her. "I want you to be *my* mommy," she said plaintively. "Will you, Car'line? Please?"

The tears broke free and coursed down Caroline's cheeks. She buried her face in Ruthann's silky curls to hide her emotion. When she finally had control again, she looked at Sam and found him sullenly poking at the fire with a stick. He darted a glance at her, then looked away, ignoring her completely.

Except for the warm body nestled against her, Caroline had never felt more alone in her life.

CAROLINE SAT ALONE outside the cabin, listening to the sound of Mitch trying to get his children bedded down for the night. Finally, he came through the door and sat beside her.

"Are you all right?"

It was a long moment before she answered. "I told you this trip was a mistake, Mitch," she said in a flat, lifeless voice.

"How can you say that?" he asked gently. "I know you've had a miserable time, but we made real progress tonight. At least now we know what's been bothering Janis and can combat it."

"How?" she asked. "There's only one way to dispel her conviction that I dislike her, and that's for me to marry you. And even then, she's going to be fighting fears of abandonment."

"But she can conquer them with our help."

Caroline shook her head. "No. I can't help, Mitch. Our whole relationship was a mistake from the very beginning."

He didn't want to hear that. "Caroline—"

"No, listen to me," she said firmly. "It was wrong for me to become involved with you, Mitch. I didn't realize that my very presence was going to raise expectations in your children."

"That was inevitable, Caroline," he told her. "It's a problem that every single parent has to deal with."

"I don't care about other parents or other children. Yours are the only ones that concern me, and I won't be a party to hurting them any more than they've already been hurt."

Mitch felt her slipping away from him and it made him sick inside. "Caroline, you're making too much of this. We'll work it out together, as a family."

"We're only a family if I agree to marry you, and I've already made it clear I can't make that commitment," she said harshly because he didn't seem to be listening to quiet words of reason.

"You will someday," he replied with more hope than conviction.

"Only one of us is sure about that, Mitch, and it's not me. Don't you see that it would be wrong for us to continue this relationship? How can I ask Janis to accept me, to try to care for me, if I can't promise her that I won't leave someday? Ruthann wants me to be her mother. The longer I stay, the greater that attachment will become, and she'll be just as devastated when I leave as Sam and Janis were by Becky's death.''

"Damn it, Caroline, why do you assume that you're going to leave someday? What makes you so certain that we can't become a family?"

She laughed shortly. "How can you look back at these last two days and still ask that question?"

Mitch's mouth fell open. "Caroline, one disastrous camping trip—"

"Is one too many," she replied. "I haven't done anything right."

"That's not true," he argued. "You're out of place and uncomfortable here, but that's my fault. I should have had someone come up here to check on the condition of the cabin before we came. No one has been here since last summer, and I should have realized that it would need cleaning and repairs. That got us off to a rocky start, but the weekend is salvageable. And so are we."

Caroline shook her head. She was numb inside from the pain of this decision, but she couldn't back down. "No, Mitch. I'll never be able to take on the responsibility of parenting your children, and I won't contribute to hurting them." She stood. "It's over. You have to accept that, because I have."

CHAPTER NINETEEN

MITCH *DIDN'T* ACCEPT Caroline's pronouncement. He loved her too much to believe that they couldn't work things out, and he also knew her too well. She was a strong, persistent woman who knew how to fight for what she wanted. In time, once the strain of this camping trip had passed, she would realize that what she wanted was a life with him and his children. She *had* to, because he didn't think he could bear giving her up. He had already lost one woman he loved; he couldn't accept losing Caroline, too.

Still, he knew better than to force the issue. Caroline didn't like being backed into a corner, and pushing her would only make her dig her heels in. He had to let the weekend play out, take as much pressure off of her as he could and hope for the best.

He wasn't surprised the next morning when she politely but firmly refused to go fishing with them. Trying to be peacemaker, Sam even issued her a special invitation, but Caroline gently assured him that they'd have more fun without her and she had some work she wanted to do on the laptop computer she had brought along. Janis had trouble looking her in the eye, and Mitch was pretty sure the girl was embarrassed by the scene she had created the night before. Eventually, she'd come around and apologize, though. And then Caroline would see that arguments were natural, human flaws were forgivable and love was too important to throw away.

Though the adults tried to paint on a happy face, Ruthann sensed the residual tension and it made her cling to Caroline even more than usual. She wanted to remain with "her Car'line" instead of going fishing. Not wanting to burden Caroline, Mitch began trying to entice the child into going along, but Caroline assured him it was all right.

"Are you sure?" he asked.

She nodded. "I thought I'd go up and sit in that glade we passed through yesterday by Pigeon Bluff. Ruthann can go with me if she wants to."

They looked at each other for a long moment, connected by the love they felt and separated by the decision Caroline had made. "All right," Mitch said finally, picking up a little cooler and the sack of sandwiches Caroline had helped make. "We'll be back after lunch. If you-know-who gets too rowdy to handle, you know the way to the stream, don't you?"

"Yes. I'll see you later. Have fun, kids."

"We'll catch a big one for you," Sam promised and they all disappeared down the trail.

"Now, what?" Ruthann asked. She was sitting beside Caroline on the edge of the porch, swinging her legs and kicking up dust.

"Now you can help me work."

Ruthann's blue eyes lit up. "Like Jannie does?"

Caroline nodded gravely and felt the persistent tug at her heart she always experienced when she was with Ruthann. So much trust... No questions, no complications... Just love, given freely.

She was going to miss that more than she had ever imagined possible. Losing the baby she had never held was going to be nothing compared to the pain of giving up this child who was ready to love her so completely.

Caroline shoved the thought away and rose. She had made her decision for the good of the children and she would not weaken. Once this weekend was over, she would be leaving this side trip into the never-never land of Mitch's life and returning to her own. It was time to focus on that.

She retrieved her laptop computer from her suitcase, packed a couple of sandwiches in the spare cooler and walked off hand in hand with Mitch's daughter. A short way from the cabin, the trail split going east to the stream, but the glade that had seemed so peaceful to Caroline yesterday was west.

The walk was an easy one through a forest of oak trees, and they played games along the way, seeing how many birds and squirrels they could spot in the trees. The path finally opened into a sloping meadowlike clearing ringed with trees on all sides that occasionally allowed glimpses of the surrounding mountains. They found a spot in the shade of a young, scraggly redwood tree and Caroline opened up her computer.

She called up a copy of the mysterious Scarlett access code and patiently explained to Ruthann that they were going to play a game of numbers and letters. The child understood none of it, but Caroline enlisted her help in punching keys and made her feel so important to the process that the little girl was still for nearly ten minutes, which was almost a record for Ruthann.

What Caroline was really doing was comparing the Scarlett code with the VIC code. It was reasonable to assume they had been constructed by the same person, and she wanted to see if she could spot any similarities other than the format. Most trapdoors weren't just random numbers. They usually included a word or a date that had some relevance to the person using it. Some of them were obvious, like a birthday or anniversary; others were often obscure like the personalized license plates that some people constructed with abbreviations so remote that they were virtually incomprehensible.

Focusing on the eight letters in the Scarlett code—yim-restp—she looked for a pattern that she might have missed. Nothing occurred to her, but then, it was very likely that at least one of those letters was incorrect. Would substituting one letter in the string make it make sense? She made mental replacements, but couldn't find anything.

"I want a new game," Ruthann said when Caroline stopped talking and asking her to do things.

"All right. Type this," she said, clearing the screen and turning the computer so that Ruthann could reach the keys. "We're going to type the letters in the VIC code, okay?"

"Okay," Ruthann agreed, though she couldn't possibly have a clue what the VIC code was.

"Type S." She pointed to each key in succession and Ruthann dutifully pushed it. "S. N. T. R. P. R. S." For some reason, that sounded familiar, and Caroline frowned. She repeated the letters faster. "SSNTRPRS." Again. "SSNTRPRS. SSNTRPRS."

Ruthann joined in the chant, reciting them, too, until the little girl shouted, "S.S. Enterprise! 'Star Trek!' I win! I win!"

"Oh, my God," Caroline muttered. "Star Trek" was her ex-husband's favorite television program.

So Evan had created Vic's trapdoor. But was he the architect of Scarlett's sabotage and the theft of the data base? She had to know.

Working quickly, completely oblivious to Ruthann, Caroline punched up the Scarlett code again. There was a clue here. There had to be. If Evan had created the code, the letters probably pertained to "Star Trek," too, or at least a science fiction concept. But what could YIM-RESTP stand for?

"Car'line? I want to play a new game."

"In a minute, honey," she said distractedly as she started breaking the word down. Yim Rest P. Yimr E Stp. Y Im

Rest p. Why I'm Rest? Well, it was a phrase of sorts, but what did it mean? And what did the P stand for? Or, and this was more likely, the code had been mistyped, which would explain why Scarlett had sounded the alarm.

"Car'line, can I pick the flowers?"

"Not just yet, Ruthann. We'll pick flowers in a minute, okay?" she said without taking her eyes off the screen.

She tried one variation after another, working so quickly that her fingers danced over the keyboard, which wasn't particularly easy since the pad was slightly smaller than a regular keyboard. That altered her normal rhythm and accuracy so much that at one point, her left hand was not positioned over the correct keys. Unaware of the problem, she typed the eight letters, then gasped when she saw the screen. The letters Caroline typed spelled TIMEWARP.

Another "Star Trek" term.

Evan had sabotaged her computer. At some point before their divorce, he had covertly inserted a trapdoor, and then waited until she was poised on the brink of success to steal her achievement and snatch that success out of her grasp. But why? Resentment? Revenge? Jealousy?

What did it matter? He had listened to her plead with him for help, he had made offers of assistance, and all the while, he was doing his best to destroy her life's work.

Caroline hadn't known it was possible to hate anyone so totally, but the emotion engulfed her, coiled through every fiber of her being, and made her feel as though she were about to explode.

She didn't have time to control it, though, because a new emotion took its place just instants later when she heard a shrill scream.

Startled, Caroline looked around for Ruthann, but she was nowhere to be seen. The scream echoed through the glade again, and the computer clattered to the ground as Caroline jumped up.

"Ruthann! *Ruthann, where are you? Ruthann, answer me!*"

She heard it once more coming from the direction of Pigeon Bluff and Caroline started running as fast as she could go.

"*Ruthann!*"

But the little girl didn't cry out again.

MITCH COULDN'T SIT still on the stream bank. He felt guilty for saddling Caroline with Ruthann after she had made her position on the children so clear last night. She had agreed to take Ruthann along to keep from hurting the child's feelings, but she probably resented the hell out of Mitch for not insisting that Ruthann go with him.

"Listen, kids, I think I'm going to go back and check on Caroline and Short Stuff," he told Sam and Janis. "Will you two be okay here?"

"Sure, Dad," Sam replied. "We got sandwiches, we got soda and the fish are biting. What more could we ask for?"

"All right." This wasn't the first time they had fished here alone, so Mitch didn't have any reservations about leaving them. "Just don't leave the stream, understand?"

"Yes, sir," Sam said with a snappy salute. "Why don't you bring Caroline back with you? Tell her she's sure to catch a fish today, and I'll teach her how to clean it."

Mitch wasn't sure how she'd feel about the fish, but he appreciated Sam's invitation. He looked at Janis. "Should I tell her you want her to join us, too?"

Janis shrugged. "I don't care."

Mitch sighed. "I'll see you later."

He headed down the trail for the glade, trying to figure out if there was anything he could—or should—say to Caroline at this point that would make her change her mind about ending their relationship. He was so lost in thought by the time he reached the point where the trails converged that he headed toward the cabin without even realizing it.

"Good, Mitch, good," he muttered when he saw what he had done and turned back. "No trailblazing merit badge for you today."

He made the correct cutoff this time, but he stopped abruptly when he heard the unmistakable sound of someone—or something—thrashing through the woods ahead of him. He also thought he heard another set of movements, but that impression was wiped out an instant later and replaced by a stab of panic when Caroline burst around a bend in the trail, her hair tangled, her face smudged with dirt and bleeding from tiny cuts, and her eyes wild with fear.

He raced to her and grabbed her. "Caroline!"

"Oh, God, Mitch," she panted, almost collapsing into his arms with relief.

"What is it? Where's Ruthann?" he demanded.

"She's fallen, Mitch," Caroline cried as a sob wrenched through her. "I couldn't reach her! I tried, but—"

"Where, Caroline? *Damn it, where is she?*"

"Pigeon Bluff," she gasped.

"Come on." Mitch grabbed her hand and they were running again.

ONLY TWICE in Mitch's life had he thought he might die, not from any physical danger, but from an emotional blow so crippling that he couldn't function. The first was when the doctor had told him Becky was dead. The second was when he burst onto the granite cliff called Pigeon Bluff and saw his tiny daughter lying at the bottom of the steep ravine like a rag doll.

"How did this happen?" he screamed at Caroline as he searched for a way down to his baby. *"How could you let it happen?"*

"She wandered off!" Caroline cried, unable to control her tears or the sobs that had been wracking her body since the moment she spotted Mitch. "I heard her scream..."

Mitch didn't want to hear. He didn't want to know. He just wanted to get to Ruthann. The cliff wasn't a sheer drop off along the entire face; it sloped steeply in places that led to small ledges. He could see where Caroline had tried to climb down to the first ledge, only eight feet or so below the rim, but it looked as though rocks had given way and she had lost her footing. She had been wise not to go farther. She might have dislodged one of the craggy boulders that jutted out of the cliff and sent it tumbling down on his daughter.

Mitch would have to find another route down. He ran down the edge of the ravine until he found what he needed—a gentler slope and enough solid footing to assure that he could bring Ruthann back up once he reached her. Caroline tried to follow him down, but he roughly commanded her to stay where she was.

Breathless, her face drenched in tears, Caroline watched as he made his way to his daughter. Not once the whole time did the little girl stir.

"Mitch, how is she?" Caroline called out desperately when he finally reached Ruthann.

"Alive," he answered.

Caroline collapsed to her knees in relief, crushing a tiny bundle of wildflowers. Little purple and yellow blossoms were scattered everywhere, and Caroline picked them up, rubbing them against her tearstained face.

"Car'line, can I pick the flowers?"

She heard the words so clearly now. Why hadn't she heard them then? Why hadn't she paid attention? Since when was a godforsaken computer more important than the life of a child?

Caroline clutched the flowers and prayed as she had never prayed before.

At the bottom of the ravine, Mitch ran his trembling hands over Ruthann's body. Her left leg was broken, but it seemed to be a clean fracture. She had cuts and scratches everywhere, but the ones on her abdomen didn't look too bad. It was her head that worried him. There was a deep cut on her chin and a widening bruise on her temple that signaled a serious concussion.

How could Caroline have let this happen? Why hadn't he listened to her? She had told him so many times that she didn't want the responsibility of his children. He hadn't believed her, and now Ruthann was paying for it.

Using his belt and a dried piece of bark from a fallen tree, Mitch fashioned a splint for the broken leg. He hated to move her, but he didn't have a choice. It was an hour down the mountain to the nearest hospital, and nearly that far just to a phone where he could call for help. If he left her here, she could die of shock before an ambulance ever arrived.

Being as gentle as he could, he made his way back up the steep slope. Without his hands to steady him, he nearly fell several times until Caroline scrambled down to him and helped him keep his balance. Together, they got Ruthann to the top of the cliff.

"Oh, sweetie," Caroline said tearfully, running her hand along the child's cheek. "I'm so sorry," she whispered.

"It's a little late for that, don't you think?" Mitch said coldly. "I have to get her down the mountain right now," he said as he began striding down the path. "Can you go to the stream and get Sam and Janis safely back to the cabin, or is that too much responsibility, too?"

He couldn't have hurt her more if he'd slapped her, but it was only one more pain in the very deep well of agony inside her. "I'll take care of them, Mitch."

"That's what you said about Ruthann." He shot her a glance that was as cold as ice, then the paths separated and he disappeared into the woods.

It was everything Caroline could do to keep from running after him, but she couldn't be selfish right now. Her self-absorption had created this tragedy; she couldn't make that mistake again. Still, it was several minutes before she could move on. She had to collect herself for the kids' sake. She didn't plan to lie to them about what happened, but there was no reason to let them see her own desperate fear because it was going to be hours before Mitch could return or send someone for them.

She leaned against a tree and dried her eyes, then reached into the pockets of her shorts where she had stuffed Ruthann's wildflowers. She took them out and stroked the crumpled petals tenderly.

She didn't hear the twig that snapped behind her. She didn't hear the faint crunch of leaves. She was so overwhelmed by the consequences of her tragic failure that she didn't sense the danger.

She put the flowers back into her pocket and stepped away from the tree onto the path.

And that's when he grabbed her.

CHAPTER TWENTY

CAROLINE WAS ALREADY numb with shock and she was so startled when the man grabbed her from behind that it took a second for her to react. She tried to whirl around, but he didn't permit it. Instead, he pulled her roughly off the path and that's when she screamed.

"Shut up, Doctor," the man growled, spinning her around so that he could deliver a stinging blow to her face.

Caroline reeled, but he held on to her arm, preventing her from falling.

"Now keep very quiet, Dr. Hunter. We're going to have a nice chat, and then you can go about your business."

Caroline struggled to make sense of what was happening. He was a big man with dark hair and a tanned face. With menace oozing from his dark eyes, he was terrifying.

Clearly she couldn't fight him. His size and the gun she finally noticed stuck in his belt negated that option. Reason was her only alternative. "Who are you?"

"That's not important."

"What do want?"

"Exactly what I've got," he replied. "You."

Caroline's heart was pounding so hard she could barely think. Obviously, he knew who she was, and he wanted something very specific from her. "Why?"

"You have something a friend of my employer needs," he told her casually.

Caroline made a series of lightning-quick connections. "Would that be Howard Richmond and Sydney Grisham?"

"Let's leave names out of it, shall we? It will add to your life expectancy."

Caroline knew better than to press it. She also knew that this man had no intention of leaving her alive, but she didn't want to think about that. "What exactly does your employer's friend want?" she asked.

"Why don't we go back to the cabin and discuss it?"

She didn't see any point in protesting. At least at the cabin she might be able to find something to use as a weapon. Here in the woods she was as helpless as a kitten. He gave her a little shove and she stumbled onto the path. "You don't have to push me! I'm not fighting you," she snapped.

"True. I was told you were a smart lady. This is going to be very simple—you cooperate and I'll leave."

"Then tell me what you want so we can get it over with," she demanded.

He seemed pleased that she was being accommodating, so he returned the favor. "You put some kind of a security code on your computer Thursday night. You're going to write it down for me step by step. I've got a phone in my truck and I'll call the instructions in to my boss. If they work, I'm out of here. If they don't, you're dead."

He said it so casually that Caroline shuddered. "All right. I'll give you the security clearance," she replied, trying to keep her voice steady.

"Thank you. After all the trouble you've put me through this weekend, it's good to have a little cooperation finally. I didn't think your cop boyfriend was ever going to let you out of his sight."

Caroline came to a dead stop as a sickening realization washed over her. "You," she breathed. "You're the reason Ruthann fell."

"A regrettable accident," he replied without any indication of real remorse. "When Grogan and the kids went off by themselves, I followed them a little ways just to be sure I knew where they were going, then I doubled back. It took me a while to find you, and when I did, the kid was picking flowers by the trees."

"So you tried to kill her?" Caroline said, aghast.

"No, I tried to snatch her because I figured you'd need an incentive to give me the security codes. But she started screaming and ran into the woods. When I cornered her on the cliff, she fell."

Fury exploded through Caroline like a charge of dynamite. *"You bastard!"* she screamed, flinging herself at him, raking her fingernails across his face. *"She's just a baby! How could you hurt her?"*

The attack surprised him so much that he stumbled back, but he kept his grip on her arm until another voice caught him off guard.

"Caroline? Caroline!"

Sam's voice cleared the red haze of fury from Caroline's mind. Mitch's son had stumbled into the middle of this deadly situation, and no matter what Caroline's captor said, she knew he wasn't going to leave any witnesses behind. Rage, fear and the knowledge that she had to protect more than herself gave her the strength she needed to seize the slight advantage she had.

"Run, Sam!" she screamed, pummeling her captor with her fists. He was already off balance, and the renewed attack was enough to send him staggering into a brier bush. He swore, tried to extricate himself, and in so doing, lost his hold on Caroline. She pushed again and he went toppling into the bush.

Caroline whirled and found Sam and Janis on the path, staring in disbelief.

"Run!" Caroline screamed as she headed for them.

Sam didn't have to be asked again. He turned on his heel and sprinted down the path, but Janis was frozen.

"I said run, damn it!" Caroline shouted, grabbing the girl's arm to propel her into motion. Together they darted along the trail, dodging overhanging limbs as they ran for their lives.

No one looked back, but Caroline knew that the prickly bramble bush wouldn't detain her assailant for very long.

MITCH PACED the waiting room in the hospital. What the hell could be taking so long? He'd been here over an hour already and no one had told him a damned thing.

Ruthann hadn't stirred once in the car on the breakneck ride down the mountain. He had delivered her into the hands of the hospital staff, called Pop to ask him to come to the hospital immediately, then he'd started pacing. He hadn't stopped since.

"Mr. Grogan?"

Mitch turned sharply as the ER doctor came toward him. "How is she? How bad is the concussion? Are there internal injuries?"

The doctor smiled patiently. "No internal injuries, just the broken leg, which we've already set. The concussion is pretty bad, but I don't think it's life-threatening. Your little girl should be fine in a few days. She's very lucky."

Somehow, Mitch's legs did what they were supposed to do and held him up. "Did she regain consciousness? Can I see her?"

"Yes. To both. She came around right after we started an IV. She's been asking for her daddy and someone named Caroline."

Mitch would have given anything if he could have transmitted this news to Caroline right then. Her negligence had caused this, but he didn't doubt that she was sincerely concerned. "Caroline is—" He stopped. There wasn't any point in explaining the cast of characters to the doctor, and besides, he didn't know exactly what Caroline was to him anymore. "She's with my other kids up in the mountains."

"Well, you can go in and see Ruthann now, just to put her at ease, but then I want you to let her get some rest. She's going to sleep for quite a while, I expect."

"Thanks," Mitch said. "My father will be here in a few minutes. Will you send him to her room?"

"Sure."

The doctor had a nurse show Mitch to Ruthann's room. He entered quietly and found his little girl engulfed in a sea of white bed sheets, tubes and wires. A pristine-white cast decorated with brightly colored teddy bear stickers stuck out from under the sheet.

She looked so small and helpless that Mitch felt tears stinging his eyes. He choked them back and went to the bed.

"Hi, there, Short Stuff," he said quietly, bending so that his face was close to hers. He smoothed her tangled hair and gave her a kiss.

"It hurts, Daddy," she whined.

"I know. Does it hurt bad or just a little?" he asked, worried about whether or not they had given her the proper dosage of pain killers.

"Just a little. Not like before."

"Well, you go to sleep and it will stop hurting, I promise."

She nodded sleepily. "Where's Car'line? I want my Car'line."

Mitch stiffened his jaw. Ruthann was so sweet and trusting. She didn't realize that this was all Caroline's fault. "She had to go find Sam and Janis," Mitch told her.

"Fishing?"

"Yes. They were fishing. But when Pop gets here I'm going to go back and get them."

She licked her lips as her eyes drooped closed. "I haffa tell Car'line I sorry. She said don't pick the flowers, but I didn't mind her. Did the bad man go 'way?" she mumbled.

Mitch frowned. "Bad man? Did you have a dream about a bad man, honey?" he asked, concerned that she was delusional.

Ruthann shook her head just a little. "No. The bad man...chase me to Pigeon Buff," she said, her speech painfully slow and slurred. "I did...like you told me and yelled real loud...but he didn' go 'way. I kick him...and then I falled down. A long way." She opened her eyes and a worried frown came over her face. "The bad man didn't get Car'line, too, did he?"

Mitch felt his heart slam into his chest. "No, honey, he didn't get Caroline," he said comfortingly, but inside, his head was pounding. This wasn't a drug-induced delusion. Ruthann hadn't fallen because of Caroline's negligence. She had been chased away by someone intent on doing her harm.

And Mitch had left that someone alone on the mountain with his children and the woman he loved.

"You sleep well, honey," he told his daughter quietly. "I have to go now, but I'll be back with Caroline real soon."

Mitch dashed out of the hospital room, praying that it was a promise he could keep.

CAROLINE LEANED against the damp cave wall, struggling to catch her breath. To her right, Sam was on his hands and knees panting heavily and Janis was on her left, huddled with her arms clasped around her knees and tears streaming down her face. Less than five minutes ago, they had been out in the open on a rocky trail where their pursuer might have spotted them at any moment. Now, at least they had a safe place to hide. For a few minutes, anyway.

Caroline squinted in the shadowy darkness to check her watch. She wasn't exactly sure what time it had been when Ruthann's horrifying scream had set this whole nightmare in motion, but Caroline guessed that Mitch had been gone for nearly two hours. He had Ruthann at a hospital by now, and she could only pray that the little girl was all right. At least Ruthann was getting help and was safe, which was more than she could say about Mitch's other two children. They had been running for what seemed like hours, and the man Howard Richmond had sent to kill her was still out there searching for them.

Escaping him had been nothing short of a miracle, but they'd had just enough of a head start to put some distance between them and her assailant. That and their strategic advantage—the fact the kids knew the woods and their assailant didn't—had saved them so far.

Mercifully, the kids hadn't stopped or tried to ask questions. They had seen enough of Caroline's struggle with the man to know that their lives were in jeopardy. With Caroline prodding them on, Sam had led them to his fishing hole, but instead of crossing, they went upstream and doubled back onto a second trail that led into the same hills they had traversed yesterday. He led them across a ridge that Caroline remembered only too well because it had scared the living daylights out of her. She barely noticed the sheer drop today.

From a sheltered spot on the top of the ridge, they had been able to look back and see their pursuer in the distance, picking and stumbling his way carefully along the trail.

"Another city dweller. Thank God," Caroline had murmured breathlessly. "All right, Sam. Where to now?"

The boy nodded, and as soon as he caught his breath, he said, "We gotta make for the caves. Is that okay with you?" he asked cautiously.

Caroline managed a weak smile. "I'd rather face a bear than our friend back there any day."

"Who is that guy, anyway?" Sam asked.

"It's a long story. I'll tell you later."

"He had a gun, didn't he?"

"Yes."

"Where's Daddy?" Janis wanted to know. "Why isn't he helping us?"

Caroline didn't want to tell them, but she had to. "That man caused Ruthann to have an accident, but your father and I didn't know about him. Mitch took Ruthann down to the hospital and I was coming to find you when he grabbed me."

"Is Ruthann okay?" Janis asked with alarm.

Caroline reached out and touched her hair. "I don't know, honey."

"Oh, God," Janis moaned as tears sprang into her eyes. "I want Daddy."

Caroline reached for her and held her for as long as she dared. "We've got to do this ourselves, Janis. I need you to be strong for all our sakes, all right?"

The teenager nodded and tried to dry her eyes, leaving dark smudges on her cheeks.

"Let's go, Sam," Caroline said. "You lead the way and everybody stay low."

They were off again, scrambling up trails and crisscrossing rocky plateaus in the hope of losing their pursuer. They climbed for nearly an hour until Sam finally led them off the trail, up a sheer rocky slope to another ledge, then into a cave.

"You know, kids, it's ironic how your priorities change," Caroline said quietly, striving for a light tone so they wouldn't see how desperately frightened she was. "Those drop-offs didn't look nearly as scary as they did yesterday."

Sam raised his head and looked at her. "I'll bet the cabin would look pretty good to you, too."

"Spiders and all."

"How come your blisters aren't hurting?"

"Liquid bandage. Great stuff."

He nodded and sat beside her, his body pressed close. A long silent moment passed before he said in a very small voice, "It's not like in the movies, is it? Being chased, I mean."

Caroline put her arm around him. "I don't know, Sam. You haven't gotten around to showing me any chase movies yet."

"Next week we'll rent *River of No Return*."

"It's a date."

"Why are you two babbling about movies?" Janis cried, and Sam immediately shushed her.

"We're babbling because we're scared," Caroline said softly.

"You can't be scared," Janis whispered fiercely. "You have to get us out of here. That man's going to find us and kill us."

Caroline shook her head. "No. He won't. I promise you, Janis. I won't let him hurt you."

It was so clear from the look in her eyes that she wanted to believe, but she had lost all her trust in Caroline months ago. It wasn't going to come back in a few hours. "How are you going to stop him?" she asked defiantly.

"I don't know that yet."

"We're safe here, aren't we, Doc?" Sam asked nervously.

"Yes," she told him, but she didn't really believe it. Mitch had no idea they were in trouble and it might be hours before he returned. Even then, he would have no idea where to find them.

On the other hand, the man somewhere below had a pretty good idea of the direction they had taken and nothing short of an accidental fall down one of those drop-offs was going to keep him from searching until he found them. Caroline could recognize him. Moreover, he was aware that she knew who had sent him.

But the kids had gotten only a glimpse of him, and he knew that, too. If he found Caroline and got what he wanted, he might not waste time looking for them.

If it was the only way to save Mitch's children, she would do it, but there had to be a more creative solution than offering herself up as a sacrificial lamb. She just had to find it.

Caroline tried to visualize where their assailant was now. Just outside the cave, or far back on the trail? Had all of Sam's switchbacks and crisscrossings confused him? Was he lost? Had he, indeed, fallen? Had a rock slide— Caroline sat up straighter. A rock slide. They had started a half dozen of them on their hike yesterday and their mad dash to safety today. Could Caroline start one more?

"All right, kids. I want you to listen to me very carefully. I'm going back out there to see if I can tell how far he is behind us."

"No, don't," Sam pleaded. "We're safe here."

"*You'll* be safe here," she said, coming to her knees in the low-ceilinged cave. "I'm going to try to lead him into a trap."

"Caroline, don't!" Janis gasped.

"I'll be all right, Janis," she assured her.

"But you don't know the trails," Sam argued.

"I know up from down, and I'm not likely to forget this place. I'll let you know just as soon as the coast is clear."

"But what if you don't come back?" Sam asked.

"Don't worry," Caroline said, then managed a grin as she lowered her voice in an imitation of Sam's favorite Austrian action hero. "I'll be back."

Sam threw his arms around her neck and hugged her tightly. "I love you, Doc," he told her.

"I love you, too, Sam," she said fervently. "You're the best teacher I ever had."

She pried his arms from around her neck. "You and Janis take care of each other."

"Be careful, Caroline," Janis said in a small voice.

"I will, Angelface. See you later."

"I'm really sorry, Caroline."

Caroline reached out and touched her cheek, soothing away the tears there. "No matter what you may think to the contrary, Janis, I love you, too."

She turned and ducked out of the cavern before the girl could respond or Caroline could change her mind.

THE CITY DWELLER wasn't having an easy time of it on the rocky trail below Caroline. He was much closer to the cave than she had hoped, but she heard him long before she ever spotted him, and that gave her ample opportunity to keep herself out of sight. As soon as she had him pinpointed, she realized that all she had to do was wait and he would pass directly under her.

It was almost too easy. Except for one small problem. All of the boulders overhanging the trail seemed to be securely fastened to the mountainside, leaving nothing but small rocks and pebbles that wouldn't do much more than call attention to herself if she showered them down on him.

So much for her brilliant landslide idea.

She had to find a better point from which to attack. She looked at the craggy rock face that rose above her. Too steep to climb, and too visible. He would spot her in a minute. If she went south on the ledge, she would be moving closer to him and it was more likely that he would hear her. She had to go north.

Crawling like an infant, she quietly edged her way along the top of the escarpment until her "road" took a sharp turn to the right. That gave her the cover she needed and she felt secure enough to stand and move more quickly. A quick peek over the edge told Caroline that her pursuer's trail would still lead him under her, but her own path suddenly came to a dead end. An old landslide blocked the way, cutting off any hope she might have of escaping higher into the hills...but also providing her with exactly what she needed.

With her heart thundering in her ears, she crouched behind a small boulder that was resting on a bed of loose stones and waited.

WHEN MITCH arrived at the cabin, four rangers from the Big Sur Mountain Rescue Service were already there, and two sheriff's deputies were right behind him. He had stopped long enough at the hospital to place the two strategic calls because he knew better than to go into a dangerous situation without backup. Also, he had hoped that the rangers would be able to get there quicker than he could. He had been right, but so far they'd had no luck in finding Caroline or the kids.

"We found a pickup truck hidden off the road about a mile from here, but we haven't found anything other than the signs of a struggle I told you about just up ahead," Luke Clancey, the chief ranger, told Mitch as they hurried up the wooded path.

Mitch tried to think like a cop instead of a father and a man in love. "Any traces of blood?" he asked tersely.

"None."

"What about the registration on the truck?"

"I called it in to the sheriff's department. They checked the Department of Motor Vehicles and found out that it's registered to a man named Wilson Henderson."

"Does he have a rap sheet?"

Clancey drew a blank. "Rap sheet? You mean a criminal record? I don't know yet. I guess they're still checking on that."

Mitch had forgotten he wasn't dealing with a fellow officer. Just a man he hoped was very good at search and rescue.

"He does have a record," one of the deputy sheriffs behind him said, panting as he tried to keep up. "The office radioed up a report just before we got to the cabin. Henderson has connections to some mobster named Sydney Grisham."

Mitch let go of a string of curses that turned the air blue. He had told Caroline not to worry! She was safe. Howard Richmond had no reason to harm her.

Some instincts he had. For some reason, Richmond had felt threatened and needed to get rid of Caroline. Mitch guessed that it had something to do with the trapdoor business she had told him about Thursday night, but he didn't waste time trying to figure it out. That would come later. Now, he had to find Caroline and the kids.

They reached the area where Clancey assumed a struggle had taken place. He was right. It seemed clear that two people had scuffled on and just off the trail. But Clancey was wrong about one thing. Whoever had fallen—or been pushed—into the wicked thornbush had left a little of his blood behind.

"Way to go, Caroline," Mitch murmured, choosing to believe that she had temporarily disabled her assailant, allowing her to escape. It was a logical conclusion since Wilson Henderson's truck was still nearby. If Wilson had succeeded in carrying out whatever orders Sydney Grisham had given him, he would have been long gone by now.

The cellular radio clipped to Clancey's belt squawked and he thumbed a button. "What is it, Search One?"

"We've found a trail that leads up to Widow's Peak. Looks like an adult and two kids came out of Johnson Creek and headed up the pass. We're following now."

"Any sign of someone in pursuit?" Clancey asked.

"That's hard to tell. These trails have been used a lot lately and we haven't had much rain."

"Assume the worst," Mitch said to Clancey. "Have them hold their positions until we get there."

Clancey relayed the message. "Where are you now?"

"Lobo Junction."

"We're on our way," Clancey replied, then looked at Mitch. "Come on. I know a shortcut."

They took off at a brisk jog and joined the others only minutes later. Together, the seven men headed up the rocky trail. They found spots where at least one person had stumbled and fallen, then got up and trudged on. They found an area on the ridge where three people had knelt.

One of the rangers finally found enough clear tracks to determine that Wilson Henderson was wearing a pair of fancy jogging shoes that left distinctive prints. That was fortunate, because the minimal tracks left by Caroline and the kids all but vanished shortly thereafter and the search party was forced to follow the winding, confused trail left by Henderson.

Mitch tried to put himself in Caroline's place and figure out what she would do, but he drew a blank. She had been so incompetent yesterday that he had a hard time imagining that she was being much help to the kids. But if she was holding them back, how could they possibly have gotten this far?

Sam, probably. He was a tough, scrappy kid and he knew these trails. Sam was leading them, and if that was the case, Mitch knew exactly what his son would do.

"We're splitting up," Mitch told Clancey. "You and the deputies follow Henderson's trail. The rest of you come with me."

"Where are you going?" Clancey asked.

"To the caves below Widow's Peak."

"Okay, but be careful," Clancey told him. "We had a lot of landslides up there after the last rains."

With three armed rangers as backup, helping guide him on a more direct route to the caves, Mitch picked up the pace. It wasn't easy because he was going almost straight up, while below him, Clancey's party was winding around on the easier route up the mountain. He didn't care that his lungs felt as though they would burst at any moment and the muscles in his legs were on fire. He had to find the kids before Wilson Henderson did. He had to find Caroline and tell her he was sorry for the cruel things he'd said. He had to tell all three of them how much he loved them.

As they neared the caves, Mitch tried to decide which one Sam might have chosen. He selected the most likely one in his mind, but before he could convey his hunch to the rangers, the rumble started. The sound of boulders tumbling in the distance brought them to a dead stop, then they started running.

CAROLINE LOOKED over the edge of the escarpment. Below her, the city dweller was sprawled on the trail. Blood leaked from a cut on his forehead and pebbles were still dropping onto his body, turning his blue jeans to gray. His chest was rising and falling ever so slightly.

It was the second time today that Caroline had looked down on an unconscious form, but she felt none of the same emotions that she had experienced with Ruthann. This was a jubilant victory.

"I got you, you bastard," she muttered, then turned and ran down the path toward the cave. She skittered around the corner, nearly losing her balance, and when she righted herself, she looked down the ledge and blinked her eyes.

"Mitch?"

His body sagged visibly with relief, and then somehow there was no trail between them. She was in his arms. Safe.

"I love you," she murmured fiercely. "I love you, I love you, I love you."

CHAPTER TWENTY-ONE

"CAROLINE, you're exhausted. Why don't you go back to the motel with Pop and the kids?" Mitch suggested quietly so as not to awaken his daughter.

Caroline shook her head as she lightly stroked Ruthann's arm. The little girl looked so angelic as she slept, with only a small light over the bed like a golden halo. But she also looked pale and fragile. Caroline wasn't about to leave her. "The nurse said she'd bring in a cot for me."

"There's no point," he argued mildly.

She looked up at him. "Then why are you staying?"

"She's *my* daughter."

Tears stung Caroline's eyes. "But she wants to call me Mommy," she reminded him. "That gives me a few rights, too."

Mitch stepped behind her chair and placed his hands on her shoulders. "Then we'll both stay," he said, bending down to kiss the top of her head.

Once he had found her in the mountains, the story of her adventure had come tumbling out almost as quickly as his kids had tumbled out of the cave when they heard his voice. Everyone began talking at once, and while Mitch tried to make sense out their excited chatter, Wilson Henderson regained consciousness. Fortunately, there were two deputies standing over him with guns and handcuffs, so he hadn't put up a fight.

By the time they had reached the cabin, Mitch had put all the bits and pieces together—Evan Converse, the trapdoor, the security codes that had been needed to erase the signs of sabotage and theft, all of it. Henderson hadn't been willing to name his employer, but it didn't matter. When Mitch had called the police station in Hilliard to have Howard Richmond and Evan Converse picked up and held for questioning, Evan had spilled everything, hoping to avoid an indictment for conspiracy to commit murder.

Mitch also knew that his kids considered Caroline a heroine. She had held them together like a team, comforted them and risked her life to save them. If he hadn't already loved her more than words could measure, he would have fallen in love with her on the spot.

And now she was sitting at Ruthann's bedside because she needed reassurance that the little girl who worshiped her was going to be all right. If Becky was somewhere watching all this, she had to be smiling now, because she could be sure that her kids were safe and loved.

Mitch eased onto the arm of Caroline's chair and stroked her hair. "Thank you for what you did today," he said quietly.

Caroline took her eyes off Ruthann long enough to look up at him. "I let Henderson hurt her. She could have been killed. How can you thank me for that?"

"It wasn't your fault."

"I should have been watching her," she said, her eyes filled with remorse.

Mitch nodded. "You're right. You should have. Just like I should have been watching her the day a beautiful, brilliant scientist kidnapped her at a science fair."

"It's not the same, Mitch," she told him softly.

"Yes, it is. It's called making a mistake, and it happens to everyone. Even brilliant people with PhD's."

She searched his face. "Can you forgive me for it?"

"I love you. My kids love you. My father thinks you're the best thing that ever happened to us. What kind of husband would I be if I couldn't forgive you?'' he asked, then held his breath, waiting for the inevitable retreat, but it didn't come. Instead, Caroline raised her face and pressed a whisper-soft kiss to his lips.

"I love you. I love your kids."

"But can you accept the responsibility of being their mother?" he asked.

A bright smile slowly lit her face. "Mitch, after what I did today, everything else is going to be an easy downhill slide. What could possibly be worse than protecting them from a hired assassin?"

Mitch's answering smile started in the very center of his heart and slowly worked its way outward. They were okay. They were in love. Everything was going to be fine.

Still, he felt compelled to answer her question. "Sam's first date. Ruthann's measles. Janis's—"

"Stop. Don't tell me," Caroline said, pressing her fingertips to his lips. "Let me be surprised."

Mitch leaned toward her and sealed the moment with a kiss.

"Car'line?"

Ruthann's tiny voice was the sweetest interruption Caroline could have imagined. "Yes, honey, I'm here," she said as she and Mitch drew closer to the bed. She took the sleepy little girl's hand and caressed it lightly. "I'm not going anywhere. Never."

"Promise?"

"I promise." Caroline dug into her pocket and held out a handful of crushed violets. "See what I found? Your flowers."

Ruthann gave her a sleepy smile. "I picked them for you."

Caroline felt tears on her cheeks, but she let them fall. "Then I'll keep them forever. Now, you go back to sleep."

Ruthann nodded. "Okay, Mommy."

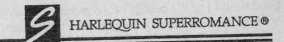

HARLEQUIN SUPERROMANCE ®

COMING NEXT MONTH

#590 KEEPING KATIE • Patricia Keelyn
Maura Anderson had no choice. Three-year-old Katie meant the
world to her and no quirk of the justice system was going to take
her daughter away from her. So she ran...right into Alan Parks's
arms. The small-town sheriff offered her a future. But how could
she trust him when he represented the thing she feared most—the
law!

#591 TWILIGHT WHISPERS • Morgan Hayes
Claire Madden couldn't believe her good fortune when she
inherited a sprawling mansion in Maine. Not only was the house
gorgeous, but it came with its very own handyman, the irresistible
Michael Dalton. It also came with a mystery—a murder mystery—
that Michael was dead-set against her solving.

#592 BRIDGE OVER TIME • Brenda Hiatt
Kathryn Monroe wanted to make a difference. She'd spent years in
politics, but it had only left her feeling empty. She went home for a
rest, and, through some twist of fate, ended up in 1825. Here was
her opportunity to liberate the slaves...and the women. She'd
switched places with her own ancestress, Catherine Prescott. And
she wasn't sure she wanted to let Catherine's beau in on the secret.

#593 GHOST TIGER • Janice Carter
Meg Devlin's only chance of finding her father lay with
Conor Tremayne. He was the journalist who'd shot the film in
which Meg recognized the face she hadn't seen for nineteen years.
Conor seemed more than willing to help but, as their search took
them through northern Thailand, Meg had the distinct impression
the handsome reporter had his own agenda.

AVAILABLE NOW:

#586 SINGLE...WITH CHILDREN
Connie Bennett

#587 DANCE OF DECEPTION
Catherine Judd

#588 LUCK OF THE IRISH
Sharon Brondos

#589 CANDY KISSES
Muriel Jensen

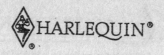

HARLEQUIN®

MARRIAGE BY Design

Harlequin proudly presents four stories about *convenient* but not *conventional* reasons for marriage:

- ◆ To save your godchildren from a "wicked stepmother"

- ◆ To help out your eccentric aunt—and her sexy business partner

- ◆ To bring an old man happiness by making him a grandfather

- ◆ To escape from a ghostly existence and become a real woman

Marriage By Design—four brand-new stories by four of Harlequin's most popular authors:

CATHY GILLEN THACKER
JASMINE CRESSWELL
GLENDA SANDERS
MARGARET CHITTENDEN

Don't miss this exciting collection of stories about marriages of convenience. Available in April, wherever Harlequin books are sold.

HARLEQUIN®

Don't miss these Harlequin favorites by some of our most distinguished authors!
And now, you can receive a discount by ordering two or more titles!

HT#25409	THE NIGHT IN SHINING ARMOR by JoAnn Ross	$2.99	☐
HT#25471	LOVESTORM by JoAnn Ross	$2.99	☐
HP#11463	THE WEDDING by Emma Darcy	$2.89	☐
HP#11592	THE LAST GRAND PASSION by Emma Darcy	$2.99	☐
HR#03188	DOUBLY DELICIOUS by Emma Goldrick	$2.89	☐
HR#03248	SAFE IN MY HEART by Leigh Michaels	$2.89	☐
HS#70464	CHILDREN OF THE HEART by Sally Garrett	$3.25	☐
HS#70524	STRING OF MIRACLES by Sally Garrett	$3.39	☐
HS#70500	THE SILENCE OF MIDNIGHT by Karen Young	$3.39	☐
HI#22178	SCHOOL FOR SPIES by Vickie York	$2.79	☐
HI#22212	DANGEROUS VINTAGE by Laura Pender	$2.89	☐
HI#22219	TORCH JOB by Patricia Rosemoor	$2.89	☐
HAR#16459	MACKENZIE'S BABY by Anne McAllister	$3.39	☐
HAR#16466	A COWBOY FOR CHRISTMAS by Anne McAllister	$3.39	☐
HAR#16462	THE PIRATE AND HIS LADY by Margaret St. George	$3.39	☐
HAR#16477	THE LAST REAL MAN by Rebecca Flanders	$3.39	☐
HH#28704	A CORNER OF HEAVEN by Theresa Michaels	$3.99	☐
HH#28707	LIGHT ON THE MOUNTAIN by Maura Seger	$3.99	☐

Harlequin Promotional Titles

#83247	YESTERDAY COMES TOMORROW by Rebecca Flanders	$4.99	☐
#83257	MY VALENTINE 1993	$4.99	☐
	(short-story collection featuring Anne Stuart, Judith Arnold, Anne McAllister, Linda Randall Wisdom)		

(limited quantities available on certain titles)

	AMOUNT	$
DEDUCT:	**10% DISCOUNT FOR 2+ BOOKS**	$
ADD:	**POSTAGE & HANDLING**	$
	($1.00 for one book, 50¢ for each additional)	
	APPLICABLE TAXES*	$ _____
	TOTAL PAYABLE	$ _____
	(check or money order—please do not send cash)	

To order, complete this form and send it, along with a check or money order for the total above, payable to Harlequin Books, to: **In the U.S.:** 3010 Walden Avenue, P.O. Box 9047, Buffalo, NY 14269-9047; **In Canada:** P.O. Box 613, Fort Erie, Ontario, L2A 5X3.

Name: _____

Address: _____ City: _____

State/Prov.: _____ Zip/Postal Code: _____

*New York residents remit applicable sales taxes.
Canadian residents remit applicable GST and provincial taxes.

HBACK-JM

Fifty red-blooded, white-hot, true-blue hunks
from every State in the Union!

Look for MEN MADE IN AMERICA! Written by some of
our most popular authors, these stories feature fifty of
the strongest, sexiest men, each from a different state in
the union!

Two titles available every other month at your favorite
retail outlet.

In March, look for:

TANGLED LIES by Anne Stuart (Hawaii)
ROGUE'S VALLEY by Kathleen Creighton (Idaho)

In April, look for:

LOVE BY PROXY by Diana Palmer (Illinois)
POSSIBLES by Lass Small (Indiana)

You won't be able to resist MEN MADE IN AMERICA!